CHECKING YOU OUT

GREEN VALLEY LIBRARY BOOK #10

ANN WHYNOT

WWW.SMARTYPANTSROMANCE.COM

COPYRIGHT

Print Edition
ISBN: 978-1-959097-55-6

To my partner, Pat.
You know why.

CHAPTER 1

LOIS

"Peily, you holding up over there? Your magic is running low," came a male voice through my headset, the warning implicit. I leaned forward in my computer chair and bit my lower lip, watching the floor my avatar was standing on go up in flames. To avoid becoming extra crispy, I scooted Peily to the left and kept on task. This was my big shot to show this group of elite players that I had what it took to join their guild as a healer, and if I let the guy the dragon was snacking on die, well, I could kiss my spot on their roster goodbye, too.

"Don't fuss; I've got it, Deathdrop," I replied, calmly clicking through my healing rotation. I eyeballed Deathdrop's health points like they were my own lifeline. The tide had turned in what had been a rocky fight, and now the dragon was going down, and it was a race to see if my healing could outlast the beast. A scant moment later, as my magic points ran dry, the dragon fell and the battle was won. Phew!

"Great job, kiddo!" Deathdrop yelled. I threw my hands up in the air and whirled my desk chair around, helplessly tangling up my headset cord. I didn't even care—I had shown the most badass group in the online role-playing game *Guilds of the Ages* that I was ready to join them, and I had saved the virtual life of the guy I was crazy about. I mean, sure, I didn't really *know him* know him, but we talked online all the time, for at least an hour or two a day for the last two months. I knew his name was Norman, and he was from a little town in the middle of nowhere, just like me. We were both almost eighteen, seniors, and wanted to move to New York City as soon as freakin' possible. In fact, my Swedish-born grandmother, my Mormor—my mother's mother—who socked away money in her chest of drawers, had already secured an apartment for Norman and me and we could move in right after graduation.

I couldn't wait to meet Norman in person. He was so kind, funny, and loyal. As far as I knew, he never divulged the secrets I shared with him to anyone. It was a favor I reciprocated, never even telling this other girl I played with, Maxine—Max—that Norman and I were sort of a *thing.* I banished thoughts of Max from my mind at that moment, a twinge of guilt hitting me at the thought that I was joining a guild—a group of players who banded together to take on big challenges in-game—she personally hated because of their leader, some guy named Wrath. Well, I was signing up for Norman, and any drama could bugger off. I hated drama; I had enough of that in high school.

My place in the guild assured, I went to an impromptu party the players threw to welcome me. Norman and I swapped to private voice chat where we could use each other's real names if we wanted. Though rarely did he call me Lois; he always had a nickname up his sleeve. His current favorite was *kiddo*, which drove me nuts because I was only two months younger than him. Though he was insistent that he only called me that not because of my age, but because his favorite movie was *Kill Bill*, and I was so badass that I reminded him of the heroine who I guess was called kiddo a lot, too. I couldn't weigh in on the appropriateness of the nickname because I was saving the movie to watch with Norman.

"You were so awesome tonight, kiddo," he said, his voice full of pride and affection. "I shouldn't have bothered to question you at all during that fight; you were on point the whole time."

I whirled around in my desk chair again, butterflies having long since taken up permanent residence in my stomach and chest. "Thanks, Norm. You know, you were pretty great, too," was all I could think to say. I was so damn flattered every time Norman said something kind to me. I wondered if he felt the same way when I said something nice about him. Did guys get all giddy over how much they loved someone? I looked over to the photo Norman had emailed me that I had printed out and stuck to the front of one of my computer speakers, gazing into brown eyes and a mop of shaggy dark blond hair on a pleasant face. Graduation was two months away and the city was beckoning me. Freedom from this quiet, stupid town full of quiet, stupid people. I wanted loud, I wanted fast, and I wanted adventure. And to experience it all with Norman by my side! We even had a plan to meet for the first time at the top of the Empire State Building, like in *Sleepless in Seattle*. What could be more romantic?

"Do you think they'll let one of us in the building late, after their last run, like in the movie?" I mused.

He chuckled. "I love your imagination, Lo. Of course they won't, but I don't think I'll have any trouble picking you out of a crowd. I'll know you the moment I set eyes on you. I'll look for the fiercest, most beautiful, black-haired goddess of a woman ever made."

Those butterflies flapped their enormous wings against my breastbone, and I felt like I could take flight just on the strength of his words. I was convinced Norman and I were a perfect match; he was so full of excitement, energy, and positive thinking, like I tried to be but so often failed at. According to my Mormor, Norman and I were like halves of a whole, and when we finally met, it would be like fireworks. She fancied herself a bit of a mind reader—ha! More like an email hacker.

One evening, while I was making lists of stuff Norman and I would need to buy to furnish our apartment, I got a short email that changed my world forever.

Lois:
I have to tell you something that will hurt you, and for that I have many regrets. I will not be joining you in New York. I turned eighteen and the first thing I did with my mother's encouragement and support was enlist. She always told me that enlisting at eighteen after high school would be the biggest favor I could do for myself. I know this will bring my mother peace in the knowledge that I am serving a purpose bigger than myself and will learn valuable life skills that I couldn't gain bumming around New York City. There will be no point in waiting for me, as I've put aside childish dreams. Please don't reply. I leave in the morning and drawing this out will only hurt you.
Regards,
Norman

He didn't want to "bum" around New York? He was supposed to take one year off and then apply for Computer Science at NYU, where I was headed! And I got that his mother sometimes smothered him, but this… Enlist at eighteen when we were at war? And why did this email read like it had been written by an AI pretending to be Norman?

My heart felt torn into pieces as I lay on my bed and stared numbly at the email on my laptop, willing the cruel words away. He had just spoken to me about our rental not three days ago, and now the very concept of us having a life together fell under the category of "childish dreams"? What the hell! Did he even know that the enlistment age was seventeen, and he could have avoided meeting me altogether if he'd done this last year? Why did he have to drag me through his crisis of dreams and duty?

Two weeks later, I walked across the stage in my high school gymnasium, graduating with tears blurring my vision. I was still leaving for NYU, but according to that email I'd gotten, I would be going it alone. In a move I hadn't dreamt of and still couldn't understand, Norman had bailed on me. Now I wouldn't be surprised if I never saw that pleasant face in person for as long as I lived.

As for the game, and how hard I had fought for my spot? I never hit uninstall so quickly. In my heartbroken disappointment, I had learned fast that life isn't a game, and I quit the guild and never played again.

Ten Years Later

I wiped down the bathroom counter and looked at the gleaming surface with intense satisfaction before turning back to my maintenance cart and whistling as I straightened up my cleaning supplies. My feet and back were a bit sore, but it was a good sore, like after a decent jog or that goat yoga my best friend Max had dragged me to last weekend. Max was the reason I found myself here in Green Valley, Tennessee instead of my old apartment in Queens. And while she claimed she had nothing to do with my employment at the Green Valley Public Library—where she also worked as a cataloguer—I had suspicions she may have pulled a string or two. Or five. Working as a library janitor wasn't my dream career, but it paid a decent wage and money seemed to stretch further here in Tennessee. At least it did when you got the ultra-cheap "friends and family rent" deal I had at my new place. All my landlord, Rose, asked for was that I pitch in on the groceries and utilities, which I tried to argue was unfair to her, but she wouldn't take no for an answer. My coworkers at the library were also beyond friendly, and it was good, honest work that was satisfying at the end of the day. I'd had an office job at a PR firm in New York, but it often brought migraines, anxiety, and homicidal tendencies every time someone grabbed my ass or ordered me to grab them a latte.

My exodus from New York was compelled by a few reasons. But my fate was sealed when, on a particularly vulnerable night for me, I confessed to Max that my job was on the chopping block and that managing to raise a daughter solo in the city was a task I worried I was failing at. I wanted her to have the opportunity to experience wide, open spaces like I did growing up, and with just me at the helm and no car, day trips out of the city were few and far between.

Why was I raising a daughter solo? Well, to put it bluntly, I got knocked up and married too young to someone who didn't know himself well at the time. Now David, my ex, with his new love, Philippe, on a French vineyard. He sent regular child support, but we still always seemed to be up against it with bills, and I felt like a failure for not making more money.

I wasn't being fair to myself or David, really. He worked hard on the vineyard to support Elsa, and he was a great dad to her, even paying for trips back and forth to bring her to France for summers and alternating Christmases, like he was going to do this year. He was also like family, once I'd gotten past the initial shock and heartbreak of finding out my husband was gay. Now that was no easy task—it took two years of therapy and some deep introspection to decide if I wanted David to be part of our lives in a permanent way.

I pushed down the stab of pain at missing my baby's sixth Christmas and hummed my favorite carol as I wheeled my cart to the maintenance closet, fished the keys out of my pocket, and unlocked the door. Pushing the cart inside, I checked over my inventory, made a note of what was running low, grabbed a rubber glove, and then smiled as the clock hit five.

Max would be down in the basement with headphones on, cataloguing her heart out, so I continued our usual ritual and, after locking the closet up, went to fetch her. Until I could afford my own car, Max was providing me with rides to and from work. Now, this temporary solution I could handle in the short-term, considering we worked in the same building with the same hours, and I lived with Max's mother in her big Victorian house. However, aside from what I needed for Elsa, nothing but the essentials were being bought before I picked up a used car.

I had my eye on one at the Winston Brothers Auto Shop and, with this month's paychecks, it was within my reach. I'd been told that the Winstons sold classic cars, and while my heart ached for a 1965 Mustang Fastback, Beau Winston, one of the owners, had told me they had wound up with a 2018 Nissan Sentra in excellent condition that they were keen to sell. Well, I was keen to buy. A car, I knew from growing up in the country, was freedom. And this relocation of mine? It was partly about needing room to breathe.

I waved to Sabrina, a library assistant who had squeezed in the cleaning here at the branch before they could budget for a full-time janitor, and to Finley, who ran the local special collection. They both smiled back, and

Sabrina gave an enthusiastic wave. Finley did a rather frantic hand gesture when she saw me, and I grinned and made my way over to her. I'd bet anything she didn't get the book club reading done.

"*Psst!* Lois!" she hissed. "I didn't get the book club reading done. Max is going to kill me; this is the second time! You have pull with her. Can you make sure she doesn't kick me out?"

I smiled wide and shook my head. "I have 'pull' with her? You make her sound like a mafia boss."

"When it comes to book club, she practically is. You haven't been to a meeting yet; you don't know," Finley pointed out.

"Okay, okay. I'll talk to the big bad dragon lady about it. But you know she would never actually expel anyone from her club. There's a LEGO portion most evenings, for Pete's sake."

"Which is one of the reasons I don't want out!" she replied sensibly.

I laughed and made my way to the basement stairs, waving as I went. I crept down, trying not to make the third step from the top squeak just in case her headphones were off, because scaring the hell out of Max was one of the small joys of my day. Of course, it was all in jest; we'd been best friends ever since we'd met in the online roleplaying game *Guilds of the Ages* way back when I was seventeen. In fact, I had never "met" Max before this relocation to her hometown. But I had been desperate, and when a friend reaches out to offer a helping hand, well, sometimes you've got to take it… Whether you know them offline or not. As I saw it, the only good thing to come from my foray into online gaming had been meeting Max. She'd been my rock more than once, and this invitation to Green Valley was so Maxine. I loved her to bits, and she was a sister of my soul.

As expected, Max was at her workstation, a new book in one hand and her other clacking away at the keyboard. She was in a perpetually happy mood these days because her boyfriend and his best friend were moving here from Florida tomorrow, along with their computer business. Whenever she talked excitedly about it, I simply clenched my teeth and smiled, burying the feeling in my gut which incessantly nagged at me. I was completely, one hundred percent, supportive of her relationship with Jonathan. It was the hanger-on that bothered me.

Deathdrop.

No, *Norman Grant*.

All the times I searched for the name Norman Grant amongst the casualties in the news, all the times I lit candles for him in churches praying for his safety, I whispered that name. He was my first love; my first broken heart.

Okay, so maybe I was being a wee bit dramatic. The falling-out with Norman—with him leaving to enlist instead of coming to New York with me after graduation—was a pain I had buried deep down underneath other pains, other joys. Joys that no longer included gaming, a former passion of mine, and how Max and her former enemy, Jonathan, got all twisted up together to start with—not to mention Norman and me. I may be loyal to my best friend, but I held that part of my life close to my heart and never shared it. Now I wondered: what would happen when the Wonder Twins arrived tomorrow? I felt those darn butterflies in my stomach and got lightheaded if I thought about it too much.

Would he apologize to me? Still care for me? He'd have to connect the dots if I didn't tell him outright that I was the player formerly known as Peily. But then, how many people named Lois from Nebraska, then New York, played *Guilds of the Ages* back then alongside our mutual friend, Max? I mean, okay, I had kept my married name, but unless he was a total dolt, he'd have to know it was me, right?

There wasn't that big a difference between Lois Jensen and who I was now, Lois Washington. I would be lying, though, if I denied there were *any* differences: when I was seventeen, I had a goth phase, and my now long, red hair was cut short and dyed midnight black. I wore the chunkiest black-framed glasses I could find before discovering contacts, and I always had a full face of makeup, something I didn't bother with now. I also weighed a bit more back then and since had lost the round shape to my face.

Banishing all thoughts of Norman Grant from my head, I crept down the steps and, quiet as a mouse, made my way over to Max. Dangling the rubber glove from one hand, I snuck up behind her and let it brush over her shoulder. Looking over, she shrieked, dropped her book, and mashed the keyboard. Cackling evilly, I took in her not-amused expression and forced myself to rein in the smile at her expense. But honestly, she was too easy!

"Lois, is it in your long-term plans to scare the crap out of me at every available opportunity? I'd like to know while we're still getting into the groove here," Max asked in a slightly waspish tone. I knew not to take it too harshly, so I put my hands up in an innocent gesture and gave her my best impression of Elsa when she did something wrong. Head slightly down, eyes wide and eager, hands open and imploring. "Ugh, not the lost puppy look again, Lo! You know that slays me. Fine, you're forgiven."

"And I'm sorry. Oh, and you're no longer officially on duty. It's past five and my cart is tucked away. You ready to hit the road?" I knew the answer, but I asked it each day anyway.

"Just this last entry..." Max trailed off, lost back in her data. I sat in an empty chair next to the pile of weeded books and poked through them, wondering if there would be anything decent to take home for Elsa. She was precocious, and though she was only six, she was reading at a fourth-grade level. So, I kept my eye out for chapter books as well as picture books, which she still loved based on her blooming appreciation for art.

Seizing a book from the pile, I brandished it at Max and said, "You're getting rid of *Sulwe* by Lupita Nyong'o? Why?" I asked, offended on the book's behalf. "It's gorgeous." I flipped through the tale of a girl born much darker than anyone else she knew until I saw where a page had been ripped out. "Oh, sorry. I didn't see that." Suddenly, inspiration struck. "Hey, could I have this for Elsa? I was thinking I could frame some of the pictures and hang them on the walls. She could use a little more Black Girl Magic in her room." My daughter had beautiful brown skin, darker than my pasty white. She had also inherited her father's impish grin, dimples, and from somewhere got stunning grey-blue eyes. Say what you want about a man who abandoned me for someone else in French wine country, but we had made an incredible child together—in intelligence and looks.

At Max's hum of assent, I tucked the book into my bag and waited for her to finish her cataloguing record. Our plan for tonight was to get the boys' rental stocked with things like toilet paper, cleaners, and some essential groceries. Nothing too extravagant, but enough so that they could manage the first few days they were here until they got the lay of the land. I had found the same kindness extended to me when I moved in with Max's mother three weeks ago. Much to my shock and delight, two bedrooms upstairs with a connecting bathroom had been cleared out of most of their possessions, save furniture, and made up with brand new bedding. Elsa's room was a little girl's dream, done with purples and yellows and butterflies on the walls. And with these pages from *Sulwe*, it would be perfect.

As Max finally turned off her workstation and rose from her desk, I smiled and banished all thoughts of Norman Grant. I'd have enough of him tomorrow when they arrived, so why worry in the meantime. I felt the butterflies fly away for now. My daughter was waiting to be picked up from daycare, and no doubt Rose would have gone ahead and put together a delicious supper for us all, despite my repeated attempts to help with meals. With pleasant things to look forward to, I marched out of the library and into the crisp December air.

CHAPTER 2

NORMAN

I blasted one of my favorite playlists as I snaked through the Appalachian Mountains; my target the small town of Green Valley. My truck was loaded up with my best friend Jonathan's and my things as we made our move from our adjacent trailer parks in Florida to our new home, him leading our caravan with a U-Haul holding the equipment and parts from our computer shop.

It had been an exhausting day, with my truck getting a flat an hour out of Florida while I'd been singing along to "Georgia on My Mind." By the time we reached Tennessee, "Great Balls of Fire" played as we had to stop again because my truck was overheating. I really did need to replace or repair this rust bucket. It was #goals now that our business was taking off, and I hoped that we would be able to set up shop quickly in our new location. As "Highway to Hell" began to blare, I reached out and swapped to the next song, my superstitious mind not letting anything tempt fate. And thus, I descended into Green Valley with "MMMBop" as the soundtrack to my new life. So I enjoyed Hanson now and then. I didn't stress too much over what was or wasn't currently popular; I liked what I liked.

I cranked up the dial on my music and let excitement roll over me as I thought about embarking on this new adventure. Was I sad about leaving Florida? Not really. Okay, not at all. Jonathan would never know how selfish it was of me to suggest that we relocate Supernatural Computers from here-there-be-dragons Florida to Tennessee so he could be with his girl. I wanted a change probably more than he did, just for different reasons.

Jonathan and I had been best friends since the sandbox, and I'd miss his family, the Owenses, but my own kin had all hit the road running or passed on years ago. I kept my mother's trailer as a place where we could stay when visiting the Owenses. I had boxed up many of her things before leaving Florida, but it was hard. I think part of me was convinced that if I kept it like it was while she was living there, she'd walk in through the door one day, groceries in hand, and cluck at the sight of me plopped on the couch playing video games—a taco in one hand and a controller in the other. Not that it was feasible to play that way, but I'd made it work a time or twelve.

Maxine, aka Max, aka Maximus_Damage, had come into our lives through a more convoluted path. All three of us were gamers, into massive multiplayer online roleplaying games where you create a character and play online with people from all over the continent or even the world. We'd known her since an old game, *Guilds of the Ages*, was popular, and she and Jonathan, aka Wrath, had been like oil and water in there. Beginning a rivalry that would span a decade, lead to an epic romance, and take us on this journey to a new state to start over—this time as a team. Well, okay, *they* were the team.

I was Norman, aka Deathdrop, aka The Third Wheel. But online, we were still playing together as members of the same guild in the awesomesauce game *League of Magecraft*. Think of a guild like your squad in the game. They were the ones who were there for you, in good times and in bad. Like when they celebrated your birthday and gave you sweet loot, or booted you out for a month as a lesson when you pushed a wee prank a bit too far.

As much as I loved *Magecraft*, I didn't like thinking about its predecessor, *Guilds of the Ages*. A lot of crap went down in that game that not even Jonathan knew about, and if I let myself go back there and linger, I saw a confused, deluded seventeen-year-old boy facing a future of fighting on some foreign shore, who desperately wanted to pretend it wasn't going to happen. That there would be another path for me somewhere, somehow.

But no, I'd followed in my father's footsteps like my mother wanted and enlisted right out of high school—for all the good it did me. My mother was from a military family: her father was a war hero. She had married a military man who became a war hero. And with me? I'm sure she wanted to go three for three.

And then there was *her*. An amazing girl who was regrettably hurt by my fantasies, and she was the main reason I didn't let my thoughts stray back there too often. I didn't like feeling like scum, and hurting her like I did put me firmly in that territory.

As we entered Green Valley proper, my GPS let me know we were less than five minutes from our rental. It was as cheap as we could find and I wasn't expecting much, but I didn't need much. I'd lived in far worse places than a possibly moldy one-bedroom with a pull-out couch. Jonathan had insisted I take the bedroom, which I assumed was because he was going to be spending a lot of nights at Max's place, and to assuage his non-necessary guilt over the move. I'd told him we'd *Mario Kart* it out for who got the bedroom, but he was holding firm on me having it.

As I scratched my beard and sang along to the music, I bopped my head and took in the sights. Objectively, it wasn't a hopping town, but compared to where I was from, it was practically a booming metropolis. And there was a charm about it, all decorated for the holidays. We finally stopped beside a place called The Dew Drop Inn. The proprietor also owned the house beside the inn for long-term rentals, and it was just our luck that she had a first-floor apartment available.

We had to stop in front of the inn because parked by the rental house was a well-loved—okay, ramshackle—blue Jeep, and standing near it, two women and a kid playing jump rope. One of the women I recognized instantly. She was a beautiful, curvy, fair-skinned brunette, jumping up and down in excitement. I watched as my best friend leapt out of his truck, ran over to meet her and grabbed her around the waist, kissing her passionately. Feeling rather uncomfortable spying on their happy reunion, which I have to say was a tad enthusiastic for broad daylight on a public street, I turned my attention to the other woman, the one who was shooting daggers in my direction.

She was tall, lanky even, and had red hair that flowed straight down over her shoulders. I could tell she was pretty from even back here, but why the hate-stare? Women usually saved that for our first date. If I could find a sweet girl with a tolerance for gaming and patience with my disability, I'd be set, but I seemed to get matched up with every harpy in Florida when I'd waded into the online dating pool. I'd given up dating altogether years ago because not even my puppy eyes could hold up against the wrath of a woman like the one in front of me. I broke off eye contact, on the off chance she decided to turn me to stone with her glare.

Knowing my hip and left leg were going to give me hell when I put weight on them after sitting for so long was delaying me from joining the group, but I couldn't put it off any longer and be a creeper in my truck. Eventually I'd need to go to the bathroom if nothing else. I grabbed my cane from the back and slowly made my way out, wincing as I touched down on solid ground.

Yeah, that hurt even more than I had thought. Fuck. I put my right hand onto my left thigh and rubbed it, not able to stop the nerve pain, but at least it felt like I was doing *something*. What I really needed right now was to get inside, do some stretches, maybe lie down, and pop some painkillers. Nothing hard, though. I'd fought too long to get off those, so some acetaminophen or ibuprofen, mixed with some gabapentin for nerve pain, would have to do. I closed my eyes and heard the laughter of a child nearby. Must be the kid who was using the jump rope near the woman who looked at me with loathing in her eyes.

Despite the pain, it was hard to keep my trademark grin off my face for long, returning when I heard a familiar voice shout, "Norman! Get your ass over here for your hug."

I started over toward the group and a body slammed into mine. I wrapped Max up in both arms, my cane bobbing in the air behind her back. She was soft in my hold and felt nice, and at that moment I hated myself for thinking so. This was my best friend's girl. There were rules, and they didn't include thinking of your best friend's girl as anything but a friend, too.

Ah, it had always been hard with Max and me. I was beyond happy for her and Jonathan, but there were twinges of jealousy that bled through at times. Like when we were all eating dinner and I saw how they gelled together, and I wanted a girl just like her. But not *her*-her. She would never be mine, and that was that. I was thankful for our friendship, because it was one of the most important of my life, and I would forever be grateful to her for everything she'd done for Jonathan. And me.

The sound of the child's laughter increased in volume, knocking me back to reality. I let Max go and she beamed up at me, taking me by the right arm and winding her arm through mine, lending me some support as I walked over to the group by the rental. We stopped beside the tall, pretty, redheaded woman with the sour expression who had her arms wrapped around a little girl that looked five or six, with tawny brown skin and some beautiful natural black curls.

Max nodded at the pair and said, "I want you to meet my best friend in the world, Lois Washington, and her daughter, Elsa. Lois and Elsa, this is Norman Grant—Jonathan's best friend and business partner. Now that y'all are acquainted, I'm going to spend some quality time with my man while you get to know each other better. Sound good? Great!" She clapped me on the back and took off toward the front door of the rental, following Jonathan inside.

CHAPTER 3

LOIS

I paced as we waited for the boys to arrive, keeping one eye on Elsa and the other on the street they would likely be driving down. I could see the proprietor of The Dew Drop Inn peeking out through her curtains, as though waiting for something gossip-worthy to occur right there on the sidewalk. I'd forgotten this charming aspect to small-town living, and it wasn't something I had missed. All that was happening here was a librarian getting revved up to see her sweetheart, a library janitor getting fired up to see her sort-of ex, and a six-year-old playing jump rope on the grass.

I paced on the sidewalk. Max gave me a curious stare, asking, "What's with you today, Lo? You've been off all day. It's Saturday, the sun is shining, it's not freezing, and tonight we're all having my mom's famous pot roast after we help the guys move in."

I scrambled for an excuse, any excuse. "I feel like we should have recruited some more muscle for this endeavor. How do we know how much crap they're bringing?"

"To a furnished apartment? Not much, I would think. I mean, all the computer workshop stuff is coming to my garage, and we can let the boys do most of the heavy lifting. Oh, which reminds me. Don't give Norman any sympathetic help carrying stuff. He hates that, and he has better strength and control with his right arm than you might think."

I was about to ask what that meant, since it wasn't cryptic in *any* way, but was cut off by Max's small shriek as a blue truck hauling a U-Haul rounded the bend, followed by a large and noisy black truck, its back covered with blue tarps. Ah, the convoy doth arrive.

They pulled up behind the Jeep, and first out of the gate was Jonathan. He and Max were all over each other within seconds. Then there was Norman, sitting in his truck, observing the scene. I waited for him to hop out and join us. Instead, he simply sat there, taking in everything. He looked as close to that scrawny teen boy as I did to that goth-girl look I rocked in high school. I could see his dark blond hair was still shaggy, but now he sported a beard which was neatly trimmed but thick enough to place him in the "lumbersexual" category of men. I could see his hands on the steering wheel, and they looked solid, capable. In fact, that was the whole aura he oozed: solid, capable, and freaking hotter than hell.

I stood stock still as Elsa ran over to me, likely curious about the new arrivals but shy, and I wrapped her in my arms and stared into that truck, waiting for him to make the first move. Those butterflies from before were back, only it felt like they were rending my insides. This anticipation was killing me!

The truck door opened and the first thing I saw come out was a leg, then a cane.

"Norman! Get your ass over here for your hug," Maxine practically yelled, and with a wide grin, the tall blond man exited the vehicle and limped over, looking as though he was leaning heavily on the cane in his left hand. Was he in pain?

Within moments, he was wrapped up in her arms. I kept my face as neutral as possible, open and friendly even, one might say. They might say it, but they'd be wrong. I felt fierce. What had happened to Norman? He hadn't needed a cane back when we were seventeen. Of course, that was before the military. The *military*! He'd been wounded. I damn well knew it, he went to God knows where and was wounded. Was it a gunshot? An IED? Was he held captive?

I had to stop the train my thoughts were on right the hell now or I would be going places I couldn't handle, especially at this moment. I had this tendency to do what, according to Dr. Google—the only doctor I could afford for myself, most of the time—was called indulging in apocalyptic thinking. Once I got started, I could be thinking about a glass half empty and end up picturing the glass exploding, sending shards flying everywhere and blinding a pack of nuns.

No more disastrous thinking about Norman and whatever happened to his leg. He was free of Max's octopus-like hug and was managing to get around well on her arm, as though he were accustomed to the cane and it didn't slow him down. He was, at present, examining the back of the truck, making sure, I guess, that the tarps held and everything was okay. That was when he looked up and made eye contact with me, flashing me a wide grin.

Max nodded in our direction and the pair walked over, saying, "I want you to meet my best friend in the world, Lois Washington, and her daughter, Elsa. Lois and Elsa, this is Norman Grant—Jonathan's best friend and business partner. Now that y'all are acquainted, I'm going to spend some quality time with my man while you get to know each other better. Sound good? Great!" She clapped Norman on the back and took off. Great? No, not great! Rewind, Max!

"Lois, hello," he said, smiling politely. "I've heard a lot about you and your daughter. Max talked about you when she visited us in Florida. She thought you'd make a solid addition to our *League of Magecraft* arena team."

"Well, I don't game anymore," I said back, sounding, even to my surprise, quite a bit salty. He didn't recognize me. I didn't realize until that exact moment how much I wanted him to, and how much it hurt that he didn't.

He nodded slowly, and stretched out his hand, saying, "It's nice to meet you, anyway." I waited for any glimmer of recognition in his eyes; seeing none, I decided to take his hand in mine. It was warm and his skin a bit rough, him obviously working with his hands. I was touching Norman Grant. How many times had I dreamt of this moment? I suddenly felt dizzy, dropping out of the handshake then shaking my head to clear it. *Focus, Lois.*

"Thanks. From both of us," I said, gesturing over to my baby who had wiggled free of my arms and resumed skipping. Okay, so six wasn't technically an infant anymore, but she'll always be my baby. I carried her under my heart for nine months of fear and terror and peace and completeness that I'll never forget. And she was not named after a character from *Frozen*. She bore the name of my Swedish grandmother, my Mormor, since she raised me after my mother's death. I never knew who my father was, so Mormor had been it for me, and it was my honor to name my child after her.

"She's a cute kid," Norman said politely, and grinned at me again. "So, do you come around here often?" He gestured to the sidewalk with his free hand.

I barked out a laugh before I could stop myself. Damn, Norman! He'd always had the ability to make me laugh. But laughter or no, this was it. Finally, after ten years, I would get my answers and I would knock the smug expression right off that handsome face. That handsome face which had no clue who I was.

"No, I'm a recent arrival in Green Valley myself. I moved here three weeks ago from New York City," I said pointedly. Still no recollection on his face.

How could he not know? Had whatever calamity that befell his leg also injured his brain? We'd emailed each other pictures, for God's sake! Of course, back then I looked what some might call completely different, but I was still the same person. I wasn't totally unrecognizable, was I?

Well, if he wasn't going to acknowledge our previous relationship, maybe I shouldn't, either. Unless he did have a brain injury. I'd have to stealthily find out. And if there was one thing I was skilled at, it was subtly ferreting out information.

~

"Mr. Norman, what happened to your leg?" Elsa asked from the couch she was sitting on, playing with her favorite stuffed bunny. It had been two hours so far unloading the truck and unpacking things inside, and we were almost finished, when out dropped that bomb from my kid's mouth. I shouldn't have been surprised; Elsa was a curious child and spoke her mind, even after I continued to do my best to teach her when and where it was appropriate.

"I'm sorry, Norman," I said, helping Max put down the last box and looking to where the guys were grabbing us all drinks from the ancient fridge. "Don't feel pressured to answer her. And Elsa! What do we say to Mr. Norman?"

She chewed on her bottom lip for a moment and then, as though guessing, said, "Mr. Norman, could you *please* tell me what happened to your leg?" I couldn't help turning my face away from her so she couldn't see my mouth twitch, then I turned back and kissed her on the forehead, running a hand over her curls.

"At least she's polite," Jonathan said helpfully.

"It's all good, I don't mind answering," Norman said, carrying his drink over to the couch and sitting down beside Elsa, handing her a juice box. "Curiosity is cool, and I appreciate that you asked so nicely." I watched as the man who was the boy I'd loved turned to my heart, my daughter, and said, "A long time ago, I was a soldier," he began. Ah ha! I knew it. The military had done this. "Well, I was sent to a country called Afghanistan. I can help you find that on the map later, if you'd like. The place I was stationed was small, but we had to go out every day on patrol anyway, to make sure that the bad guys weren't moving in on the village nearby. One day, when we were out in a Jeep—"

"Like the kind Ms. Maxine has?" Elsa interrupted.

"Not really, but sort of," Norman said. "Um, Lois, should I keep going?"

At my nod of assent, he continued, "There was an accident, a bad one, because we drove over something dangerous—a little bomb that was placed in the ground on the road. My story isn't scaring you, is it?" With wide eyes, Elsa shook her head. "Anyway, I made it out of the Jeep even though it crashed, but my hip, this part here?" Norman pointed to his left hip bone. "And my legs, especially the left one, got hurt badly. The rest of the story is boring, about how I did exercises in the hospital for a long time, and now I have to walk with a cane, mostly."

By this point I was standing beside Elsa's end of the couch, and had one hand on her shoulder, rubbing in gentle circles. Here I'd been plotting for the last two hours how to get that information, and all it took was a curious and slightly rude child. "You were lucky, weren't you? To get away from the Jeep?" she asked in an awed voice.

"You know what, I think you're right," Norman replied. He reached over toward Elsa's head and then stopped his hand just shy of her hair, pulling his hand back. "Whoops, sorry."

"Whoops, what?" I asked, genuinely confused as to what he'd say.

"I was going to tousle her curls because she's so damn cute. But I realized like, last second, that I shouldn't touch her hair without her permission."

My thoughtful Norman. I nodded but said, sharper than intended, "Yeah, that pretty much applies to all body parts for everyone." I cringed inwardly at how harsh that sounded. I was hurting, but I didn't want to be hurtful to anyone else. "Sorry," I mumbled, looking into Norman's concerned eyes.

He opened his mouth, and then closed it again and nodded. "Fair enough," he said, and smiled at my daughter, clinking his soda can against her juice box. She smiled and clinked back, and I sensed a blooming friendship. *Great. Fantastic.*

CHAPTER 4

NORMAN

The smell of homemade food was mouthwatering as we made our way into the three-story Victorian house on the other side of town. As I wedged in with Lois and Elsa in the backseat of the blue Jeep, I'd been told by Elsa that this was where they lived, with an older single woman named Rose, Max's mother. Max filled in that Rose also struggled with agoraphobia, a type of anxiety disorder which made it difficult for her to go out in public, and I got the feeling that she wasn't accustomed to large social gatherings of late. She looked overwhelmed at the barrage of people at her door, and I heard Lois lean down—seriously, the older woman couldn't have been five feet tall—and say softly to her, "If this isn't okay, we can all troop right out of here and go back to the boys' for pizza. Or we can pack up this delicious-smelling dinner and take it with us; whatever you want, Rose."

The older woman visibly swallowed, and then smiled brightly when Elsa ran up the front steps and grabbed onto her waist, almost knocking her over. Rose leaned down and kissed Elsa's forehead, then included the rest of us in that smile, giving us our marching orders. "Boys, you are just in time for one of you to put the leaf into the dining room table. I don't know why I ever bothered taking it out, but it looks like we'll need it in from now on if we're to have proper dinners every weekend. Everyone else, you get Elsa cleaned up and then help in the kitchen. I need a volunteer to set the table." She shot a pointed look at Jonathan.

I raised my hand and said, "I've got it, and the leaf." I extended that hand toward her, and she looked down in surprise and took it, giving it a firm shake. "Norman Grant. Thank you for having me—and all of us—in your home this evening, Mrs. Peters."

"Manners!" Rose exclaimed. "How nice. And none of this Mrs. Peters nonsense; you may call me Rose." She was seemingly oblivious to the snort I heard coming from Lois's direction. She'd been a tad surly ever since the moment I'd arrived. Had I dishonored her in a former life? As Rose shooed me into the dining room and then showed me the leaf and the highboy with the dishes, I wondered if I could ask Rose about her tenant while we were alone.

"Rose," I began, leaning my cane against a chair and pulling the table apart so I could heft the leaf into place, "is Lois having a bad day or something? I mean, does she seem off to you today?"

"Hmm? Lois? Why no, she seems fine to me. Sweet as pie, that one. Core of steel, though. You can feel it; she's got a strength in her. That's how she's gotten through everything she's had to deal with. Well, that, and the love of that child." I got the need to be a Mama Bear in this world sometimes, being raised by a single mother myself, but *sweet as pie?* Was she serious?

The leaf now in place, and with me laying out the napkins while Rose followed along and handed me a giant pile of silverware, the rest of what Rose said sunk in: *everything she's had to deal with.* I did some quick math. If Elsa was six, as she mentioned three times since we'd arrived, Lois must have gotten pregnant when she was in her late teens or early twenties, based on her looks. That couldn't have been easy for her, being so young. I suddenly wanted to know Lois's story, all of it. I wanted to understand why she was so prickly toward me, or was it all men? Was she shooting those death glares at Jonathan, too? What had the world done to her?

After dinner, we retired to the parlor, as Rose called it, a fancy-ish room that had seen better days but was impeccably clean. I settled into a wingback chair and Jonathan grabbed a stool from another spot and carried it over, lifting my left foot for me and placing it on the furniture. I can't say I wasn't grateful at being coddled a bit, and my best friend knew I hadn't had time to rest after the drive and moving our junk into the rental. I had been able to take some pain pills earlier, but the Tylenol didn't hold me too long when my leg acted up on days when I was sitting up for long periods or doing a lot of physical activity without resting now and then.

I saw a flash of relief on Max's face when she saw me set up with the stool.

I couldn't help but look to Lois next, to see if she'd noticed what Jonathan had done. She was staring straight at me, her head cocked to the side. Caught looking at me, her cheeks turned pink and she abruptly turned her head to Elsa, who was playing on the floor with a *Star Wars* LEGO set. She seemed like a great kid. Charmingly chatty, and smart—if how fast she assembled that kit was any indication of intelligence.

While Max and Jonathan set about making a fire, I checked out the room. I loved big old houses like this one, ones that had a sense of history and where the walls practically whispered to you if you listened closely. I grinned when I caught sight of another subversive cross-stitch that was hanging over the fireplace. They were sprinkled throughout the parlor, kitchen, and dining room, and I knew Rose had a sense of humor from that if from nothing else. This one was copied from that internet meme about the cross-stitch being proof of having the patience to stab something ten thousand times.

Rose walked in carrying a tray with a pot of tea, a stack of cups, and cream and sugar on it. As she set it down on the coffee table, she said, "The sink is dripping in the kitchen. We've tried everything, but it keeps making that drip-drip noise all night. Think there's anything you can do?"

While I knew she was talking to Jonathan, I jumped in. I didn't know why I was so eager to spend more time around the redheaded sour puss, but I couldn't seem to help myself. There was something magnetic about her, from her angry flashing eyes to the blush when she was caught staring at my leg. I wanted to know what her deal was when it came to me, and I figured the best way was the direct approach.

"I've got it," I said, nodding at her and Rose. "That is, if you don't mind me poking around with your plumbing. Er, that sounded wrong. I mean, your pipes. If you don't mind me poking your pipes. I have experience if that helps. I grew up learning chores like that from my uncle. He was a handyman."

"That would be fantastic, wouldn't it, Lois?" Rose asked as she poured the tea. She handed me the first cup, and I accepted it gratefully while Lois murmured, "Yes, fantastic." From her tone, I could tell she'd rather have a colonoscopy than see me again in their home.

"Mr. Norman, can I play with your cane?" Elsa asked, scooting across the floor, clutching her X-wing in one hand. She looked up at me with wide, earnest eyes in a gorgeous shade of blue-grey and flashed me a smile that revealed dimples. How could anyone say no to this kid, like, ever?

"Honey, canes aren't toys," Lois said, sitting down cross-legged on the floor beside her daughter. This close to me, I could make out more clearly the splash of freckles across the bridge of her nose and under her eyes, which were a stunning green. Her skin was pale, and she had what looked like a natural peachy glow to her cheeks. It was supremely bizarre how every time I looked at this woman, she became more attractive to me, even if she obviously didn't like me without being bothered to get to know me first. Lois picked up a bowl of bricks and asked her daughter, "Why don't you play with your tauntaun instead?"

"I don't like putting together the tauntaun—he winds up as a sleeping bag anyway," Elsa stated. I let out a burst of laughter which I quickly covered up with a cough at Lois's disapproving glare. But hey, I wasn't the one who let my six-year-old watch *Star Wars*. I mean sure, the Ewoks and the droids were cute and all, but what about all the hands getting cut off? Or the gigantic space worm? That shit was traumatizing if you saw it too early. I'd had nightmares as a kid that Jawas were going to kidnap me and sell me for parts.

"Hey, kiddo," I said, and both Lois and Elsa whipped their heads in my direction. Odd. "Um, Elsa, I mean. Would you mind if I put together your tauntaun for you? With your mommy?"

Lois looked like the last thing on Earth she wanted to do was put together a bowl of LEGO bricks with me. I waggled my eyebrows at her to get her goat, and she narrowed her eyes at me while Elsa replied, "Sure. I'm going to blow up the Death Star." She got up and made *pew pew* noises, advancing around the room, flying the X-wing with her right hand. With the daughter now gone, maybe I could get to what was bothering the mother.

I carefully lifted my left leg off the footstool, and then slid down onto the floor with an ungraceful plop. Wincing a little, I covered it with a smile and clapped my hands together, facing Lois. "Okay! Bring that bowl this way, madame, and a tauntaun shall we have."

"And a Han and Luke," she said softly, with a small sigh of resignation, handing me the instructions but keeping the bowl planted firmly beside her. I got the sense that Lois liked being in control of things, even if it was merely a tauntaun that was destined to become a sleeping bag. Well, no problem there; I scooted a bit closer and spread the directions out on the floor between Lois and myself. This was kind of cozy, and as she and I put the figures together, I tuned out the buzz and chatter of the rest of the room. Though I did notice Lois looking up frequently and keeping an eye on Elsa, who was, rather disturbingly, pointing her X-wing at a globe of Earth and making even louder *pew pew* sounds.

"She's a good kid, huh?" I asked, hoping to start on the right foot with her this time.

"Well, obviously," Lois replied, one side of her mouth pulling up into a grin. "She's only attempting to blow up the very planet we live on." I knew it; the key to defrosting Lois's icy exterior was to talk about her daughter. I scrambled for what I could say about a child I'd known for a few hours, and the most interaction we'd had was sharing war stories and then I'd helped cut up her pot roast at supper. Think, Norman, think!

"She sure put that kit together fast. And it was brand new. That was impressive for a kid her age. I think so, anyway."

"Mmhmm," Lois murmured, and slapped the head on the tauntaun, placing the completed creature back in the bowl. "So, should you do the honors, or should I?" she asked, mischief in her bright eyes.

"The honors?" I asked, genuinely confused, and also taken aback by the smile I saw break out on Lois' face.

"Of getting your lightsaber ready and having mini-Han slice that open. And voila! We have a sleeping bag."

I couldn't help it; in that moment, it was the funniest thing I'd ever heard, because it was Lois and she was talking to me like a regular person, not like a pebble in her shoe. We both burst into laughter and shared a smile. Just when I thought we might be getting somewhere, though, she swerved a one-eighty on me.

"It's time for Elsa's bath, actually. You'll excuse us." And with that she was up and away, off to grab her kid and head up the stairs. I sat there dumbly, wondering how fortunes could change so fast, and practically shrieked when Jonathan's hand landed on my shoulder, taking me by surprise and making me almost piss myself.

"Don't take it personally, Norman. I've heard that she's a ball of sunshine wrapped up with a layer of common sense. You must bring something special out in her. So hey, you should take it personally. Sorry."

I swatted his hand away, irked at my failure to figure Lois out and discover what her problem with me was. Well, at least there was still a dripping sink in my future.

CHAPTER 5

LOIS

As I sat on the edge of the tub watching Elsa meticulously count bubbles in her bath, my angst was deep. What had I been thinking, bailing on Norman like that? I'd been raised with better manners than that. And I had shamelessly used my daughter as an excuse when it wasn't even her bath time. I'd been scrambling, because sitting there on the floor with Norm—no, *Norman*—I had felt like I was starting to enjoy myself when I was damn well supposed to be feeling like ripping his face off.

I swear, it was like when he slid down on the floor beside me and wanted to do LEGOs together, I was transported back to my seventeen-year-old self, feeling all fuzzy in my head and nervous in my stomach because Norman wanted to spend time with me. Common sense had fled, and I was overcome with all that leftover teenage longing. And hormones. God, he had smelled good. All earthy and piney and… Okay, he smelled like soap and a splash of cheaper cologne, but it called to me in a feral way. His mischievous eyes, so wide and brown, had met mine over the bowl of bricks and, as the cliché goes, my heart skipped a beat. A beat! More like I felt like I was going into a full arrhythmia. And so, I had done the only reasonable thing: I grabbed my daughter and fled for the hills.

I knew I needed to decide what to do about Norman and this whole odd situation. I didn't want to draw it out into this big awkward *thing*, but I also wasn't sure I was ready to pounce on him in all my justified wrath, either. I knew what I needed, and it wasn't the sage wisdom of a six-year-old or Rose's well-meaning motherly advice. I needed my best friend, and I needed to finally tell her the secret I'd kept all these years.

~

"You *what*?!" Max screeched over Skype that night. Yes, we lived in the same town, and I could have told her this at any time, but I preferred to do it when I wasn't chasing after Elsa or tired right after work on one of our drives home. I was presently snuggled down in my bed in my favorite flannel granny nightgown—a gift from Rose—while Max was across town similarly attired, but in flannel kitten-print pajamas. We both had our tablets in bed and were chatting while Jonathan was spending the boys' first night in Tennessee in the rental in solidarity with Norman.

"I said," I replied calmly, "that I used to have a long-distance relationship with Deathdrop. Norm."

"Oh, don't call him Norm; he hates that nickname."

"But that was my special… Oh," I said, letting that sink in. I guess he wanted as little to do with me as I had to do with him after everything went down and he had taken off for boot camp. I didn't know how I felt about that, except so embarrassed I stuck my head under the blankets and moaned.

"Lois, stop being a turtle! Come out and tell me the story. I won't judge, okay?" Max's voice floated from the tablet, and I let out a grunt of frustration and peeled the blankets back, poked my head out, picked up the tablet, and told my story. All of it, from meeting him in *Guilds*, to keeping our friendship a secret because I knew Max barely tolerated him and Jonathan, to our on-the-down-low Romeo and Juliet—minus the deaths—love story.

"And he sent you a breakup email out of nowhere one day? When you'd even

already found an apartment for both of you in New York? That doesn't sound like Norman. He's a prankster at times online, sure, but he's also *so* responsible offline. And he's the best friend anyone could hope to have, other than you, Lo. So, what changed?" Max's brow was furrowed, and she looked as confused as I had felt off and on for ten years.

I thought back to that damn letter, and the never-forgotten words danced in my head. *I have to tell you something that will hurt you and for that I have many regrets. I will not be joining you in New York… There will be no point in waiting for me, as I've put aside childish dreams. Please don't reply. I leave in the morning and drawing this out will only hurt you. Regards, Norman.*

"I don't know, honestly. He *had* been getting distant with me in the game, popping offline when I'd pop on, saying things about how his mom needed him, or he had chores, or some excuse. I thought he was getting nervous about graduation and the move to the city, you know, meeting offline. I mean, hell, *I* was nervous until I got that horrible email. I mean, he signed it: 'Regards, Norman.' Who in the nine hells tells the girl they are supposedly in love with, 'regards'? I was so angry, Max. Part of me still is. I think he's noticed the death glares I've been sending him. And I don't want to carry all this ugly anger again after I've moved on and put it behind me. But I guess if my reactions to him have meant anything, it's that I couldn't have really put it all behind me, right?"

Max was quiet for a moment. Then she said slowly, "Lois, do you know anything about Norman's parents? About why he went into the military?"

"His parents? Not much, other than he admitted his mother smothered him and practically shoved him into the service, and his father had drowned in the swamp near their home when he was a kid. What does that have to do with him and that email?"

Max scrubbed a hand over her face. "I think you need to talk to him, Lois. Have a real talk; tell him who you are. You look so different now, there's practically no way he would recognize you. There's no way *I* would even recognize you. And you have a different last name now. There are things about Norman's past that I think you should know, that I learned when I was down there staying with him and being there for Jonathan when he had his bipolar episode. But I don't think it's my place to tell you. It's like, serious stuff, Lo. I think… I think perhaps Norman was using *Guilds of the Ages*, New York, and his relationship with you to escape from the reality of his situation."

My stomach roiled. Max thought that our relationship was just an escape for Norman? How could I accept that when at the time it meant everything to me? "I need to go to sleep, Max. I can't… I can't digest any more of this tonight. I don't know exactly what to do, but I do need some time to think about it. Will you keep my secret, even from Jonathan, until I'm ready?" I asked in earnest.

"Of course, silly-pants."

"I'm not wearing pants."

"Hawt."

And so, with a smile, I logged off Skype and turned off my lamp, letting the darkness hide my inner conflict and ease my heartache.

CHAPTER 6

NORMAN

We had planned to spend Sunday at Max's garage, unloading the U-Haul and getting Supernatural Computers at a functional stage. Well, as my mom used to say, God loves it when you make a plan—so He can screw you over. She was cynical after my father's drowning and had moved away from the church, as if it weren't obvious with that pithy gem. Anyway, my Sunday plans were a bust when I awoke with my leg screaming at me, the feeling of fire and deep-seated ache stretching from hip to ankle. Speaking of my hip, it felt like it was being crushed in a vise and the pain shot across my lower back, which made me aware I'd have to be incredibly careful moving around today.

As luck would have it, I had anticipated this might happen because of yesterday's long-haul trip, so I blearily reached around to the bedside table where I'd stashed a glass of water, a cocktail of pain meds, and crackers to take the edge off my churning stomach. Man, how part of me wished I were still on the morphine at times like this. Or that I still drank too much. Anything to kill the pain, or at least numb my mind to it.

But I'd been down those roads, and I wasn't going there again after all I'd been through to get off morphine while in rehab for my broken body. Then it was my friendship with Jonathan that got me away from drinking too much beer when I'd returned home. He'd suggested a different outlet for my frustrations and my pain: a newer game at the time, *League of Magecraft*.

Once I'd had a bit of time to settle into that, I rebuilt Lucille, my computer, for the first time. And after an epiphany by either Jonathan or myself—who could remember when we practically shared a brain at times—Supernatural Computers was born. "Supernatural" because our hallmark was crazy custom builds, several of which had gone viral and brought us a steady business.

Which brings us to today, and officially moving our headquarters from Jonathan's garage in Florida to Max's garage in Green Valley. An upward rather than a lateral move, as far as I was concerned. A knock sounded at my door, and I answered for Jonathan to come in. He stood in the doorway, looking at me and letting out a puff of air.

"I see your bedside pill collection is gone and so's the water, so I'm guessing you're in hell," he said, leaning against the doorframe and crossing his arms. It would be so easy to be envious of Jonathan, with his perfectly fit body and easy stride. But I never could let myself go there, because bitterness would take me down to a dark place in my soul. Besides, he was my brother in all but blood, and I knew about the demons he had to fight living with bipolar disorder. Jealousy was a fool's game.

"My leg is messed up, and my hip and back. But it's fine. You know I can push through it. I need some time to let my meds work and I'll be ready to go to Max's. You said she and Lois actually already cleaned out the garage for us?"

Jonathan chuckled. "Yeah, those women are all about getting shit done. And I think they really want to see our business succeed, you know? I mean, I don't know about you, but I don't want to work out of a garage forever. But this is such a great shot for us for now. It's also one that doesn't have a firm date attached to it. We can wait to set everything up until you don't feel like crap, Norman."

I peeled back the covers and sat up, twisting until my legs were hanging over the edge of the bed. Ouch. I felt like someone had taken a baseball bat to my left ankle and hip, and once again cursed the fool who had gotten me into this situation—me.

"Well, for starters, we *are* paying a rental fee on that U-Haul. We can't keep our junk in there forever. Besides, I think that Max was getting pizza for us and trying to make a day of it. Let's get it over with. If you and Max have to carry a few more boxes and I have to sit and direct the flow of traffic in and out of the garage, then that's how it will have to be." It sounded good in theory, but I knew today was going to be rough. Jonathan looked at me with blatant skepticism, but nodded. Okay, it was on. We were so doing this.

~

"That is *so* enough for today," Max said. "Even my back is starting to hurt after this. The U-Haul is empty and it's just unpacking, which you guys can handle tomorrow, which is the start of the work week anyway. I think it's time for pizza and a movie. I'm officially pressing pause on this quest."

I leaned over toward Jonathan and said, "She's going all Maximus_-Damage on us. Who put her in charge, anyway?"

"I think she did, considering it's her garage and we're getting it rent-free," he replied.

"Fair point." I turned to Max. No sooner had the words left my mouth when a sharp stab of pain hit my lower back and my hip started to throb. "Actually, would you mind if I took some of the pizza to go? I think I need to rest for real, and if I head back to the apartment, I won't be in your way if you two want to get cozy." I winked at Jonathan, and Max snorted a laugh.

Max told us to wait a minute and dashed off to the cottage, only to reemerge holding a pizza box. Man, my friends were awesome. See, the thing about awesome friends was that you didn't find them that often. So when you did, you had to hold on to those unicorns tight and care for each other, through thick and thin. Max and Jonathan were that for me. The thing that troubled me about our situation is that I knew Lois was in that small circle for Max, and Jonathan had warmed up to her over some joint Skypes before we moved here. I didn't want to make waves when it came to one of my bestie's unicorns, who seemed to want to trample me to death. Okay, so maybe I was digging too deep into the metaphor, but I *had* wanted to be an English major. I liked metaphors.

Jonathan took the pizza box from Max, and she gathered me up in a hug. Then, with a wave, we were off, and I was left pondering my problem: how would I get Lois to hop on board the Norman Friendship Train?

By the time I'd made it through the pizza and half a season of *Bridgerton,* I had a foolproof plan. I knew how to get Lois to like me. All I had to do was convince her to join our arena team and play with us as a foursome. She said she didn't game anymore, but once a gamer, always a gamer. So maybe Norman Grant could get on people's nerves. But everyone loved Deathdrop. Online, I was charming, I was mischievous, I was *fun*. Maybe if she got to spend time with me in-game, she would want to socialize with me out of game, too. Get to know more of the real me, and we could all come together as a tight group of friends. I would love that, given that I knew exactly two people I could depend on in this whole state.

Plan forged, I was ready to put it into action. But when would I get to see her again? There was that going away party for Elsa tomorrow night Max had told me about this afternoon and invited me to. Hopefully my leg and back would cooperate and I would be there, ready to win Lois over and sway her to our team for some Deathdrop time. I rolled over to get a sip of water and hummed "Hammer Time" as I did so. This was going to be great; I knew it. I was kind of psychic like that.

CHAPTER 7

LOIS

I softly whistled "It's Beginning to Look a Lot Like Christmas" as snow slowly fell outside the library window I was cleaning. Granted, there wasn't a lot of snow, only what my Mormor would call a "light dusting," but it was enough to make me nostalgic for Christmases up North, or in Nebraska. Satisfied with the state of the windows—which I had cleaned thoroughly after finding some teenagers dry humping up against one—I prepared to do final checks and get things on my cart reset for tomorrow.

I was whistling to cheer myself up because I was morose that this was my last day with Elsa. It was time for our bi-annual tradition of me hauling her out of school (or preschool, as the case had been last time) and sending her off to France with her father. David would be flying into Knoxville tomorrow morning and staying overnight before flying back out with Elsa on the following day.

I had gotten permission from our head librarian, Thuy Nguyen, to take a later shift both days to run back and forth to the airport in Max's Jeep. I'd chatted with Beau Winston on my break earlier in the day, and he confirmed that the Nissan still had my name on it and that everything was fine with them receiving the down payment. I'd been terrified that the check wouldn't clear even though I knew I had the money, which I think was a leftover from my days of juggling bills and always being in over my head.

I'd refused to take the car until I had all the cash to buy it outright, and he was fine with that arrangement if I had reliable transportation in the meantime.

He had offered me the loan of a Dodge Neon until I was ready to take the Sentra, but I had refused lest someone else needed it. Two weeks from Friday, and it was an early Merry Christmas to me with my own car. By the time Elsa got back from France, I'd have a booster seat installed and all our favorite road songs loaded up and ready to go.

For Elsa's last night, everyone was coming over again, even though they'd just been on Saturday. The boys were bringing fried chicken and sides from a place called Genie's Country Western Bar, and Rose was making sweet tea. I was going to make a salad, and Max was bringing a stack of board games that were family-friendly, even though Elsa was precocious enough that I was sure she could play Scrabble or Carcassonne.

The first thing I wound up noticing, though, was that Norman wasn't in tow with Jonathan and Max. They explained that his hip was acting up too much after the trip here and the unpacking-palooza, and he needed another day to rest and recuperate and then he'd be fine. They said that he normally moved so smoothly you hardly noticed the cane, but the long car ride—around 500 miles—was too much all at once.

I nodded in understanding but felt disappointed that he hadn't come. I didn't know why; I should hate everything about Norman Grant. And yet, I thought of those wide, kind eyes; his rough hands and neatly trimmed beard in contrast to his shaggy head of hair, and part of me melted. While we had a fun time the other night my mind kept straying to him, hoping he wasn't in too much pain. Why did I care? I guess I didn't like to think of anyone in pain and alone. Yeah, that had to be it, and the reason I loaded up some Tupperware with food in it for Jonathan to take home to him.

I instantly recognized the figure of my ex, his six-foot-four-inch frame towering over

the others in the arrival hall in the Knoxville airport. His hair was cropped close to his head, which shocked me, because the last time I'd seen him, which had been last week on Skype, he'd had locs halfway to his waist. His eyes were a warm brown that held humor in them, and his rich, dark brown skin was as beautiful as ever. God, how I had loved David. I did love him even now, in a different way.

My counselor that I had seen after the breakup had told me that when you love someone like I had loved David, you can continue to carry them in your heart throughout your life. It doesn't mean you're still *in* love with them, only that they will always be a part of you, and that's okay. Back then, I had to give myself permission to carry David in my heart, because he had broken it so badly.

We had met when we were both freshmen at NYU, and had both come from small towns; me from Nebraska, and he from Georgia. We had an instant connection, and while I was still grieving Norman, I was making fast friends with David. We had so much in common—except gaming. David had no interest in it whatsoever. In my book, that made David the perfect friend.

By sophomore year, we had moved in together and that kicked off a whirlwind romance where we took each other's virginity. We experienced all the other great firsts of falling in love—except, it wasn't *really* the first time I'd been in love. But Norman was God knew where and David was there with me, so I let myself put Norman on a shelf way in the back of my mind and plowed headlong into a serious relationship. By junior year, I was unexpectedly pregnant, and we were hastily married. By David's senior year I had dropped out to care for Elsa, vowing to finish my degree later, only to be faced with the tearful admission of David's true sexuality and a stack of divorce papers which he insisted was for our own good.

When we started our relationship, David had promised me everything I had ever wanted in this world: friendship, partnership, and a home filled with children and pets and love. And then one day he ripped it all away over something he couldn't control, over something I couldn't argue with and neither of us could change. It still didn't stop me from resenting him and feeling that he should have known somewhere, deep inside, that he was gay all along and not stolen my heart. I was twenty-one, had no living family of my own to offer support, Mormor having passed on not too long after I discovered my pregnancy, and now was going to be a divorcée with a child. A baby I would be raising alone for the most part because David had met someone new, an exchange student, and with his graduation looming, he would be free to follow Philippe to France.

I shook off the past and smiled wide, walking over to meet him. "David," I said, reaching up and grabbing him into a hug. He laughed his deep, familiar laugh and leaned down, kissing my cheeks and then laying one on my forehead.

"The cheek kisses were from Philippe. That last smack was from me."

"As I assumed." I looped my arm through his and we comfortably walked together; David only having his carry-on, as this was a quick stop to get Elsa and not a long visit.

"So, what's new with my favorite girls, other than this snap relocation?"

"It wasn't snappy, and it was very necessary," I said, my hackles rising. I didn't really know why his question made me instantly angry, except for the fact that it almost felt like he was questioning my parenting decisions, and here I was, trying to do everything I could so that Elsa would have a good life. We were almost out of the airport, and I didn't want to bicker with David in the car. It was the Christmas season, and I wanted this short visit to be jolly, dammit.

David stopped walking and took my hand in his, looking down at me with what I thought was a deliberately neutral expression on his face. "I don't know what to think, Lois. You don't call me for help, you don't talk with me for advice about what's best for Elsa's future. You don't know what it's like to be Black in a small town in the South, Lolo. I do. I don't know if this is the right place for Elsa. She's more my color than yours. There could be… difficulties for her."

I thought about that for a moment and fumbled around for the right words. "David, I appreciate what you're saying, and your own experiences. You're right that I don't know what it's like to be a person of color living down here. But I'm going to remind you once: you lost the right to have input on where Elsa and I live when you left us," I said, my voice as even as I could make it. "There are several Black families and Black-owned businesses in Green Valley. Everyone we've met so far has been kind to both of us, and I've talked to Elsa's teacher and principal, and even though she's only been there for a few weeks so far, she's fitting in at school, making friends. And she's not the only Black or biracial child in her class. I know this move may have seemed sudden, but I was drowning in New York. We needed a change, and the place that offered us refuge was here in Tennessee. I'm not sorry I chose to take it."

"You would have all the refuge you need in France, at the vineyard. There's a caretaker's house on the property no one is using. Please think about it. We could raise Elsa together full-time: you, me, and Philippe."

I sighed. I knew that despite David and me verbally agreeing that I should have full custody, David wanted Elsa to live in France, but this was the first time I was included as a package deal. I was a little stunned at his offer, and caught off guard at the phrase, "you, me, and Phillipe."

"I'll think about it, okay? But don't expect me to say yes. I'm happy here, and Elsa is settling in nicely, getting used to the people."

David nodded and leaned down again and kissed my cheek. "I'm sorry,

Lolo. I just wish things had worked out differently with all of this. I hate that I'm not a full-time father to Elsa. When I left, I didn't know how much it would hurt to be apart from both of you. Letters and Skype and holidays are a decent compromise, but not great. But it's not fair for me to try to guilt you into moving across an ocean because I'm not happy. I made my bed and now I'm lying in it, I suppose."

"With a sexy vintner," I said cheekily, bumping him with my hip and changing the mood of the conversation.

"Yes," he said, laughing. "How about you? Anyone new in your life?" he asked as we resumed our walk toward my borrowed transportation.

"Sort of; not exactly," I said. "I'll explain on the way home. Do you remember I used to play a video game called *Guilds of the Ages*? Before we met?"

He stopped beside Max's Jeep and a pensive look came over his face. "Wait a minute," he said slowly. "You don't mean the guy you used to light candles for, what was his name… Norman?" At my nod of assent, he practically gasped, "Norman's back?! Why didn't this make the family newsletter?"

"Uh, because we don't have a family newsletter?"

"We will by the New Year," David promised.

"Daddy!" Elsa squealed as she ran across the yard at Rose's place, practically leaping into David's arms as he climbed out of the vehicle. He held her and planted kisses all over her face and tickled her belly. She laughed and wiggled to get down, but then changed her mind when she realized he had shaved his head not too long ago, and there was new, short growth. "Your hair is all gone," she said, her eyes wide. She reached up a hand and gingerly petted the hair that was there.

"And your hair has gotten longer since the summer," David said, touching her bouncy curls.

"We're both different," she said.

"But not where it really counts," I offered, wheeling David's carry-on behind me and starting up the path to Rose's front door. She had graciously opened her home to David for the night, offering up the final guest room which was on the rarely used third floor. I did some cleaning up there and made the already-spotless room extra-spotless for my neat freak ex, though he would never complain about the accommodations. David was good like that, not a snob in any way. When he found out I had become a janitor after working as a PR assistant, he simply asked if I was happy about it. I was so thankful I could tell him—without lying—that I was.

Dinner, prepared by new BFFs David and Rose, was a delight, and conversation flowed smoothly, mostly around Elsa, with David sneaking in questions about Green Valley. He stopped trying to play Sherlock when I gave him a look across the table followed by a swift kick underneath it, and from then on out it was all fine. We did the dishes as a group, except for Rose whom David and I insisted watch *Jeopardy!* and rest a bit.

For Elsa's bedtime, we decided to divide and conquer, an approach that worked well in co-parenting. David got Elsa her bath, while I went through the packing checklist I had made up and meticulously went over her luggage and carry-on to make sure she had everything she would need. I got teary-eyed as I put her fluffy bunny into the carry-on, knowing it would be as hard as ever to say goodbye in the morning, but this was simply the way it was.

Elsa came barreling into the room in her favorite fuzzy purple pajamas and smelling of coconut body wash. She climbed up onto the bed and, practically bouncing, asked, "Why did you cut off your hair, Daddy?"

David sat down next to her and tickled her side, Elsa bursting into shrieks of delight.

"I wanted to make a change, little bird. Like you and Mommy and this change from New York. Are you happy here, *ma cherie*?"

"*Oui,* Daddy," she answered in the affirmative. "Mommy and I shared a room in New York, and now I have my own, and there are butterflies and pretty pictures. And the library where Mommy works has a lot of books I like. It's smaller than the one back in New York, but the people are as nice."

At the mention of books, I hoped she got some sleep tonight and didn't sneak in reading under the covers with her flashlight. I gave her carry-on one last go-through, and asked Elsa if she was sure she didn't need her rabbit to sleep. She got under the covers and I leaned down and kissed her goodnight, a mix of joy and wonder running through me that this beautiful, smart little girl was mine.

When we'd first gotten married, David's parents had flown up to New York to meet me, and his parents felt like family right away. His mother in particular was a godsend and a wealth of information about being pregnant. When things started to fall apart in New York, I was on the verge of asking my former in-laws if they would take us in. They had stayed in contact with Elsa and me over the years and loved their granddaughter to bits. David, however, was estranged from his father after coming out of the closet, and I didn't want to make things awkward by moving in when I was on Team David.

Then Max had extended an offer to live with her in her cottage, which morphed into an invitation from her mother, Rose, to live in this big, practically empty Victorian. Rose said we had brought new life into the house and into her heart. I was more than happy to do so.

~

The next morning, we were up before dawn to get Elsa and David off to the airport. Their long day of travel started early, and we knew from a few years of doing this to always overestimate how long it took to get an animated child ready in the morning. Elsa was chatty and got wired whenever it was time to travel. Too young to remember when it was me, David, and her, she loved Philippe and the various farm and garden chores there were to do on the vineyard. It was like a big, sprawling playground for her. Even in winter, there was something to keep her occupied outdoors most of the time. Not to mention she was on cloud nine that it was almost Christmas.

While David made sure Elsa got dressed in her travelling outfit and checked that she hadn't unpacked anything from her carry-on overnight, I made up a full breakfast. I set the food in the oven to keep it warm and walked back up the stairs, hearing Elsa's high voice and David's deep one as I advanced on her bedroom. They were both sitting on the bed, the carry-on in between them and Elsa looking ready to fly. When Elsa saw me, she smacked a kiss on his cheek and then leapt off the bed to run to me, flinging herself at my waist and giving me as large a hug as she was able.

"What was that for?" I asked, leaning down and kissing her forehead.

"Because I love you and I won't see you for a long, long time," she said seriously.

"It's only a month, sweetheart. You know how fast that will go on the vineyard. Right, David?" I said, feeling good in these moments when we were together as a family. All we were missing was Philippe, but even he was here in spirit when Elsa and David started spouting off French to each other. So, it was a non-traditional family, but it was still a family. We had worked hard to make it that way, putting aside hurt feelings, guilt, and self-loathing to make it as happy a family we could for the sake of the little girl we all loved.

"Yes, and there's a surprise waiting for you," David teased.

"Did the baby horse get borned?" Elsa asked, clutching her hands to her face like she was trying to contain her elation over the possibility of seeing a new foal.

"My clever little bird. Yes, there's a brand-new baby horse for you to help us take care of, if you think you can handle the responsibility. And something you can think about on the plane is what you want to name the foal. She's a girl."

"I can name her! Oh, *je suis très heureux*. I mean, I'm so happy, Daddy. Sorry, Mommy."

My considerate daughter. She was going to be bilingual, I just knew it, spending so much time in France. She was already far more proficient in French than I was, but she knew the family rule was that it was rude to exclude someone from the conversation if they couldn't speak the language you were talking in.

I was learning French, mostly as a hobby, but also so Elsa could speak either French or English when she was home with me. I didn't want to stifle her because I couldn't pick up a language. And who knew? Maybe when Elsa turned eighteen she would decide to move to France, and I would be the one traveling back and forth, or moving there, too.

I shelved those thoughts, refusing to think of my baby as a teenager spreading her wings and flying on her own. For now, she was mine—and David's and Philippe's—and that was that. I reached down to grab her and tickle her, making her squeal and run laughing into David's arms. After watching them together for a long moment, I took her hand and led her down the stairs to our last meal together before the New Year.

CHAPTER 8

NORMAN

My body felt great, the sun was shining, and the birds were chirping, all making for a fantastic day in my world. Supernatural Computers was up and mostly running, with almost every box unpacked, tools and parts meticulously arranged by Jonathan and Max. Go figure, having a cataloguing librarian around was useful for classifying all our shit. I focused on getting everything we needed for our current order on the workbench so I could do what I did best. Build.

I hummed "Iron Man" as I installed a motherboard and envisioned a workshop like Tony Stark's, complete with Dum-E on fire extinguisher duty. As it was, Max's garage was a step above what we had in Florida in terms of comfort, though we'd had more time to make the Owens' garage our own. With a little more time and elbow grease, this place would be near perfection. The single drawback was that we had temporarily stopped offering custom desks until we came up with a more permanent build site.

Max had offered up her backyard for us to expand the garage and put up a small building, but we weren't sure we wanted to intrude on her property more than we were. The same deal went with Rose's house; she had an outbuilding no one was using but she was already hosting two Tennessee newbies. Did she need the buzz of a saw and the thwack of a hammer going all afternoon on top of that? Nope, not if we were running this operation, anyway. That woman was what my mom would have called a "real lady," and both Jonathan and I were charmed by her. Neither one of us wanted to make life more difficult for Rose.

Thinking of Rose, that brought me around to the Case of the Dripping Sink. As soon as I was done working on a few more parts of this project, I was going to take off early if it was cool with Jonathan and head over to Rose's place. I had found my uncle's toolbelt, given to me when he died, and all I needed to do was raid the toolbox and load it up.

I full-on sang "Iron Man" now as I worked, because even though I knew Lois wouldn't be there, I would get to spend some time with Rose. She had promised cookies in exchange for the sink repair, which excited me. The last time I had homemade cookies was when Olive, Jonathan's oldest sister, had made us some, and they were more like briquettes than anything else.

Once I got to a natural stopping place, I poked my head up and turned to Jonathan. "I'd like to run over to Rose's to fix the sink like I promised, since I'm feeling good today and am capable of crawling under a countertop right now."

"Sounds fine by me. I'll finish up the project you were working on here in the meantime. And hey, call me if you need help."

"Ha! You want to get your mitts on my cookies!"

"Are you kidding? Of course I do. Have you tried Max's baking? Good lord, there's nothing she can't burn to a crisp. She tries, bless her heart, but she's a frequent flyer at the Donner Bakery for a reason." Jonathan placed an empty chassis on his workbench, and I knew he was organizing things in his head to get the next two orders straight.

With the move, we were backlogged, but we could catch up if we worked a weekend now and then, and especially if we could wrangle Max into helping us when she wasn't working at the library. That woman could build a mean machine when she had the time or inclination.

I arrived at Rose's place at around noon, fully expecting to find her buzzing around her kitchen or watching a soap. However, when I'd knocked on her door, nothing. No bright and cheery face greeting me, no one shouting for me to come in. I surmised Rose must be out for one of her short walks. She was gaining ground in her battle with agoraphobia and walks around her block were one way she was doing it. Figuring she'd be home in short order, I decided to follow her instructions should I pop by when she wasn't there and use the spare key under the flowerpot by the side door, which led directly into the kitchen.

Whistling some BTS because I felt so fine today, I sang the English parts of "Fake Love" while I found the ceramic flowerpot hand-painted with blue flowers. I'd had a thing for Korean pop bands for a few years now. Well, ten to be exact, when the girl from *Guilds of the Ages* introduced me to them. Peily… Why did I keep thinking of her lately?

Sloughing off feelings of guilt today, I took the key in hand and first peered through the thick curtain lest I find Rose naked or something. Seeing nothing but fabric, I turned the key and opened the door, to be greeted with the slim figure of someone standing in front of the open fridge, their back to me, only covered by a towel. A tiny towel. A tiny, pink towel. Holy shit, I *was* psychic.

Then it hit me: no way was this Rose. Rose wasn't even five feet tall, and this beauty was at least five ten. Even though the unmistakable red hair was up in another pink towel, it was Lois. Lois practically naked. Shit!

The floorboard creaked and she swung around, earbuds now ripped from her ears and held in one hand, another hand holding a sandwich. She did what I suppose any reasonable person would do in her situation: she screamed, just as her towel went sailing to the floor. I yelped, and turned around as fast as I could, closing my eyes lest I get a glimpse of her reflection in a window. Backing up slowly, I got down on my hands and knees and put my cane down on the floor and continued to back up until I felt a towel. I reached behind me, and unfortunately, got a handful of smooth calf instead.

"Don't touch me!" Lois, seemingly back into her body from wherever she had fled in her startlement, almost shouted.

"I'm trying to help you!" Where the hell was that damn towel? And why was it so small?

"Well, stop!" She reached out with a foot and pushed at my right leg, gently, I noted, but firmly. I felt around some more, and aha! As the door swung open again and Rose entered, I held the towel aloft, triumphant. I wondered at the image we presented: Lois naked in the kitchen with me kneeling at her feet, facing away from her and holding up a towel. She made a huge noise of frustration and snatched the towel from me, and I heard a rustling noise and then, a pained, "I swear, Rose, whatever this looks like, it isn't."

"Well honey, I have no problem with you entertaining a male visitor while Elsa and I aren't around to see it, but I would expect it not to be in the middle of the kitchen in the middle of the day." Rose sounded tickled, but I knew Lois would not be.

"Trust me, Rose, no one here is being entertained," I piped up, grabbing my cane and getting to my feet. I pointed to the handyman's belt around my waist, and then to her sink. "I'm here strictly on business. Truth is, whatever that… was, happened so fast I couldn't even begin to describe what Lois looks like naked."

"Norman!" Lois hissed at me, and I knew she was tempted to kick at me again. I moved slightly away from her and kept my eyes on Rose, who broke out into a peal of laughter.

"Lois dear, why don't you get a plate for that sandwich and head back upstairs? I can handle our houseguest here," the older woman said, grabbing a mint-green apron from a hook and tying it around her waist. Yes, focus on the apron, Norman. Not on the gorgeous, nearly naked woman moving around the kitchen behind you. The apron, with its embroidered woodland creatures and sprigs of ivy, look at that. Look anywhere and at literally anything except—

"Lois?" Rose called up the hallway. "Do you prefer snickerdoodles or chocolate chip?"

"Snickerdoodles!" she called back, and I couldn't resist the laughter that descended upon me.

Rose and I sat down at the kitchen table, eating warm snickerdoodles with cool milk. With the plumbing monster slayed and the drip destroyed, Rose was happy. But I was not. Lois still hadn't come back downstairs after her flight from the kitchen, and I worried that she was embarrassed when she had nothing to be embarrassed about. It was a situation that could have happened to anyone, and I didn't see anything, because I respected a person's right to not be seen naked against their will.

"So, what is it you're chewing on?" Rose asked as she polished off her milk.

"A cookie?" I replied, unsure of where we were going with this.

"Not in your mouth, Norman, in that handsome head of yours. You've been quiet ever since I got home, and that's not like you—or so I've heard. So come on, spit it out. You'll feel better about it."

I ran a hand through my hair, one of the things I did when I was nervous. "Why doesn't Lois like me? I mean, has she dropped any hints that you could tell me? I'm not exactly asking you to break any secrets she's told you, but there has got to be something she's holding against me, and it is driving me up the wall, because…" I trailed off, realizing something myself.

"Because you want to get to know her better. Because you like her? As in, how do you kids say, *like her*-like her?"

A small but troubled smile fell across my face. "Yes, I think I do. I know I've spent a short amount of time around her, but she's magnetic, isn't she? I mean, she draws you in with those eyes and freckles and that death glare. I want to know more. I'm interested. Intrigued."

"Infatuated?" Rose teased, and she wasn't that far off the mark. I practically was.

"Rose, do you know what her plans are for the holidays? Now that her daughter is gone, I mean. She staying here with you, or does she have family to go to somewhere?"

"No, no family for her, other than that beautiful child. Her mother died when she was young, and the father was never in the picture. She was raised by her grandmother, who passed while she was still pregnant. Her only family was David. And then, well, I'm sure Jonathan has filled you in on why that didn't last, poor lamb. But God has a plan for us all, and we are born who we are. There aren't many of us brave enough to live our truth, knowing we will hurt those we love in the process. David is a decent young man. I liked him very much."

"And the holidays?" I prompted, wanting to get away from the lovefest for Lois' ex and back to the topic at hand.

"Oh! Yes, the holiday. She has been invited to have Christmas here with me. Maxie and I kind of go nuts with the food, but we enjoy it. It took us a while after my Maximillian died to realize that we were allowed to be happy even though he was gone, so we always make a big thing of the holidays, even though it's just the two of us. Of course, this year Lois, Jonathan, and you are all invited. You can even spend Christmas Eve sleeping over if you like, and we can all be here to have a big breakfast and presents on Christmas morning."

I gulped, honored at being included in the group. "I-I don't know what to say. Thank you, Rose. For thinking of me."

"Of course! You're one of my Maxie's unicorns, aren't you?"

With Elsa gone, the dynamic of our group shifted, and that week saw Max, Jonathan, Lois and me hanging out almost every evening, usually at Max's cottage for joint cooking and a movie, or sometimes at Rose's place for the same thing. I felt like I was starting to break through Lois's shell when it came to however it was she felt about me.

Tonight, we were on double duty in the kitchen—no doubt an arrangement contrived by Jonathan—and I was keen on making enchiladas. I had brought all the ingredients, and when Lois looked at the pile I was pulling out of the shopping bags, she turned to me and said, "This looks like the makings of something delicious."

Startled, I stammered out, "Uh, yeah. Yeah, they're my mom's recipe for enchiladas. You've never known bliss until you've got your mouth wrapped around one of these." Realizing the possible double entendre to what I'd said, I turned a shade of red and grabbed the chopping board, while Lois, no longer able to remain stoic, burst into laughter. It was a sound that reminded me of everything good in my world: the ringing of bells at Christmas, or the laughter and happiness I brought my mother the first time she saw me back from my time overseas.

"I've never known bliss until I've had my mouth wrapped around your enchilada. Is that what you… You know what, forget it. Free pass on the most awkward statement of the evening."

"Hey, the evening is still early. And Jonathan can be at least as socially awkward as me," I replied, chopping up a red bell pepper. She stood beside me and snatched a piece of bell pepper to eat. I grinned and raised my eyebrows at her, but she only looked like she was feeling around twenty percent guilty.

"Madame Thief," I began, in a bastardized English accent, "if we are to have supper anytime this side of the New Year, you are going to get the chicken from the fridge and prep it while I keep working on the veggies."

"Fine," Lois complained a little, but I knew it was to get my goat, because she couldn't conceal her smile altogether. We worked well as a team, and I filed it away as a success.

A few nights later, we newbies got our feet wet at Genie's Country Western Bar. I danced with Max, then, at her prompting, I braved the potential wrath of Lois and extended a hand to her. Next thing I knew, we were slowly moving around the dance floor and she was smiling at me, for the second time in just three days.

Good Lord, had I accidentally triggered the Apocalypse? Or was she coming around to the conclusion that I wasn't a total asshole? We had gotten off on the wrong foot, and I was happy to see her warming to me long enough to dance and laugh in my company.

Even though all this socialization was taking away from my gaming time, I found myself happily settling into life here in Tennessee. The first time I'd run into Lois since the Flying Towel Incident was when she had stopped by Max's after work, and we were pulling in some extra hours in the garage-slash-workshop to make up for lost time. I had walked up to her to take a bag of groceries from her, when she leaned in close to me and said, "You don't say anything about what you did or didn't see. Got it?" Oh, I got it all right. I tried once again to tell her I hadn't seen anything, but she didn't seem in the mood to hear it. Or in the mood to fork over her heavy bags from the Piggly Wiggly. But that was then, and she was obviously trying to protect herself from further humiliation. Now, I had the beginnings of what I thought was a friendship.

Tonight it was wings and a movie, I think. I felt like we were leaving out Rose, but Max let me know that her mom could use the downtime from the constant press of having houseguests. She'd been living alone for so long that it wasn't a hardship for her to have an evening here and there to herself.

After Jonathan and I had finished up in the shop, we entered Max's cottage to the amazing aroma of baking wings and coffee. We all settled in for some serious eating, and to argue about what to watch tonight. Lois looked like she was enjoying the night out—until the topic turned to gaming. Then her face turned cross again, and she got up from the table to pick at her food at the counter. I seemed to be the only one who noticed the rapid downturn of her mood and her obvious discomfort, and I suddenly wished that I'd never had the idea to coax Lois into gaming again.

There was a story there, there had to be. How could anyone look so down at the mere mention of videogames? Had they somehow annoyed her beyond the realm of what an ordinary non-gamer would feel? Hurt her, even? I didn't know, but as I went through a mental rolodex of reasons Lois was upset, I got pulled back into the conversation by Max.

"She's got to join our arena team in *Magecraft*; help me convince her, guys. You know what a great healer she is, she *was* in your guild for a while in *Guilds of the Ages*, the traitor," Max teased, and the Coke I was drinking came snorting out of my nose.

I furiously wiped my face with the sleeve of my sweater and said, "Excuse me? Lois, that Lois, Lois *Washington*"—I pointed—"was in *our* guild?"

Max turned a deathly pale and looked to Lois, biting her lower lip. "Lo—" she started, before getting cut off.

"I guess the cat's out of the box, and it's very much alive," Lois murmured, sighing heavily and putting her plate down on the counter.

I felt lightheaded. It all came back, everything I'd shoved into the deep recesses of my mind. The rush of pure joy seeing *my* Lois pop online; the notification saying "Peily" was there. And now I knew *my* Lois was *this* Lois. This wasn't some random, often-prickly-around-me woman from New York, this was the girl I'd loved from Nebraska who dreamed of New York like a castle in the sky, and somewhere along the way wound up pregnant and living in small-town Tennessee. Why had I not made the connection before? So her last name was different; she had been married. I was such a fool.

I wiped my hands with a napkin and then got up, walking over to where Lois stood by the counter, staring at the floor and chewing on her lower lip, her eyes closed. I reached up with my right hand and cupped her cheek, my arm slightly shaking as the enormity of the moment rolled over me. Her eyes looked straight into mine, wide and liquid, and she ever so slightly leaned into my hand.

The single greatest regret of my life was standing there staring back at me, and for a moment I swore time warped and I was seventeen, looking at the emailed picture she'd sent me back during our *Guilds of the Ages* days. So her hair wasn't short or dyed black anymore, and she wasn't covering up her eyes with black smudges or those chunky plastic black frames; it was still her, and I hadn't seen it. Non-goth Lois was a stunning redhead with the same face under all of that seventeen-year-old girl makeup, and I'd been stupid enough to look right past the real her.

I thought back to those loaded statements she would make, and those cold stares when I first arrived, despite being all sunshine with her daughter and becoming fast and firm friends with everyone else in our little group. There was only one explanation: *she knew*. She knew who I was this whole time, and I hadn't recognized her right away as I should have. She must be so pissed. As if she had the same thought as I did at the same time, she batted my hand away, and took a step backward.

"Hey, kiddo," I said softly, putting my hand back down. I always called her that, because she reminded me of The Bride in my favorite movie, *Kill Bill*. The woman with a spirit so strong she could overcome any enemy, win any battle, and live on her own terms. "Looks like I screwed up. Again."

"I don't know what you're talking about," she said haughtily, even as her lower lip trembled.

"Don't do that with me," I implored, knowing I had no right to ask anything of her but hoping she would give me a chance I didn't deserve. "You knew I was Deathdrop from the start, and I didn't recognize you. I looked past you, and failed to recognize a woman who was a girl I lo—"

"No," Lois said, crossing her arms in front of her chest. "You don't get to say those words to me. You ditched me in an email! I walked my high school graduation in tears because of you. I went to New York alone, when it was supposed to be our dream we had together. For what? So you could get your Jeep blown up in Afghanistan!"

I saw Max and Jonathan get up and move to the bedroom and heard the door click, understanding they were giving us our privacy. Good. This would be easier without an audience. I swallowed hard and figured I deserved whatever tongue-lashing she was going to lay out, for the breakup email if nothing else. But if she would only listen, maybe I could make her understand. And if I listened to her, maybe I could understand what she was feeling, too. Time for honesty.

"That email was the shittiest thing I have ever done in my life, kidd—er, Lois. But I wrote it because I thought… Oh, hell, I thought it would be better, like ripping off a Band-Aid, instead of not showing up in New York to meet you. We were going to meet at the top of the Empire State—"

"I remember," she said brusquely. "That has nothing to do with this."

"It has everything to do with this," I countered. "We cared for each other, deeply. We were going to reenact one of your favorite movie endings because it was so darn romantic, and because I wanted to give you the world, including an epic romance like you deserved. But I couldn't, Lois. If I had been free to do what I wanted, I would have."

Confusion flashed in her eyes. "But that's what going to New York was all about! It was about us being free to make our own choices! All you needed was the cost of a bus ticket. I had enough from my Mormor to keep us afloat for a few months; plenty of time for you to find a job. We talked about all this! So what's your next excuse for lying to me and breaking my heart?" She shifted her gaze downward for a moment, as if she'd said too much, but then met my eyes dead-on. She wasn't letting me escape another second of this.

I ran a hand through my hair and exhaled loudly. "I never, ever wanted to break your heart. I'm not going to lie and say I didn't know you had feelings for me, because I know you did, but I'd hoped they weren't as deep as the ones I had for you. I thought that I could share New York with you as a dream we had together, not something that would actually happen. Because, for me, it never could. I *had* to enlist, even though I didn't want to. Fuck, I *really* didn't want to. The pressure from my family was huge, Lois. You have no idea. My grandfather served and got a box full of medals; my father was awarded a Purple Heart for his service during Desert Storm. They were freakin' war heroes. And then my dad drowned back home in a stupid accident in the swamp when I was still a kid.

"My mother had his picture and that Purple Heart on display smack in the middle of the living room, where you could never not see it. She wanted with all her heart to have me follow in his footsteps, and thought that the military would teach me how to, I don't know, be a man? Ugh, that's sexist as fuck, but she was old-fashioned in her thinking. Or she'd seen *Mulan* too many times, whatever. I loved her so much, and we were all the other had in a lot of ways. I mean, I was always welcome at Jonathan's house, but they weren't my family. Mom doted on me to the point of suffocation because she had no one else. And being a single mother isn't easy, as you know, and I wanted—I *needed* to make her happy. To fulfill her dreams, instead of mine, because I felt like she deserved it after everything she'd sacrificed raising me. So, after I turned eighteen, I sent you that email because I knew my time of living in a fantasy world was up. And I made it short and to the point because I thought if you hated me, at least you wouldn't miss me. Or mourn me."

She let out a loud huff. I noticed her eyes were wet, but I pretended not to. I reached out with my right hand, hoping she would take it. She looked at my hand at length and then nodded once, took it, and we did this awkward sort of handshake before I pulled her into a one-armed hug. We were almost the same height, so I pressed my cheek into her hair and said softly, "You look amazing, kiddo. I'm sorry I didn't recognize you, but in my defense, you *were* all gothed up in the photo I still have of you." God, her hair smelled amazing; like coconut and some flower I couldn't identify. I knew I loved it and I breathed it in deep, hoping she wouldn't notice.

"You look almost the same, hair all shaggy. A fair bit more ripped than back then. The beard is a nice addition," she commented, the first kind thing she'd said to me since we arrived. "But of course, I knew who you were for ages; that you were playing *Magecraft* in the same guild as Max. She would tell me tales of pranks and the idiots who pulled them. The name Deathdrop came up more than once. Who else is named after that dance move and had a bit of conflict with her? It didn't take a genius to figure out it was my Norman." I shuddered as I held her against me, at hearing her call me "my Norman."

"I would light candles for you, in churches I'd walk by," she said, her voice gone soft, and it was almost hard to hear her. "I'd say a prayer, and at home, I would check around news sites for casualties. If your plan was to make me forget about you, it failed."

I squeezed her tighter and breathed in deep the scent of her, pressing my lips to the side of her head for a scant moment. How many times had I longed for this all those years ago? And, to be honest, in the time since?

"I wrote to you, you know," I said cautiously, unsure if I would break our embrace. "In Nebraska. You wanted me to send you water from the Atlantic when we were kids, remember? It was about… five years ago, now. I guess I was checking in, seeing how you were, what you'd done with yourself. I figured your Mormor would know where you were and pass it on."

"You figured wrong. Mormor died while I was still pregnant with Elsa. I never got the letter."

"I'm sorry you went through that, Lois. It must have been so hard on you, the relocation to New York without any family to depend on with your mom and your grandmother gone."

"You remembered that?"

"I remember everything. Well, maybe not everything, I don't have a perfect memory, but I remember almost everything you ever said to me. Because it was all important."

She laughed, and looked absolutely freakin' radiant when she did so. "I call bullshit on the 'all important.' We talked about crap all the time that wasn't worth the bandwidth it was sent over."

I grinned. "Yeah, so maybe we did. But wasn't it fun?"

"Remember the time we worked out how we'd get to each other in the event of a zombie apocalypse?"

"I still think a *Cloverfield*-like event is more likely," I countered.

"Not that *Cloverfield* theory again!" She reached out and gently pushed at my chest, laughing. I got all aflutter in my stomach when she did, because she was initiating physical contact. And I wanted physical contact with Lois, even after all this time. But more than anything, I wanted our friendship back. I knew she was no longer the farm girl who dreamed of bigger things, and I was no longer the boy from the swamp dreading his future. We were in completely different places in life now. But the woman in front of me, she was someone I wanted to get to know—as Norman and Lois, not Deathdrop and Peily. And I would dedicate every iota of free time I could to it. In a non-creeper way, of course.

CHAPTER 9

LOIS

He knew. Norman knew who I was, and instead of me wanting to slap him silly for being such an asshole and hurting me all those years ago, I simply felt a kind of catharsis in the coming out process. It felt *good* to be there with him out in the open at long last, a fulfillment of a dream I thought would never happen. But I couldn't, wouldn't, let myself get carried away by schoolgirl dreams of romance again. Norman had let me down before, and I had next to zero immunity to his charms, even though I was no longer that teenager in an old farmhouse in Nebraska, longing for my guy in a trailer park so far away. So, now what? I guess it was time to stop the awkward silence that had descended upon us.

He obviously had the same idea, because he said, "So after Nebraska, you went to NYU? And Elsa? How—"

"Topics for another time, I think. I will tell you, but I've been so busy processing the fact that it's *you* and we're *here*, and before Elsa was born, you were the most important person in my life, after Mormor. And then you were just… gone. Can you respect that I might need a bit more time before dropping my whole life story?"

He huffed out a small sigh, ran a hand through his hair, and nodded.

"I have an idea," he said. "Come out to dinner with me. Like a real sit-down dinner, so we can talk."

I considered my options. Dinner, with Norman? Could I last that long around him, the two of us, and keep my walls up? I would not allow myself to go tumbling ass over teakettle for this man! A potentially romantic dinner was like step one on the path to certain doom.

"Coffee and a doughnut," I countered, remembering the out of this world doughnuts that had been brought to the library staff by a happy patron last week from a place called Daisy's Nut House. At my suggestion, Norman's eyes lit up, and a grin stretching from ear to ear broke out on his face.

"Really? Fantabulous!"

"I'm not sure that's actually a word," I said, smiling despite myself.

"Does tomorrow work?"

"Pick me up from work at five and maybe we can grab a sandwich, too. I'll need a ride home afterward. Deal?"

We shook on it, and I noticed how sweaty his hand was. Hell, he was nervous about all this. But then, so was I. Me and Norman Grant. Going out for food. To talk, like normal people. Adults. *Oh, my God.* I suddenly needed my best friend, and I dropped Norman's hand to head down the hall to knock on Max's bedroom door. When I knocked loudly, I heard a muffled "Ouch!" and let out a snort as I realized that Max likely had her ear squashed against her side of the door right where I hit it, trying to listen to what was going on in the kitchen.

"Ahem," I said as the door swung open and I met the sheepish face of Max. Jonathan shook his head, an innocent expression on his face.

"I swear I told her to come make out with me on the bed, but she had to eavesdrop."

I grinned and not-so-gently punched Max in the shoulder. "Snoop. So, what were you able to hear?"

"You're going on a date to Daisy's tomorrow after work!" she almost shouted.

"Yeah, we are!" Norman's voice bellowed from the kitchen.

"Well now that the whole neighborhood knows, I would appreciate it if we got back to our dinner," I said, heading back to where I saw Norman sitting at the table, a triumphant grin on his face, piling more wings onto his plate.

As I pushed my cart around the library the next day, I ruminated on the animated conversation that Max, Jonathan, and Norman were having last night about *League of* freakin' *Magecraft,* and I have to say I was a tad envious. It all seemed so easy with them, like they shared a hive mind. And then there was me, friends with them all in different ways, in different times in my life, and unsure of where it all fit together now. I also was nervous about my "date" with Norman after work, because this would be the first time we'd be alone together that we both knew who the other was. No more secrets, no more lies by omission.

I reflected on how I had felt about Norman, convinced that after a few months of talking for around an hour or two a day I knew him in all his complicated facets. I hadn't known shit, apparently. I hadn't known about his family pressure to enlist. I hadn't known his dead grandfather and father had been war heroes. And I hadn't known how much he wanted to be with me, instead of where life took him. I guess all of that was why I was giving this another shot, or at least a chance to talk in relative privacy.

I wasn't ashamed to admit that I was anxious enough to worry about what to wear for the big event. I decided on dark-wash jeans, a Beatles T-shirt, and a pink motorcycle jacket over it. I wore my red Converse and my sloth socks. I had blow-dried my hair extra carefully that morning, so instead of looking like a bird's nest, my hair fell straight down my back. With a tiny bit of eyeshadow and some red lip balm applied at the end of my shift using the mirror I'd hung in the maintenance closet, I felt ready to go.

I had expected him to wait in his truck in the parking lot, but nope, there he was, perusing the DIY display I'd suggested to Sabrina. He picked up a few books and looked through them as I watched him from the door to my closet, admiring his broad shoulders and the shape of his toned arms through the tight maroon sweater he was wearing. His beard looked freshly trimmed, and his hair was as adorably shaggy as ever. Okay, Lois, time to stop checking him out and go over there. One foot in front of the other.

I awkwardly made my way across the main room of the library, my face feeling hot as I reached up and tapped Norman on the shoulder. "I'm ready when you are," I said, trying to sound cheerful when everything inside of me was suddenly questioning if this was the worst idea in the history of ideas.

"Hey, kiddo! I mean, Lo. Um, I don't know what you'd like me to call you." I understood what he meant; when we were alone on voice chat, he always had a nickname for me. He only called me Peily, or now Lois, around other people. So, how did I want to play this?

"I think we'll go with Lois and Norman for this evening, if you don't mind. Easier that way." Yeah, easier because it created distance between us, and removed the intimacy of a special name.

"Sounds fine."

"So, have you had a chance to have anything from Daisy's yet?" I asked as we emerged from the building. Norman pulled on and zipped up his coat, and I guessed it was his Floridian background making him think it was cold. I was used to a New England winter and found it just fine with my pink motorcycle jacket hanging open.

"Nope, but I've heard from Max that the food is great," he replied, playing along with this small-talk routine.

Ugh, this was so awkward; what did I say to my Norman? Had I any right to think of him as "mine" anymore? No, I decided. We got to the black truck and Norman rushed ahead of me at the last moment, opening the door for me and helping me up into the vehicle, though both were unnecessary. Not that I didn't appreciate a bit of chivalry from time to time. And it was so… *Norman* to want to be helpful in any and every way. At least the Norman I remembered. It was nice to see that he wasn't completely gone as I had feared after that breakup email, which had been so out of character for him.

I remembered how he had assisted me with the towel incident, and the corners of my mouth twitched. Maybe he hadn't changed that much over the years, after all. And that day, when he'd turned up at the house looking like every virile, horny handyman fantasy I'd ever had in his tight white shirt and toolbelt had, embarrassingly, played a part in my willingness to go out tonight. Now ensconced in his old truck, I felt my cheeks heat again.

"So, um, what's on your playlist?"

"I am glad you asked, madame," he replied, steering us through the streets of Green Valley. "In honor of the festive season, I am currently working my way through the *Glee* Christmas albums." He hit a button and a holiday mashup began to play. I found myself smiling and singing along by the time we got to Daisy's.

"Carols are totally your kryptonite," he said, shutting off the truck. "You can't help but come out of that shell of yours when one is playing, can you?"

"Guilty," I replied, because he was right.

"Stay right there," he said, grabbing his cane from the back and climbing out of the truck. I knew what he was doing, but again, if it made him happy, why not? Within about thirty seconds, he was on my side of the truck and opening the door for me, extending his right hand for me to grasp as I climbed down. As we walked to the entrance, I couldn't help but notice that he never dropped my hand, and so we made our way inside holding hands, swinging them a little between us. He helped me out of my pink faux-leather jacket, hanging both coats on the rack by the doorway.

We opted for a small table in the back, where we'd have some element of privacy. My stomach was churning, and I honestly didn't give a fig if I had a doughnut or not. I wanted to talk.

"So, how weird is this?" Norman asked, pulling out my chair for me. "I mean, we didn't exactly make it to the top of the Empire State Building together, but small-town Tennessee ain't bad, is it?"

I raised my eyebrows. "Too soon, man," I said, half-smiling. He sat down.

"Fair point. So, Lois, I know you said you didn't want to do memory lane with me. And I can understand that. But can you explain how you wound up in Green Valley? Unless I haven't earned the right to that story yet."

Our waitress popped by right then and I ordered a coffee, the only thing I thought my stomach could hold down at this point. I didn't even pay attention to Norman's order, I was so twisted up in knots. "Well, it's not much of a story," I began as the waitress returned to pour me a cup. I added sugar and cream as I continued, "I was living in a shoebox in Queens with Elsa and working as an assistant at a PR firm for peanuts. I mean, peanuts was my salary, not what the firm was for. Um, but you probably got that. Okay, moving on. David was doing all he could for us, but it got too hard to juggle everything. I was going to lose my job due to 'downsizing,' and Elsa's daycare costs were going up. Maxine and I have been best friends ever since we played *Guilds* together, so when I confessed to her that things were getting too tough, she offered up her cottage's gaming room for me and Elsa. That's friendship, knowing how much she loves that room." Norman chuckled.

"Then she or her mom had a brainwave, and they decided that Rose's place would be a better fit for us. And so, I loaded up a U-Haul like you guys did, and after two days of driving—because you can't keep a kid entertained by yourself for a twelve-hour-straight drive—here I am." I took a long sip of the delicious coffee and closed my eyes, breathing deeply to slow my racing heart.

Norman reached across the table and asked softly, "Can I take your hand?"

"Yes," I replied just as softly. He put his hand around my free one, and him holding me felt right. It felt true. We sat there wordlessly for a few minutes, until a plate and a bottle of sparkling water were deposited in front of Norman.

"Feel like a bear claw?" he asked, pointing to the two different doughnuts on his plate. How on earth did he remember that a bear claw was my doughnut of choice? Mind-boggled, I shook my head.

"I'm sorry, I can't eat right now. I thought I could, but I can't."

He looked concerned. "Is this too upsetting for you?"

"No," I said, leaning forward and taking another sip of my coffee. "It's just bringing up a lot of feelings. I keep having flashbacks to being a kid and wanting this more than anything in the world. And then I remember what happened to me when I went to New York, and I feel hurt. I mean, I do not regret David, and especially not Elsa. I love them both. But I thought it would be you and me, and it wasn't, and I—"

"Hey, it's okay," he said, squeezing my hand. "I wanted all of that with you. I never wanted to learn how to shoot a gun, to take a life. To be shipped off to the middle of nowhere in another country and wind up disabled because someone put an IED in the road that we happened to hit. All I wanted was you, Lo. Lois. And I'm so, so sorry I wasn't there for you. I can't apologize enough."

I thought for a long moment, draining my coffee cup. "I have an idea. How about we put the past on hold? It's going to color everything if we don't. Why don't we try to get to know each other as Lois and Norman *now*, not as Peily and Deathdrop, not as Norm and Lo, and all of that." I put the cup down on the table and hoped the waitress would be back with more coffee. "And I heard that you hate the nickname Norm," I said, kicking him under the table while giving him an impish grin.

"Only because it reminded me of the most shameful thing I've ever done," he said, poking at the Boston Cream doughnut on his plate. "One person is allowed to call me that, and she's sitting in your seat. I'm going to attack this doughnut now," he declared, dropping my hand. "It may not be pretty. Please don't judge me by my eating habits."

"Dude. I saw you and those wings last night. After that, nothing will shock me."

"Itsh a good idea," he mumbled around the huge bite of confection in his mouth. He swallowed and washed it down with a huge mouthful of his drink. "You and me, trying to start over. I'm game if you are."

"Considering I suggested it, I'm on board." I extended a hand to him. "Hi there. I'm Lois Washington, formerly Lois Jensen. I'm twenty-seven, from Nebraska and New York City. I like books, coffee, crafting, and I'm rediscovering my love of games. I have a six-year-old daughter named Elsa and am about a week away from owning my own car."

We shook hands, and he said, "Shall I?"

"Please do."

"Okay. I'm Norman Grant, I'm twenty-seven, from Florida. I like building things, not destroying them. I like animals, computers, and gaming. I don't have any kids, but I have a rust bucket of a truck and two best friends I would lay down my life for. I hope one day soon to be able to say that small circle has expanded to include everyone at this table."

We sat in silence for a few moments, absorbing what the other had said. I was curious about something else that neither of us mentioned, so I figured the hell with it, and I went ahead and asked. "Well, Norman Grant, is there anyone special in your life?"

He let out a small choking noise and quickly took a drink. "In my life? Special? No. No, nope, nada. Women usually give me one date and then run like they were being chased by a wild boar. I don't know if it was the chronic pain and cane that scared them away, or if it was my glowing personality. I would get nervous around women, talk about video games too much, or the shop. Or I would get uncomfortable because they would ask about my time in the service, and I don't like to discuss it with folks I don't know well. Hell, I don't like to discuss it with anyone. So, it never really went anywhere. I gave up on dating a while ago. The dating pool in our dot on the map wasn't that big, and I tired of using internet dating sites to find women from farther away who were terribly unsuited to me."

"It sounds like you just hadn't met the right person. I'm sure there are women out there who wouldn't care about your chronic pain, in a negative way I mean, and who would love to talk video games with you." He flushed red and did that thing where he ran a hand through his hair when he got nervous.

"Yeah, well. So it goes. Um, how about you? Anyone special?"

"Not since David," I replied, taking a swig of my second cup of sweetened coffee. I was never going to sleep tonight at this rate. "I kind of figured with a track record like mine, I had horrible taste in choosing men. I decided to focus my energies on my daughter instead."

"Smart," he said, polishing off the Boston Cream and reaching for the napkin dispenser to wipe off his sticky fingers. He was so cute in that moment, I couldn't help but take a jab at him.

"But hey, I heard that you have a special relationship, anyway. With Lucille, right? Max says you keep hand lotion beside her on your desk."

His eyes bugged out and he coughed, turning into nervous laughter. "I swear, it's not what it sounds like. Lucille was the first computer I built when I got out of the military, and I finally did a full rebuild this autumn. She does have a lot of sentimental value. The lotion in question is for my fingers. I have mild eczema, and I get kind of picky if I don't keep them well moisturized. But try explaining that to your best friends when they're intent on maligning your name and turning everything into a joke." He looked wounded for about two seconds, and then broke out into genuine laughter. "I'm not surprised that story made its way around to you, honestly. Those two are terrible."

"And yet you're the one with the reputation for pulling pranks, hatching schemes?" I raised my eyebrows.

"Exactly! I'm a simple victim here." He wiped even more vigorously with the napkin, but the stickiness from the doughnut wasn't budging.

"I thought you ruined a guild meet-up like two and a half months ago so that Jonathan and Max would be alone together and fall in love."

"And look how well that turned out," he finished, his voice victorious. "I think I need to run to the bathroom to wash my hands. You'll still be here when I get back?" he joked, and I nodded.

I watched as he left and reached for my cell, frantically texting Max, who I knew would be waiting for updates.

Me: This is crazy, I feel like I'm in a time warp. And I half hate him, but he's so cute and sweet, and he ordered me a bear claw, Max. He remembered my favorite doughnut after ten years. Who does that?

Max: What about the half that doesn't hate him? Is it telling you to jump his bones? It is, isn't it? Tell me I'm wrong!

Me: Max!

Max: It's a perfectly valid question. Think about how perfect it would be. You, reunited with your long-lost love, who's war wounded but still brave, noble, kind, and charming. And hot. But if you tell anyone I said that last part, I'm telling them about your third nipple.

Me: I don't have a third nipple, and so what if I did?

Max: Okay, yeah, that's being mean to people who have nubbins. Sorry I said that; I take it back.

Me: Good. I swear, sometimes I think you're as bad as Elsa!

Max: I can't help it if your daughter reminds you of me.

Me: No, you boob, you remind me of a six-year-old. Hey, gotta go, he's coming back.

"How's Max?" he said, sliding back into his side of the table and gesturing at the cellphone I was trying to stealthily put into my purse.

"I swear, you're a witch," I replied. "How did you know I was texting Max? And she's fine, by the way. We had a teachable moment about what is and isn't appropriate to make fun of, so it was a useful gossip session."

"Teachable moment, hmm? Why do I feel like I'm in store for a few of those?" he asked, holding up the plate with the bear claw on it and shaking it gently in a tempting manner. "You know you want it, Lois. I've seen you eyeing this bear claw ever since it arrived. Why think about it? Take what bit of joy is in front of you, even if it is merely a doughnut." And then he winked at me!

"Is it just a doughnut, though?" I said, almost whispering, and cocked my head to one side.

"I'm not offering you a pomegranate so you'll be my underworld bride. Sometimes a doughnut is just a doughnut."

I snickered. "Fine, I'll take it if it means that much to you," I said, and reached out, taking the plate. I took a bite of the pastry and moaned involuntarily, and Norman sat back and smiled, nodding his head.

"Good, right? I knew you'd like it. Do you still hate pizza? I swear, you better have hidden that shit while you were living in New York."

I swallowed the ginormous bite I had taken and nodded, putting the rest of the bear claw back on the plate. "Yes, I still hate pizza. Elsa has had it before at friends' houses and picks off the toppings, like me. It's got to be genetic."

"You must miss her a lot," he said, leaning forward and crossing those gorgeous forearms on the table.

"I do," I said, grabbing a wet-wipe from my purse and wiping down my hands and mouth. Geez, I should have offered one to Norman earlier; I wasn't thinking straight. "She has been the center of my world ever since I found out I was pregnant. I was starting my junior year, and scared shitless, but she was there, she was real, and she was *mine*. And when David left us after his senior year, she was all I had. I gave up a lot for her, but I'd do it again in a heartbeat. That child *is* my life. She comes first in everything, and I wouldn't have it any other way." He nodded, and reached for my hand again, covering it with his warmth.

"I love how much you love her," he murmured. "Is she gone for long?"

"This year is her year to be with David and Philippe for Christmas, obviously, and she goes for a month. It's such a long way that two weeks doesn't seem worth it, almost. And it is only once every two years. Then she spends about six weeks every summer over there. It's hard, but it's good for her to be raised by all her parents, not only me, even though I carry the load of it. She learns all kinds of things from David, and from Philippe, and their parents. The only extended family she's missing is mine, but she never knew them, so she doesn't feel the loss of it. She has asked me before why she doesn't have grandparents in Nebraska, and I had to break down and tell her that she did once have two grandmothers there—my mom and Mormor—but they both died. I always want honesty between us, and I think a painful truth is better than a sugarcoated lie. I learned that the hard way."

"Ouch," Norman said, chewing on his bottom lip. "I messed you up, didn't I? I swear I didn't mean—"

I put up my hand. "No, Norman; I mean yes, but no. I'm more referring to what happened with me and David, and how he handled revealing his sexuality to me. Let's say I wasn't Philippe's biggest fan for a while, until I realized that he had nothing to do with David and me breaking up. It would have happened eventually, and the longer it lasted, the messier it would have gotten. And Philippe loves Elsa so, so much. He is determined to teach her proper French cuisine instead of the 'American slop' we eat." I snickered.

Our waitress came by with more coffee, and I shook my head and smiled up at her. "No more for me, thanks. Norman, did you want to order anything else? I'm happy to stay if you are. Otherwise, I'd like to get going."

"We'll have the check, thanks," Norman said, much to my relief.

Why I was so relieved, I wasn't sure. In fact, everything about being with Norman again made me unsure. I felt like I was at sea, each wave more turbulent than the last, each movement tossing me about until I felt like hurling over the side of my little boat. I had no oars, no compass, no GPS. I was utterly lost with this man, and I had the sinking feeling that what lay ahead was more confusion and possible heartbreak.

CHAPTER 10

NORMAN

After I paid up—I insisted—and we left Daisy's, I had an epiphany. I didn't want this date to end, so maybe she didn't either. As I popped the holiday album back on and pulled away from the parking lot, I decided to turn toward Max's place and then reached out to squeeze Lois's hand.

"Do you mind if we pop by Max's garage before I take you home? I would love to show you Supernatural Computers, 2.0." *Come on, say yes.* God, please let her say yes. I was totally falling again, I could feel it, but this time I wouldn't fuck it all up under the weight of other people's expectations or childish fantasies and lies.

She stopped singing "Last Christmas"—a cover; I was winning Whamageddon this year, dammit, which was an informal competition to see if you could make it to Christmas Eve without hearing the original version of "Last Christmas" by Wham!—long enough to say, "Yeah, sure. I mean, it's not like I have to rush home for Elsa. I was feeling, I don't know, overwhelmed? I think I'll feel less whelmed in private. That's not even a word, is it?"

"I don't think so, kiddo," I chuckled, then corrected myself. "Lois, I mean." It grew quiet in the truck, save for the stereo, and I mentally kicked myself. Lois and Norman. Not Kiddo and Norm. Not Peily and Deathdrop. Get it through your thick head!

"Do you still love Christmas?" I asked her, certain that the enthusiasm she was putting into that song was proof enough.

"Not really without Elsa. I still love the music, though. Um, about the shop, I'm actually excited to see what you've done with the place," Lois said, and I took it for the peace offering it was.

"We had a heap of help from Max, and from you, I hear. Getting it cleaned up enough for us, I mean. We appreciated that so much. And Max went bananas on the organizational front when it came to our parts and tools. I mean, that girl even has a label maker! Our shop in Florida was never this neat and professional looking."

"You sound proud."

"You know what, I am. I'm proud of what we accomplished. It took a lot of elbow grease from all four of us, but it was done in record time. The part that sucks is we can't offer the custom desks anymore, but we'll find a proper shop somewhere, sometime, and let Max have her garage back eventually."

"From all five of us," she said, letting out a small giggle. "Elsa carried a box or two, and then she found Max's old handheld consoles and it was off to play games while we worked."

"A chip off the old block, I see," I teased.

"I'm actually not letting her game very much until she's older; that was a one-off treat to keep her out from underfoot. I don't want her to grow up with tons of screen time."

"Was that a Lois decision or a David decision?" I asked, curious at how they managed to make things work co-parenting across the ocean.

"That was a mutual decision," she replied. "We actually Skype every week to discuss Elsa and then she gets to have a virtual visit with David and Philippe. They want us to move over there permanently, you know, so we can raise her together, the three of us."

I inwardly swore. No way in hell did the universe itself conspire to reunite Lois and me—in Green Valley, Tennessee, of all places—only for her to go off to live with her ex and his new partner all the way in France. No, this was my second chance with her, and this time I wasn't giving up on us before we even had a chance to know each other again as adults. I composed my thoughts as we pulled into Max's driveway. "That would be a lot to adjust to. And what about you, do you even speak French? Do you want to live in the same house as your ex?"

She shook her head. "No, and hell no are the short answers. Now, are you going to show me that workshop?"

I nodded, gesturing for her to stay put. I got out of the truck and walked around to her side, opening her door and helping her down. I kept her hand in mine, hoping she wouldn't pull away. She didn't. Sweet!

We held hands as I walked her to the shop, waving to Max through her kitchen window on the way. I saw Jonathan's hand come up but not the rest of his body and decided not to dwell on it. I noticed Lois's cheeks were a bit pink after we passed by Max, and realized it was because of the handhold.

"Are you comfortable with this?" I asked her, gesturing with my head toward our linked hands. She stopped on the path to the garage and faced me.

"I wish I were more comfortable with it, Norman. I mean, I don't mind touching my friends, but I don't want you to spin dreams about what it all might mean. Because I'll be totally honest, I have no clue in hell what it might mean. All I know is that when we hold hands, whenever we touch, it's like whatever anger I had toward you fades away and I can't even remember what I was angry about to begin with."

Well, shit. I turned my hand over in hers, picked it up, and gently kissed the back of it, then let it fall away. "Let's save stuff like hand holding for later, okay? I don't want to mess up rebuilding a friendship with you, or even more if that's where it goes."

She was quiet for a moment. "Is that what you're hoping for? More than friends, I mean."

I grimaced inwardly. The truth for the win, always. I'd learned that the hard way when I'd lost her the first time around. "Um, I don't know how to properly answer that except with absolute honesty. I respect that you don't know if you're ready. But I am. I am so ready to get to know this strong, brave, fierce woman in front of me, and see if we fit together now as well as we did when we were teenagers."

"We were a good team, back then. Now, I want to see the shop. I was promised a tour, and damn it, I want a tour!"

A smile plastered itself on my face and I lifted my cane, pointing at the garage side door. "Right this way, madame."

After Lois acted thoroughly impressed with the shop, I dropped her off at Rose's place, stopping in briefly to say hello to the other woman, whom I found to be warm and motherly. She reminded me of Mrs. Owen, Jonathan's mom, when she was having one of her clear days. Unfortunately, Mrs. Owen's anxiety disorder was severe, and she was heavily medicated for it.

During the rare times when she wasn't foggy, though, she was supportive, kind, and authoritative. Just like Rose. With a promise to bring by some Donner Bakery banana cake on a future visit and stay for a while, I left the women and drove back across town, softly singing the carols under my breath and wondering if it would be worth it to get a tree for our rental.

Now that I thought of it, hadn't Mrs. Potter said no trees because of the mess? Yes, she had! Well, damn. I'd have to be content to mooch off the holiday cheer at Max's and Rose's homes, then. I mean, I could do a fake tree —I always had in Florida—but I was in the Great Smoky Mountains, for the love of Charlie Brown. I wanted a real tree, with a real smell.

I imagined that Max and Jonathan were going to decorate Max's cottage together as a couple thing, but I wondered about Rose's place. I know! I'd pop by tomorrow and ask them if they wanted me to pick up a tree for them with my truck. That way, I would be bound to be included in the setting up process in some way. Though, I imagined if anyone could wrangle an eight-foot fir tree solo, it would be Lois.

Was I scheming? Oh, hell yes. But judging from the sad expression that came over Lois's face whenever Elsa was mentioned, and how she said she didn't enjoy the holiday without her daughter, I was determined to infuse the next few weeks with as much Christmas cheer as possible for her. I mean, I couldn't fill the space in her heart left by Elsa, but I would certainly do everything else I could to make sure she had fun this month. Rose, too, while I was at it. Why not? I could play Santa Claus to the two women, if they'd allow it.

I sat down on the couch in the stale little rental unit, eating cold pizza from the fridge and wishing I had ordered something else at Daisy's. I could eat like a machine, and it wasn't always pretty. But I also liked to eat healthier than this, preferring salad or wraps or soups. And tacos, but didn't that go without saying?

The point was, by the time the last cold slice was gone, I felt no fuller and no more satisfied. I wondered if I would ever feel satisfied until it was Lois that I tasted on my tongue, her delicious scent drawing me in every time we were near. I wanted to kiss the hell out of her, but I also wasn't an asshole and wasn't going to push for anything she wasn't enthusiastically ready for.

Not expecting Jonathan home at all that night, I locked the door to the unit and didn't tuck down his bed on the pullout. I instead went into the sad-looking bedroom and got undressed for the night, hatching my plan for tomorrow. Operation Christmas Tree was going into effect.

~

Jonathan gave me a strange look the next day when I asked if he minded if I left work at twenty to five instead of five or five-thirty per usual, but I had leveled him an even glance and said, "It's for the greater good, man." With that he waved a hand at me and I was off, back to the library.

Now, there were only so many times I could circle around that DIY display near the library entrance without looking like a weirdo—who was also in desperate need of home reno advice. I couldn't control this blanket of nervousness that had enveloped me, and I didn't want to wander through the library at the moment.

Lois had let me in a bit at our Daisy's date, and I wanted this evening to be a pleasant surprise for her, not me being an unwelcome intrusion. I chickened out about seeing Lois while she was on duty and decided to build up some courage and regroup in my truck. This time, I had parked right next to the blue Jeep of Max's, so I was sure not to miss them.

When the girls emerged from the library, laughing and smiling, I knew I wouldn't be able to stand it if I saw Lois' face fall at the sight of me. *Casual, Norman; act casual*, I told myself. I grabbed the small handful of pamphlets and other detritus of leftover mail in the dash and started flipping through them at random, not paying attention to what I was reading, just that I was doing something other than sitting here staring at the library doors, waiting to put my grand plan into action.

I heard a knock at my window, and the leftover mail went flying everywhere. Lois was there on the other side of the glass, eyebrows raised and a smug expression on her face.

I rolled down the window and she got the jump on me, saying, "Fancy seeing you here. Again. And parked right next to Max."

"Yeah, that's quite the coinkydink, don't you think?" I put on my most charming smile.

"It's quite stalkerish, actually," she retorted, and my face fell, not even considering that angle. "Oh, stop looking like a kicked kitten; I'm teasing you." She reached in through the window and poked my shoulder. "To what do we owe the pleasure of your company?"

"I thought I would bring my truck over and drive you to Rose's place, to see if she wanted us to go pick out a Christmas tree. I could transport it and help set it up."

Lois and Max shared a look, like they were communicating telepathically as I've often thought female best friends could do through some kind of sorcery, and Lois turned back to me and nodded. Max jumped in, as expected.

"You know my mother has had an artificial tree since the '90s. It might take some convincing to get her to give up all that silver. Good luck, though; this is a Deathdrop scheme I actually like."

I gave Max a salute, then opened my door. Before I could grab my cane, Lois, quick as an antelope, had made her way around the truck and was opening the passenger door. Well, then. I suppose maybe I had gone a wee bit overboard with the door opening thing. I had wanted to show her that I cared for her, and part of caring for someone is showing them in various ways that you want to make their life easier. But I guess I got it: she wasn't a child and could handle opening and closing her own door. Point taken.

Man, I think I needed to talk to my friend Elaine, Jonathan's younger sister in Chicago, for some advice on the woman front. I couldn't go to Max, when it was her bestie I was trying to court; she'd spill the beans to Lois. I made a mental note to Skype Elaine ASAP.

As we got going, I turned on the *Glee* holiday album we'd been listening to before, and when I was going to ask her opinion on the "Baby It's Cold Outside" controversy as the song began to play, she got in the first word. Again.

"I think this is a kind thing you're trying to do for Rose," she said, fiddling with her purse strap. "I mean, there's nothing like a real tree at Christmas. We never had one in New York; the prices were way too high for me, so I had an artificial one that I decorated with my Mormor's ornaments that she mailed to me before she died. I think she knew she was going to pass, because one day while I was still pregnant, packages started arriving, and they were things like a tablecloth of lace she had handmade, or her crystal stemware, and then the ornaments. I wish you could have met her, Norman. She would have loved you."

"Really?" I asked, a bit in shock. I knew Lois held her grandmother remarkably close to her heart, and for her to say that was a huge compliment.

"Oh yeah. That charming smile, those twinkling eyes usually up to something? And your heart of gold. All a recipe for Mormor to fall head over heels."

I smirked despite myself. "Heart of gold, huh?" I tucked that compliment away with every other kind thing Lois had ever said to me, smack in the middle of said heart.

"Don't let it go to your head," she sassed back, sticking out her tongue.

~

Rose had been ecstatic at the thought of a real tree again, saying that all of us "young people" were bringing new life into her home, and who was she to stop it? She said it was a beautiful thing and should be celebrated over banana cake. Hint, hint.

So, we first swung by the Donner Bakery—which was thankfully still open but barely—and swiped the last banana cake from their shelves. Phew. Now, we were walking through a darkened Christmas tree lot, lit up with white lights in strings in the air, and each holding a cup of outrageously overpriced hot chocolate as we perused the merchandise. It was all very Hallmark, but it warmed my insides to see the look of happiness and peace on Lois's face as we walked up and down the aisles, her stopping now and then to feel a tree, saying she was testing the strength of the needles to get an idea of how long it would last in the house.

Finally, after we'd covered the whole lot, Lois grabbed my arm and said breathlessly, "There it is! Our tree!"

Our tree. I felt like preening like a peacock when she said that. And she was right, the tree was beautiful. Upon inspection, we found it was an eight-foot-tall Fraser Fir monstrosity that made me glad for those high ceilings in Rose's parlor. I got out cash for the proprietor, who looked down at my cane and back up at my perfect posture, and asked, "Did you serve, young man? I did, back in Vietnam. Lost me a leg for it in an ambush." he said, ringing up our purchase.

"Afghanistan," I replied a tad tersely. "Kept the leg, but the hip gives me fits." I tried to simmer down, but I knew what people thought when they heard about my service and saw this cane. They thought I was some kind of hero, not some asshole lucky enough to escape a burning Jeep.

"Well, thank you for your service, young man. Twenty percent off, from one old soldier to you," he said, and I felt awkward as all hell as I handed over the cash. But I couldn't think how to say no without insulting the man's kind gesture. I thanked him, and he asked if we needed help with the tree, which I politely declined. Lois and I lugged the tree to my truck, a slow process with me limping along, but using the tree for support and having fun, which was all that mattered.

After a quick stop at Eager Beaver's Hardware and Lumber to pick up a Christmas tree stand, we were headed back to the old Victorian. Getting the tree through the house was a bit of a challenge, and in the end, I called Jonathan on my cell and asked him to drive over and help get this big beast of a tree inside.

Rose decided she'd be better suited to warming us up some apple cider than trying to help haul a tree through her narrow hallways. I winced whenever we brushed up against a family photo or a cross-stitch, but eventually, after the tree had been well blessed by Lois's cursing under her breath, we made it to the parlor and wrangled it into the tree stand, finally having the tree in the right spot as Rose came in with the cider and a bottle of whiskey.

Lois and I were both sweating and panting, but even a hot drink sounded like the nectar of the gods at that moment. While Lois and Jonathan allowed a dollop of the alcohol into their cider, I shook my head when offered. I may have had a beer now and then still, but I kept away from the hard stuff.

Jonathan excused himself not too long after the tree was in position, probably keen to get back to Max. And so we stood as a trio—Rose, Lois, and I—and toasted our tree, and I felt warm inside, not only from the drink. This was what family felt like, and I loved that I was feeling it with Lois—and Rose—not only with Max, Jonathan, and the Owen clan. After we had downed our drinks, Lois said, "Oh, no! We forgot the banana cake. I mean the uh, surprise banana cake. It's still in the truck."

"I'll run and get it," I offered, sprinting—well, okay, limping, but at as fast a pace as I was comfortable with—down the hall and out to my truck. That was when I remembered that I wanted to Skype with Elaine, so I yanked my cell from my pants pocket and found her in my contacts. I dialed, as I was not a fan of texting, and she picked up on the second ring.

"Norman, my man! Why don't you learn to text?" she said, in that way of hers that was both friendly and condescending.

"Elaine, I'm in a bit of a pickle, and I need to talk to you. Think you'd be up for a Skype tonight?"

"Hmm… Well, I was going to go out with the guys, but if you need me…"

"Come on, I need you."

"Fine! You are officially on my schedule for the evening."

"Great, so we're cool for tonight? Maybe in, say, an hour or two? I'll call when I get home."

"Sure thing."

CHAPTER 11

LOIS

"Elaine, I'm in a bit of a pickle, and I need to talk to you. Think you'd be up for a Skype tonight?"

"Come on, I need you."

I turned around and ran back into the house, the image of Norman's back to me as he talked into his cellphone to some other woman frozen in my mind. He said he was in "a pickle," and yet he couldn't talk to me, he had to seek out this Elaine person? Who was she, and what made her so special? I thought we were having a nice cozy evening with Rose, and I had come out to suggest to Norman that we ask her if she wanted to play a few hands of cards and watch a movie, and instead he was getting all fidgety to get home to Skype with Elaine. Whom he "needed."

I knew I was being petty. But when David was getting involved emotionally deeper and deeper with Philippe, this was one of the hallmarks of deception. Secret phone calls or dodging me when his cell would ping. Skype meetings he swore were for work but were done in French so if I did overhear, I had no idea what was being said. And the pulling away from me—we were supposed to be each other's best friend, our everything. And it felt like he'd replaced me with Philippe, once I found out. Did Norman have a girlfriend and he didn't want to tell me? To keep from hurting me?

When I made it inside, I grabbed another glass of cider and poured in a healthy dollop of the booze Rose had offered up earlier. I downed my cup in about three swallows and tried to keep my breathing even. The last thing I needed was an anxiety attack. I used to get them over David when he was drifting away from me and I was nine months pregnant with his child. I think that's why I never dated again—my trust had been shattered by David, and I never really put it back together, despite the two years of therapy I attended. Men were like a minefield of emotional betrayal, and I did not need to go for a stroll through it.

Well, Norman was free to hit the road any time he wanted, and Rose and I could play cards and watch a sappy romcom on our own, perfectly fine. We couldn't decorate the tree tonight, because we had to give it a day or so for the boughs to relax and drop a bit. I did feel a smattering of guilt when I saw Norman carrying the banana cake in one-handed, and I swung the door open for him, plastering on a fake smile. Then I remembered Max's words, about how he was far more capable than people might assume and hated being pitied or given pity help. Well, he'd opened enough doors for me, and turnabout was fair play.

He gave me an odd look as he advanced into the kitchen and glanced back over his shoulder, only to catch me ruminating on the Elaine situation. When he put the banana cake down, he turned to me and said, "Spill it."

"Excuse me?" I said, taken a bit aback by him being so upfront.

"Something has ticked you off," he said. "I thought we were having a good time. What's wrong?"

Norman had said yesterday that there wasn't anyone special in his life, and he had no reason to lie. But then, I always thought David had no reason to lie to me, and he was chatting with Philippe at every available opportunity. Was I already losing Norman for the second time, because of this Elaine?

"You were on the phone, and I went out to help you with the cake. I overheard you. When I asked you if there was anyone special in your life, you said no," I said, trying not to sound hurt.

"And I meant it, Lois. Do you think I would lie to you when I'm trying to reestablish a connection between us? Or is this possibly a jealousy thing? Because there is absolutely nothing to be jealous over."

"It is so not a jealousy thing!" I retorted as Rose entered the kitchen. Silence descended like a black cloud over the room, and Norman shifted uncomfortably.

"Actually, ladies, I'm going to leave you to enjoy this lovely cake in peace. I've taken up enough of your time for one evening, I think. Lois, it was fun spending time with you tonight. I hope we can do it again sometime if you care to see me again."

"Well of course she would!" Rose interjected, pushing her nose in. "Why wouldn't she? Norman, thank you for bringing home the tree. It means so much to me. The last real tree in this house was put in by my late husband, you know. I do hope you will come by tomorrow evening after work so we can decorate it as a group. Ask my Maxie and her Jonathan if they want to pop by, too. The more the merrier, right, Lois?" I couldn't help but notice that the "right, Lois" was said in a pointed tone, and I nodded mechanically.

Norman promised he would pass on the invite, and that he would be back for the decoration party. And with that, he left, leaving me feeling like a rotten, jealous, ugly person. I needed some time to read and think, stat.

I sat in the parlor in my pajamas and robe, staring at the enormous tree and remembering that it had been all Norman's idea to do us this kindness. I sniffled, and Rose popped in with her tea tray, plunked it on the coffee table, and prepared a cup which she then deposited in my hands, doing a switcheroo with the wine glass I had been holding on to like a lifeline. She sat down on the other end of the couch, and turned to me and said, "I thought you could use a friend. If that's not me, you should at least call Maxie. Something went wrong between you and that boy tonight, and it's weighing on you, I can tell."

I nodded and took a sip of the chai. "What went wrong is what always goes wrong with me and good men. I keep fuc—messing up, and I don't know how to stop. I overheard him on his cell talking to some girl named Elaine, saying that he needed her. And I got… uncomfortable. Jealous, even."

"Oh, honey," Rose said, reaching out and patting my knee. "Would it help you to know that you aren't the first jealous woman in history? Would it help you more to know who this Elaine is?"

"As awful as that is, Rose, yes, it would help. I mean, we were having such a nice time and I blew it over who?"

"Jonathan's little sister who lives in Chicago, dear. She's no threat to you. Norman thinks of her as a little sister, too."

And with that, I swallowed my tears and wanted to reach for my cell to send Norman an apology, when I realized I didn't have his number. Here we were, ten years later, and I still didn't know that man's digits.

"Rose, this is lovely, but do you mind if I bail on a girls' night and take this tea up to my room? I think I owe someone an apology, and I need to first call Max to get his number." That perked the older woman right up.

"Oh, no need for that; I've got his number on the fridge. It's under the Darth Vader magnet, because until recently, I had a bad impression of Norman.

All those Deathdrop pranks on my poor Maxie! But he did bring her and Jonathan together, so it's all been for the best. And the way he put Maxie up in Florida and helped with Jonathan, well… He deserves a Light Side magnet. Do rearrange them while you're getting his number, dear."

I found the slip of paper with a phone number on it smack under Vader's head where Rose said it would be, and pulled my cell from the pocket of my robe to enter it in. Then, I swapped the Vader and BB-8 magnets, and headed up the steep stairs to my room, a tad nervous but determined. I had to make this right. I couldn't lose Norman again through a simple act of foolish jealousy, especially when it felt so damn right having him back in my life.

CHAPTER 12

NORMAN

"It was like she wasn't even herself, Eli," I moaned in front of my laptop, where Elaine's calm and practical face was staring back at me.

"I'm sure," Elaine said flatly. "Look, Norman, the truth is, she was jealous, plain and simple. And when called on it, she did what most insecure people would do and tossed it back in your face so the heat would be off her and her feelings. She's going to call you at any moment and apologize."

I snorted. "I wouldn't count on it. She'll never want to see me again, what with this on top of how I treated her when we were kids."

"Norman, don't be a goof," Elaine started to unbraid her hair and re-braid it in a different style. "She's obviously willing to move past the past, if you follow. Otherwise, there wouldn't have been two dates already. Because, yes, the Nut House and the Christmas tree lot were most definitely dates. Which means your unlucky streak is broken! It only all started to go to shit after the second date, not the first."

"Thanks, Eli. I see why I come to you for solid advice," I sarcastically intoned.

"Look, she needs a bit of time, okay? She needs the time to build trust between you two again. And as good of a sign as that second date was, it ended in the crapper because that trust wasn't there yet. But it will be, if you keep being your annoying, persistent self, and don't give up on her because of one freak-out. Be understanding. Be kind. Don't be a dope."

"I get the picture. Okay, so be freaking magnanimous as hell when she calls to apologize, because you say she will. Which, by the way, I think you are dead wrong about." Just then, the strains of "Eye of the Tiger" began to play from my pants pocket, and my eyes almost bugged out of my head. "Holy mother of dragons, Eli, I think it's her! What should I do?"

"Calm the fuck down and be kind to her. Listen to her. Give her time to rebuild that trust. Now, go!" Elaine made a shooing motion at the camera and logged off, and I grabbed my phone and answered it on the third ring.

"Yello?" I said, and cringed. "I mean, hello. Hello? Hello."

"Yeah, I got your number, all right," an amused female voice said.

"Lois?"

"Norman."

"Lois."

"Norman."

"Rocky!" we both said at the same time, ending our awkward introduction on a shared joke from our past. We had streamed and watched together *The Rocky Horror Picture Show* many times, it being one of "our" movies.

"So, Norman…"

"Yes, Lois?" I encouraged.

"I'm calling to apologize for making a fool of myself and for making you feel like you had to leave. You didn't, I was having a freak-out because… Argh, because I was jealous, okay? I'm sorry, but I was. I didn't know who this Elaine person was that you were calling on our date, and I kept getting flashbacks to my time with David when Philippe moved in on my man, and my inner wrath beast was unleashed. Can you forgive me? I don't want things to be awkward when we decorate the tree."

"They won't be," I reassured her, thrilled she had referred to tonight as "our date." "There's nothing to forgive, Lois; we're good. We're always good, as far as I'm concerned. Okay?"

"Okay," she said, her voice sounding less small, more confident. Mission accomplished! "So, what are you wearing?" she practically purred into the phone, before giggling like a crazed hyena. Lois always had this bizarre laugh once she got going. I secretly loved it.

"Oh, you know, work boots, jeans, tight white T-shirt. I look like I climbed out of a photoshoot for GQ, per usual." I settled back into the pillows behind me, my laptop having been open on my bed. I was in fact wearing pajama pants and nothing else, but I wasn't telling her that. Or wait, what had Elaine said earlier? *Show her your vulnerability. Let her see that you've changed by being absolutely honest.* "Okay, fine, you tore it out of me. I'm wearing red pajama pants with Christmas trees on them. They're hideous, but they were also given to me by my mother, who had no taste at all, but I love them to bits because they remind me of her. They are getting a bit threadbare, actually."

"Oh, Norman, I'm sorry. How long ago did she pass? We've never talked about her since reconnecting."

"That's because I don't talk about her," I said, wetting my lips and biting them. "It was four years ago. Aneurysm—she went to sleep and didn't wake up. I found her in the trailer when I was on my way to work; she was always up before me to make me breakfast. No matter how often I said I didn't need to be babied, that woman would coddle me something fierce. And I loved her something fierce. And now she's gone."

"I wish I could have met her. Even if I'm not impressed that she pushed you into the service."

"I wish you could have, too." My voice was growing thick. "Maybe on my trip down to Florida with Jonathan and Max to visit the Owenses in the spring, you could come with. We could even brave the long drive and the tourists and take Elsa to Disney, if she's never been."

"I lived in an apartment the size of a walk-in closet in New York her whole life, Norman. No prior trips to Disney World."

"Well, I didn't know if David and Philippe had taken her to Disneyland Paris. I have no idea how well-off they are, but with him flying all over to get her and escort her personally, I assumed they were rolling in it."

Lois let out a bark of laughter. "They're okay, but no. David saves up all year for those trips, and eventually Elsa will be old enough to make them solo. She's not a spoiled child, and she's learning the value of hard work from all of her parents."

"It's nice that you include Philippe, but honesty time here: how do you *really* feel about him stepping up onto your man?"

"Oh, they were too remorseful to make me too mad, Norm." I noticed the nickname slip out but said nothing. "Eventually they came to me together, after David came out, and swore that they hadn't done anything other than talk while David and I were still a couple. And Philippe, as much as he was in love with David, still felt terrible that David would be following him to the family vineyard instead of staying in New York with me and Elsa. Now that, that was a tough pill to swallow. But apparently Philippe's parents were ill, and he couldn't stay here, so… Anyway, it's all in the past, now."

"Yeah, sorry; I'm too curious sometimes," I admitted.

"You always had to know all the things, when it came to the game and the guild anyway, since that was mostly what we talked about. Are you still like that? Are you an officer in your guild?"

"Ha! Like they'd want me in a leadership role. They think of me as the court jester. Now that's a role I play well."

"I remember. You're still probably the best at your character class, though. Let me guess… You play a rogue and have found practically every hidden treasure in the game."

I preened a bit under her words. "Well, yeah—wait a minute! How do you know there is hidden treasure to be found in *Magecraft*? You said you had no interest in the game!"

"I lied," she said bluntly. "Of course I'm interested in the game. It's only, gaming ended badly for me before. Going back to it, it's a tough decision."

"Join our arena team, Lois. With your skills, if you played for, like, a week to get a feel for your class in this game, you could tear through other players with us in player vs. player mode. Come on; Elsa's away, why not have a *League of Magecraft* Christmas?"

There was silence for a long moment, and she sounded embarrassed when she said, "I don't own a computer powerful enough to handle the graphics requirements. My laptop is nine years old, from when I was a student."

Oh, well that wouldn't do. "That's not a problem; I have a spare laptop I can loan you until we can build you a new computer at the shop. No charge for labor, and the parts will be my Christmas gift to you. No arguments, no take backs, it's done." I felt like a hero when I said it.

Then she responded, "No, I can't accept that. It's too big a gift; I know parts aren't cheap. And I know that Max's new computer was one of these friendship deals you pull, and it was free labor and parts at cost."

"Yeah, but now it's *Christmas*," I said, as if she was completely missing the point.

"Oh Norm, what am I going to do with you?"

"Whatever you want, kiddo."

CHAPTER 13

LOIS

The boughs hadn't dropped on the tree as quickly as we thought, so the decoration party was delayed until Thursday; something I was secretly glad of, as it gave me some space from Norman to sort out my jealous feelings of the past with David and this new flare-up with Elaine. I was taking a cheese pie out of the oven when I heard the front door open, and a loud familiar "Ho, ho, ho!" at the door. Norman.

It was officially what I was referring to in my head as Date Number Three: The Decorating. The plan was simple; we would decorate the tree, have a cheese pie and mulled wine or hot chocolate here, and then the two of us would go for a walk downtown to see the window displays at night. Checking out the window displays downtown was always something I'd loved doing in New York, and while I knew Green Valley wouldn't have quite the glitz and glamour of the big city about it, the town was growing on me. Tomorrow night we were going to the Community Center for a jam session, and while I'd never been a fan of country music, I was willing to give it a go.

I had brought down Mormor's ornaments, which Rose had said I could most definitely use to decorate the tree, though we'd still be using some of hers, given the beast's size. It would be a mash-up of memories, and that sounded fine by me.

I couldn't Skype Elsa in for the party, given the time difference, but I wanted to show her what we had done tomorrow, and I decided to include a tradition everyone disliked doing but looked nice when it was done: the popcorn chain. I'd already popped two enormous bowls full, and they were waiting in the living room for some industrious hands to get to work.

I bustled to the living room, checking my hair in the hall mirror, pleased with how it hung long and shiny after my lengthy attempts to tame it earlier. It was frustration with the way my hair would turn into a rat's nest that had compelled me to chop it off in high school. I had little patience back then, and I remember what a steadying, calm influence Norman had been on me.

I'd hated my father for being invisible in my life, even hated my mother for dying, hated school—not the academic work, but the bullies—and was generally not a joy to be around. I wondered what exactly had attracted Norman Grant to me back then, and what on earth he was doing with me now. But here we were at date number three. The kissing date. That's how I always saw it anyway, and I was a slow mover.

Giving my V-neck green sweater and jeans a once-over, I made my way to the parlor, where Norman was espousing the virtues of the fir tree we'd picked out, dressed in a Santa jacket and hat. How could I not smile, standing in the doorway, watching him across the room, dressed like that? His eyes were lit up, and with his shaggy hair peeking out from under the lopsided hat and his beard trimmed neat, he looked like a naughty holiday fantasy. All he needed was to be shirtless under that open Santa jacket, and standing under some mistletoe and… Whoa, Lois. Get your hormones under control!

"He makes a striking figure, doesn't he?" Rose said behind me, scaring the bejesus out of me and making me jump. "Oh, I'm sorry, dear. I was coming down to check on the mulled wine when I saw you standing there, looking all swoony."

"Rose!" I hissed, not wanting Norman to overhear, though chances were slim given the racket coming from the parlor with Max and Jonathan in it, too.

"It's okay, Lois. I was young and in love once, too," she said, far more quietly this time. In love? How could I be in love with Norman? We were only on date three, the kissing date!

"Thanks, Rose, but I'm not quite there yet," I intoned, and she nodded.

"Maybe it wasn't you I was referring to," she said, winking. She nodded in Norman's direction as he beamed over at the pair of us; though, admittedly, most of that look was directed at me. He then looked up, and a huge smile split his face. I looked up, and bam! I was standing right under a huge clump of mistletoe. In horror, I turned to Rose.

"You didn't! Rose!"

"You bet your bippy I did."

I hid my head in my hands for a second and looked up in time to see

Norman swan across the parlor, headed for us women in the doorway. First, he bent down low and gave Rose a kiss on the forehead, saying quietly, "Merry Christmas, Rose." He next reached out and offered me his hand, which I took, and he led me around the corner. Satisfied that we were away from the mistletoe, yet feeling a slight churning in my belly, I wondered what he was going to do. He dropped my hand and reached up to take my chin in his hands. Then, ever so slowly, with plenty of time for me to stop him, he leaned in and gently pressed his lips to mine. Pulling back, he looked down at me to gauge my reaction.

"We're not technically under the mistletoe," I pointed out, feeling almost lightheaded.

"Yeah, but I figured you wouldn't want everyone to see."

"You're right," I replied, leaning up and pressing my lips to his, applying more pressure than he'd applied to mine. He groaned, and I deepened the kiss, hoping he would get on board. The next thing I knew, his hand was in my hair and his tongue was running across the seam of my lips. I parted my lips to let him in and he invaded my mouth, licking at me, our breaths coming in shared, ragged gasps. After a long moment, he pulled away and smoothed down my hair from where his hand had been in it. He rested his forehead against mine and we looked into each other's eyes, his brown meeting my green, and I knew this was a turning point in my life. After waiting ten years, I had kissed the heck out of Norman Grant.

"I think I'm cool with hand holding in public now," I gasped and, smiling, pressed my mouth to his one final time. "Come on, before they send a search party. You should know by now how nosy they all are."

Holding hands, we turned and walked back into the parlor, where everyone was suddenly looking like they were terribly busy. Uh-huh. "So, how much of all that did you hear?" I asked casually, bringing Norman's hand up and kissing the back of it before letting it go so I could show him Mormor's ornaments.

"How much of what?" Jonathan asked in a suspiciously innocent voice, and Max covered up her laughter by putting a hand over her mouth and turning around.

"Real mature, guys," Norman said, and then ruined it all with, "As if you've never heard passionate kissing before. I know you two go at it like rabbits."

"Norman!" I said, "Max's *mother* is right here!" At this point, everyone was in some state of guffawing, Rose included, and I couldn't exactly stay mad.

"Ah, young love," Rose said, pulling another ball of mistletoe from her box of ornaments. "Where should I place this one? Over the entrance to the kitchen? Or should I surprise y'all?"

"Mom!"

"Surprise us, Rose," Jonathan said, moving in on Max and pressing a kiss to her lips.

~

Mormor's ornaments hung on the tree with care, the higher ones placed by Norman, who handled them like a newborn baby. They *were* pretty old, with quite a few coming from "the old country"—Sweden. There was a wooden red Dala horse ornament which was my favorite, and was on every childhood tree I could remember at her home. The others were wooden too, mostly hearts and stars, straw reindeer and angels, and gnomes. Then there were ornaments she had collected throughout her life here in America, mostly shaped like eggs in all colors, frosted with white drizzles and curlicues. Mixed in on the tree were Rose's decorations, mostly cross-stitched ornaments, paper or clay ornaments made by Max as a child, and an impressive collection of geekery like Star Wars, Marvel, Disney, and even a mini T.A.R.D.I.S.

We all ooh'd and ahh'd when the tree was lit, all holding mugs of mulled wine and toasting our efforts. I looked around at the shining faces, and though I missed Elsa so much I could almost cry, these people around me felt like family. And family was something I hadn't had much of in an awfully long time.

While Rose, Jonathan, and Max settled in to watch *Miracle on 34th Street* and work on the popcorn chain, Norman appeared wearing his jacket and holding mine, ready to move our date along to downtown. We decided to drive and park for a shorter walk, because even though he hadn't complained, I was certain Norman had pulled something the day we brought in the tree. I mean, he had been wrestling the thing one-armed for a good chunk of the time, until he had set his cane down and used the tree itself to help support his body weight as we lugged it inside with Jonathan's help. This way, too, we'd have the truck if we wanted to make a run to Daisy's for a drink and doughnut again, which was becoming one of my favorite places in Green Valley. I loved the lattes and was giving pleading eyes to Max most mornings for us to swing by before heading to the library for work to grab one.

Norman held my jacket for me and I shrugged it on, once again appreciating his thoughtfulness. We said good night to everyone, assuming Rose would be in bed by the time I got home, and off we went into the crisp night. He let me open my own door this time without me having to pull a mad dash to get there first, and I was happy to see he was learning. Inside the truck, before we got going, I snuggled over next to him and he put an arm around my shoulders, and I said, “I keep feeling like a giddy teenager again.”

“I keep feeling like I’ve been given the second chance of a lifetime, Lois. And I’m not going to blow it. I learn from my mistakes, and I don’t make the same ones again. Letting you go was the biggest mistake I’ve ever made, and I don’t intend to do it twice. Unless you want to go, of course. I mean—”

“Shhh. I know what you mean.” I kissed his scruffy cheek and playfully tickled his

beard. He was still wearing the Santa hat but had left the jacket back at the house. I plucked the Santa hat from his head and plunked it down on mine, and he smiled as he started up the truck. I scooted back over to put on my seat belt, my excitement mounting; not only about seeing the lights, but about Norman and me.

If I could truly let the bad parts of the past go and hold on to those good times in my heart, then I think this could be that second chance he mentioned. Maybe. Hopefully? Yeah, definitely hopefully.

CHAPTER 14

NORMAN

Our walk under the stars lit up by the displays on Main Street was damn well magical, with Lois holding tightly to my hand the whole time—at one point even looping her left arm through my right so she could take some of my weight on the return trip to the truck. I'd messed up my back on the excursion to get the tree, but I had hoped neither she nor Rose suspected anything. I was getting by alternating mild painkillers. After all the years that I'd been off morphine I still craved it, and I had to constantly remind myself at times like this that a fair bit of pain was worth it to be clearheaded and present in the moment. Because, at the moment, the present was good.

Lois was sitting beside me at Daisy's and we were talking about two of my favorite topics: computers and gaming. They used to be two of Lois's favorite topics, too, and judging from the conversation, they still were. I had finally convinced her to take the laptop from me as a loaner, and I would surprise her on Christmas with the new computer, whether she wanted it or not. I had the money socked away, even after the recent rebuild on Lucille and the cost of the move. And who could say no to a Christmas present?

"All I'm saying is, *Final Fantasy Eight* was in no way better than Seven. Worse story, weaker characters, and monotonous gameplay. Period," I said, dumping some sugar into my fresh coffee.

"You're wrong," she replied, munching on a bear claw. "The graphics in Eight were amazing for their day, and both the Guardian Force and magic systems were fun, not monotonous. But please, continue to hold onto your ill-informed opinions."

"You're pissy because you could never breed the golden chocobo," I finished, taking a long sip of my hot drink. "I still play, you know. Piano, I mean. Remember when I sent you that—"

"MP3 file of you playing a selection of songs from *Final Fantasy Seven*. Yeah, I do. I still have it."

"You do?" I asked, lighting up. I would have thought she would have run that file through a shredder app by now, lest any traces be left on her computer.

"Of course I do. You played beautifully, Norman. But wait, I didn't see you bring a piano on the back of that truck of yours. Did you leave it in Florida?"

I squirmed in my seat. "No. I sold the piano after my mother died. I couldn't stand to look at it anymore, remembering all the times she had forced me to practice, and then how much fun we had on the holidays, me playing carols and everyone singing along. It hurt too much. It was one of the few things I've gotten rid of, to be honest. That trailer needs a going over and to be sold. I have a feeling that this Green Valley thing is going to work out fine." I bumped shoulders with her.

"You know, Rose has a piano in the parlor," she singsonged, poking me in the side.

"I am aware," I muttered under my breath, taking another sip of coffee. "I wasn't sure I would be welcome to play it, so I didn't ask yet. I mean, what if hers has super sentimental value, too, and that's why it never gets played?"

"Oh, poo," Lois said, polishing off the doughnut and digging a wet wipe out of her purse. "Instruments are meant to be played and enjoyed. I bet she would love some carols or something like *The Nutcracker Suite* played for her this season."

"I guess so," I said, suddenly wanting to change the topic.

Lois doctored up her own coffee with cream and sugar and, as though sensing my mood change, she asked, "I'm thinking about getting Elsa more interested in STEM. Do you think you could help her maybe once every two weeks or so? I thought the two of you could take apart an old laptop and show her how it works, the guts of it. Things like that. She might take a shine to building computers, or robotics, or coding, if we start her now. I mean if *I* start her now."

I smiled at her slip, though part of me felt like my heart had lurched into my throat with that "we." What kind of "we" would we be when we were three?

~

Friday night and the famous Community Center jam session was here before I knew it, and though I would normally be raiding with the guild in *League of Magecraft* on a Friday, I decided I could forgo a week's worth of loot to take in one of the more popular local traditions. I was trying to lay down roots in this town, after all, and besides, this was another excuse to escort Lois somewhere. Max and Jonathan were coming, too, so it wasn't like they'd be playing *Magecraft* as Maximus_Damage and Wrath and get the jump on me, gear-wise.

Jonathan had returned to the rental to get ready with me, and we were going to meet the girls at the center. As I put on a nice red button-down and dark-wash jeans, I heard Jonathan holler from the common room, "Did you remember the rule for tonight?"

"Yup. No glove, no love," I replied, brushing my hair in the mirror on the dresser.

"No, you fool. I mean, yeah, that's a good one, but I meant about the coleslaw. Do *not* take the last helping, or Max will thwack you. It's, like, a *thing* in this town. Everyone loves it, and I gotta say, it is pretty damn tasty."

"Noted. It was nice of Rose to bake more snickerdoodles for us, so we'd have something to drop off at the dessert table," I said.

"So has Lois been to one of these before? Or is this her first time, too?" Jonathan asked, still hollering. I didn't know why; these walls were as thin as paper.

"Nope, and yes. She's not a fan of country or bluegrass, which I find impossible to believe because she's usually so eclectic in her musical tastes. I'm hoping she will enjoy herself anyway." I worried at my bottom lip but decided that if the night went poorly then we'd do something else on Fridays. No one said we *had* to love the jam sessions.

"There's always an assortment of musicians playing all kinds of things, Max tells me, and that's what I saw at the one session I went to before. I wouldn't worry. Now, are you almost done checking your hair in there so we can hit the road?"

I gave a final glance to the mirror and nodded at my reflection. Not bad, I thought. I could do this. Date four with Lois. Oh, my. "Are we taking my truck or yours?" I asked, knowing what he would answer.

"Mine. That bucket of bolts of yours isn't fit for the road, man. You've got to sink your savings into getting it up to par. I heard from Max, who's friends with one of the owners, that The Winston Brothers Auto Shop is fair. At least take it in for a look over and get a quote."

I let out a ragged puff of air in annoyance. I knew he was right, but I also knew I was putting cash into Lois's computer for her Christmas present. I wondered how reasonable these Winstons were, and if I could cover both things now that I had to pay rent. When we moved to Green Valley, I knew that I would have to buy a new home eventually, which would mean letting go of my old one. I had to get myself right in the head to do that, because it would help me move on with my life and keep me solvent.

We piled into Jonathan's truck, his stereo blaring "Stairway to Heaven"—he never did like carols, the weirdo. I sang along anyway—because come on, Led Zeppelin—but my heart was only half in it. I was thinking about my mom and how much she loved this time of year. How we'd made the best of things after my father's death, and how she had these big, huge, pie-in-the-sky dreams for me.

And so it was with a morose mood hanging over my head that we arrived at the Community Center, only for it all to change when I saw Lois standing near the door, chatting with some locals and beaming a megawatt smile. And then I remembered. Friday was payday, so Monday she'd be getting her new-to-her car. Maybe that was why she was in such an elevated mood. I made my way over to the group she was talking with and noticed her attentions were focused on one individual in particular: a tall man, with a shock of red hair a few shades darker than Lois's, a beard, and quite a handsome face. I walked up to Lois, put my right arm around her waist, and pressed a kiss to her left cheek.

"Norman!" she almost yelped. "Damn, you scared me. Well, now that you're here, I want you to meet Beau Winston. Beau, this is my… This is Norman Grant."

"Ah, another new arrival in Green Valley." The redheaded man smiled at me and stretched out his hand. I took it and shook it firmly, wanting to make it clear that Lois was with me tonight, lest he get any ideas. Then I had a brain wave. The car.

"That's right, fresh up from Florida. So, it's Beau *Winston*, is it? Are you by any chance one of the brothers who owns the auto shop in town?"

"I am." He smiled wide, and damn if he didn't ooze charm. I bet he had women falling at his feet, and a few men, too. "I was discussing with Lois about picking up her car on Monday."

"That's great. My truck has been recently slandered as a 'bucket of bolts' unsafe to be on the road, and I'm hoping to get a second opinion on that from a qualified mechanic."

"Well, that'd be us. Give us a call on Monday or pop on by and we'll get you an appointment. No problem, Norman."

"Thanks, Beau." We shook hands again, and I couldn't help but see Lois roll her eyes at the male posturing she was seeing from me.

"Well, see you two inside. Enjoy the night! My brother's on banjo and my brother-in-law is on guitar in one of the rooms."

"Ah, Beau?" Lois asked quickly. "Do any of these rooms have a piano in them?"

He scratched his beard. "Well, now that you mention it, there's one in the room my brother is in, actually. Do you play?"

"No, but Norman here can tear up the keys. He's kind of shy, though, so…"

"Well, nothing to be shy about. Hop in and give it a try if you're up for it, man. Good luck—hope to hear you play!" And with that, Beau retreated inside the building, leaving Lois and me to look at each other awkwardly.

"Lois, I kind of resent being offered up for the town's entertainment," I began, but she cut me off right at the pass.

"And I resent you practically pissing on my leg! That man is my mechanic and is happily partnered off to a lovely woman who also works at his shop. You should be ashamed of yourself."

I suddenly was ashamed of my caveman behavior. What had come over me, that I staked a claim to Lois so publicly, when we hadn't defined that we were even in a relationship? She was free to flirt with whoever she wanted, even though that wasn't what she was doing in the first place. Her mechanic, of all people; who was in a relationship, anyway. God, I had to get a grip.

I held up my right elbow to her, and asked humbly, "May I escort you inside, madame?" to which she responded by taking my arm and nodding once, her saltiness obviously stowed away for now. "Jonathan has a plate of snickerdoodles from Rose for our contribution to the dessert table, in case you and Max didn't bring anything," I said, floundering for safe conversation topics.

"I know, I was home when she made them. That woman can bake. She reminds me of my mama sometimes. I don't have many memories of her, but baking with Mama when I was a little girl is one of them."

"I remember fishing with my dad. I know I had to go into the army because he did, but I stopped resenting him for it and remember the good times now. It helps. Same with my mom."

Music was pouring out of every room as we made our way through the hallways, and it was in the most packed room that I saw a piano in the corner and heard some very capable musicians pumping out some fine tunes. It was a bit bluegrass-heavy, but there was room for piano in there, I was certain. My stomach lurched. Could I jump in and keep up? Should I, to impress Lois? Maybe she'd mentioned it earlier because she wanted to see me play in person, and not just on an old MP3 file.

I decided to hell with my insecurities, and I was going to go for it. I kissed Lois on the cheek, hauled her into the room, and said, "Wait here," into her ear. Then I made my way to the front of the room and got the attention of the banjo player, pointing from me to the piano. He enthusiastically nodded his head, so I approached the old beauty and sat on the stool, cracked my knuckles, and got the feel for the tune. Then I was off.

A few of the other musicians whooped when I joined in, and then we took it down a notch, to a melancholier tune that the man on guitar sang, who was likely the aforementioned brother-in-law of Beau Winston. It had been a long time since I'd improvised with strangers like this, but it was also fun as hell. I turned and saw Lois in the crowd, having pushed her way forward a bit, her eyes laser focused on me and shining. I played for her, and if I weren't listening to the other musicians, I would have sworn we were the only two people in that crowded room.

CHAPTER 15

LOIS

After Norman wowed us with his skills on the keys, he and I had made our excuses to the many people who wanted him to keep playing and crept outside toward the back of the Community Center. Hand in hand, we giggled as we acted like teenagers hoping we wouldn't get caught but needing each other right the hell *now*, not after a drive back to the rental. I knew if I was riding an adrenaline high from watching him play, that he had to be even more keyed up after his performance. And all that energy crackled in the air between us, especially when he first got back to me in the crowd and whispered huskily into my ear, "I need you, now."

I wasn't about to argue. My emotions when it came to Norman had lately taken a sensual and downright sexy vibe. We reached the back of the center, and he backed me up against the brick wall, then cradled my chin in both of his hands and stared straight into my eyes. How long had it been since a man had looked at me with such unbridled, feral desire? Had David ever? No, definitely not. I'd never seen such raw hunger in a man's eyes and knew that I was about to kissed the hell out of.

I nodded my head once and then he was on me, his mouth fusing to mine and our tongues in a desperate dance of pent-up passion between the two of us. And holy hell, would every make-out session with him make me feel like I was about to be consumed by fire? The chemistry between us was off the charts, and I groaned in relief when he separated my legs with one of his, giving me something to grind down on.

By the time his hand had made its way up my shirt and my hand had started to unzip his pants, he stopped us, his breathing ragged.

"Lois, as much as I want this, what is happening between us is too special to spoil with a quickie in the outdoors with half the town inside." I conceded he was right, but my hormones were involved here, as well as my heart, and my body demanded satisfaction. We righted our clothes and walked around the building to Jonathan's truck, me texting Max that I was getting a ride home with him.

Luckily, the guys each had keys for each other's trucks, and Jonathan could hitch a ride with Max. We drove to Rose's place in near silence, listening to carols and my hand resting on his jean-clad thigh. Norman escorted me up to the front porch and kissed me so lightly, so gently, that I felt cherished as he held my hands in his. I held on to his hand as long as I could, with him eventually walking away, our fingers parting and my heart yearning.

The next morning, I decided before breakfast to do something I had sworn I wouldn't do. I grabbed the laptop Norman had given me and double-clicked the *League of Magecraft* icon. I created a trial account, and then spent about a half-hour making Peily, an elf druid who could act as healer. The missing piece in a four-person arena team, as I'd been told. They already had Norman as Deathdrop, the rogue who attacked from the shadows, Max as Maximus_Damage, the warrior who plain kicked ass, and her backup, Jonathan, as Wrath, the knight who could do limited healing but was not really meant for it.

They were doing well as a team, tearing up the charts so I'd also been told, but would like to move up from a three-person team to a four-person team if they ever found the right healer to gel with them. Well, I clicked on my free level up included in my new account, and suddenly Peily had max level gear and abilities. I simply had to figure out how to play this game. But honestly, how hard could it be? I was great at *Guilds of the Ages*, and *Magecraft* was considered a spiritual successor to it.

Three hours later, breakfast forgotten, I was riding my mount—a Zebrah I'd named Galadriel—into battle, killing ogres and stealing treasure. This feeling I had rushing through my veins was old, familiar, and freaking awesome.

~

It was almost noon when Rose gently knocked on my door, and I rather loudly over the sounds of fighting coming from my laptop said, "Come in!"

She entered the room carrying a tray with tea, soup, and a sandwich on it.

Bless Rose. And blast this game! I'd gotten into a fugue state where I'd lost track of time, my only focus on the next fight, the next puzzle, the next treasure. I logged off and looked up.

She stood there smiling at me and said, "My Maxie and her friends got to you, didn't they? Oh, they wanted me to play that game with them, too, but I couldn't figure it out. Too complicated for me. But you, you sounded like you were right at home when I came by earlier to check on you. Lots of yelling at the computer and the sounds of clashing swords, you know."

Oh, I knew. I could get super involved in games like this, and that would explain why I was still in my nightgown, breakfast not eaten, my teeth not even brushed. I suddenly wanted a shower very badly, and to devour what was on that tray. As if sensing my longing for the food, Rose placed the tray down on my bed and then pointed at the chair in the corner. "May I?"

"Pleashe," I said around a bite of sandwich. I quickly swallowed and, ashamed of my manners, said clearly, "Please do."

Rose pulled the chintz chair over toward the bed and then curled up in it, her feet tucked under her. "I'm sorry I wasn't here to greet you when you got back from the jam session, but I was tuckered out after cleaning the parlor and… Aw, hell, that's not true. I was in my room, my nose buried in a romance novel about a very naughty Highland rogue and the lass he kidnaps. Then she kidnaps his heart." Rose looked a bit dreamy as she leaned over to the tray and nipped one of the crackers for the soup and started nibbling on it.

"Sounds like a decent book," I said in between bites.

"Oh, it is. So how did the jam go?"

I put the sandwich down. "Rose, it was amazing. They were playing mostly bluegrass, but I think that's supposed to be all string instruments, so I guess some country mash-up once Norman got on the piano—"

"Norman played?" Rose interrupted, leaning forward in her chair.

"I think I kind of dared him to," I admitted, feeling slightly bad, but not too much. "I was talking with one of the Winstons—"

"Oh, those men are dreamy to the last one!"

"Rose!" I snickered. "I think Norman was jealous, and so I taunted him a bit. I asked Beau if there was a piano in the community center and there was, in the room with the banjo-playing Winston who it turns out is friends with Max. He's in her book club. And fuck it if Norman didn't get right up there and start killing it on the piano. I mean, um, sorry for my language, Rose."

"Honey, this might surprise you, given the graying hair and the motherly ways, but I have heard the word 'fuck' in my life. Even used it a time or two. You aren't going to offend me. I only ask that while there is a child under my roof, we can the sailor talk. But you don't speak that way around her, anyhow."

"Oh my God, Elsa! What time is it, Rose?" I almost spilled the soup in my rush to move the laptop closer to me and shut the game down completely, flipping open Skype.

"It's okay, you've got time. That's why I came when I did; I know how my Maxie gets involved in her computer or lost in a book and loses track of what other things are important. You can eat your lunch before your Skype date. Which is in thirty-five minutes."

I let my heart return to its normal place in my body from my throat and looked at the other woman with sheer gratitude. "Why couldn't you have been my mom, Rose? You're always looking out for me—were before you even knew me—and invited me to live here."

"Well, we don't know what or why the good Lord does the things She does, Lois, but I do know I'm not the perfect mother. There are reasons why I was alone in this huge house while my own daughter chose to use part of her grandmother's inheritance to buy her own cottage in the same town as me. I think I was too tough on my Maxie, or maybe too much for her to handle after her father's death, and I stopped being able to go out."

I swallowed some of the soup and contemplated that. "But you know Max is crazy about you. She loves you very much. She goes to the Piggly Wiggly and the pharmacy for you and does whatever other errands you need. Though, when I get my car in two days, that will change. I'm taking over some of those chores, gladly."

"But Lois—"

"It would be my honor if you'd let me. You've been more of a mother to me in the last month than my own mother ever was."

Rose looked down and picked at the horrendous chintz fabric for a moment, then looked back at me, eyes soft. "All right then, dear. Now, tell me more about your date while you finish up."

~

"The foal is the smartest baby horse in the world, Mommy. I asked Philippe if he thought so, too, because he knows everything about horses, and he said yes. She knows that I'm her friend and will let me pet her nose and her flank. She's so soft. One day she will grow up and be a big horse, and when I'm a bigger girl, I can ride her. If it's okay with you, Daddy said."

"We'll definitely talk about it, sweetheart," I said into my tablet as I sat in the parlor. Elsa had been wowed by our tree and the tour I'd taken her on of the house to show her what decorations we'd put up, like the evil mistletoe bunches and Mormor's gnomes, and she bemoaned that she didn't get to make a popcorn chain this year. David overheard her and said not to fear, that he and Philippe would go pop some popcorn right then and leave the two of us some privacy for the rest of our Skype date.

"It certainly sounds like you're having a fun time," I said, smiling at her. It was impossible for me not to smile at my baby girl when she was in a good mood, which was often. She had inherited the bright, sunny outlook on things from David's side of the family, I was sure.

"Oh, I am! I never want to leave, except for I'd miss you too much, Mommy. I miss you now. And when I'm home with you, I never want to leave there, but I miss Daddy and Philippe. Do you think that's okay?"

My heart broke for her, but I understood perfectly what she was saying. She felt caught between two worlds and didn't want to miss time with any of her parents, even though it was inevitable. Because I had thought about it, and I was not moving to France. I know Elsa would have an excellent upbringing on the vineyard and have all her parents there. But I needed to think about my own happiness, too, because I knew what it was like to be raised by miserable parents. And I would be miserable, I knew, if I didn't give what was going on between Norman and me a chance.

"I think that's perfectly okay, darling. I know it must be hard, always missing your mommy or your daddy. And Philippe. But we have Skype, and we have our letters, and your trips, right? And you know that no matter how far you go, you are always in the hearts of all three of us. There's nowhere you can go where our love can't find you."

"That sounds like magic," she said solemnly.

"Well, I think love is a type of magic, don't you?"

"Yes," she replied, and then her face lit up. "Oh! I forgot to show you this book I found." She was gone for a split second and then returned, holding up a copy of David's anatomy textbook from university. We'd already explained to Elsa differences between biological sexes and various genders and where babies come from, so I was curious what had caught her attention in the book. She opened it to an illustration of DNA, and said, "Philippe told me that this is what our bodies are made of. But I told him no, that it is a picture of our soul. What do you think, Mommy?"

I teared up, suddenly missing my amazing kid so much in that moment that I wished I could reach through my tablet and take her in my arms. "I think you are a very smart person, Elsa-bear. I think there's a lot of truth in what you say." Then I heard David calling out in French, and Elsa's face fell.

"Mommy, Daddy is saying it's my bath time. He doesn't get the bubbles as nice as you. Maybe next time you can teach him how to do it right."

I covered up my laughter with a poker face I'd perfected for use around Elsa in times like these.

"Sounds like we have to say goodbye for now, sweetheart. Mommy loves you so much, always remember that."

"To the moon and back?"

"Always."

CHAPTER 16

NORMAN

I was working on Lois' Christmas present on my Sunday off, determined to get it done this weekend, when I got a ping on my cell.

Lois: *Magecraft*?

Me: For real?

Lois: Peily's back, bitches. But only until the New Year, I think. Should we round up the troops for some time in the arena?

Me: Hell yes! I'll get them since I'm at Max's and they're both inside.

Lois: Why are you in the shop on a Sunday? Backlog? We can always do this later.

Me: Oh, fuck no, we're doing it now. I'll come pick you up and you can set up with me in the rental unit. I have to go there to play on Lucille since someone is borrowing my laptop :)

Lois: Okay, I'll be waiting. Xo.

"Xo"? She was xo'ing me in a text? Yes! Go, Team Norman! I made sure that I was at an okay stopping point with the project and then put away my tools at record pace, practically flying to the cottage to tell Max and Jonathan to mount up for arena time. I was the leader of our arena team, and it helped us with our group dynamics in general when we really needed it back in Florida during Max's visit during that terrible time when Jonathan wrestled with his mental health.

They were both in, and I was excited as I drove across town to Rose's place. Then my heart lurched when I saw Lois on the front steps, holding a bag. A bag too big to hold the laptop. It looked more like an overnight bag. Oh, good God above, please let it be an overnight bag! I'd give up tacos for a month if it were, I swore.

She walked toward the truck, a smile on her face and her hair a riotous color of reds in the fading sunlight. She opened her own door, and as she climbed in and stuffed the bag into the back of the truck, she explained, "I thought I would invite myself over for a sleepover if that's okay. I brought some DVDs. Jonathan is spending the night at Max's, so I know your pullout couch will be free."

My heart lurched and my stomach roiled, and I momentarily forgot how to drive as I stared at her. She looked back at me in a quizzical fashion. "Is that okay, Norman? Did I overstep by inviting myself?" Overstep? There was literally no way this smart, gorgeous, perfect woman could overstep anything when it came to me.

"No." I shook my head, mouth still slightly gaped open. I got it together and continued, "No, not at all. Let's hit the road, Peily," and she beamed at me as I turned on another album of carols, this time *Elvis' Christmas Album*. No one did Christmas like the king, and there was no better music to get us in the mood for a relaxing and hopefully romantic evening.

~

"Get off my best friend, you jerk-faced troll!" came Max's voice through the headsets we were all wearing. Lois's Peily was under major attack because everyone knew to go for the squishy healers first. I crept through the shadows as Deathdrop, coming up behind the troll player and bam! Stabbed him clear in the back while he was distracted by Max attacking from the front. The troll went down, and now we had two of these other players to contend with. Jonathan was making short work of their healer, who was nowhere as badass as Peily, and soon, with a bit of teamwork, the battle was won.

It was our third victory in a row as a team, and personally, if it weren't for the amazing woman sitting in my living room, I could have skirmished all night. I typed into the chat box to Jonathan, privately.

Me: Dude, she's SPENDING THE NIGHT. As much fun as this is, get Max on board with us ditching for now. I want the rest of the night with her.

Wrath: What?! Go, Norman! Don't worry about Maximus_Damage over there, I'll take care of her. No biggie. Now shoo! Enjoy. Remember the rule!

Me: Don't eat all the coleslaw?

Wrath: No glove, no love, you fool.

Me: I don't think it's going to be that kind of sleepover.

Wrath: Well, enjoy it, whatever it is. If you don't log off in like 3 seconds, I'm going to tell everyone about how you always cry during *Titanic*.

"Why are the boys being quiet?" Max said over the voice chat. "What are you plotting? Spill!"

"My guess is they're talking about how I'm spending the night at the rental with Norman," Lois chimed in.

"What?!" Max screeched, like an excited teenage girl.

"Yeah, and to be honest, I've had my fill of the game for the evening. I brought DVDs and I want to have time to watch one. Oh, and Norman?"

"Yes?"

"Will you drive me to the library in the morning? So Max doesn't have to pick me up?"

"Of course."

"Okay, logging off. This was fun, guys. I can see the appeal. I'll keep playing with you until Elsa gets back, but after that, I make no promises."

We all said our goodbyes and logged off at around the same time, leaving me sitting in my room, wondering what was going to happen next. Then I began a frantic tear around my room to make sure it was reasonably clean, with no boxers in the middle of the floor or anything. I was usually neat as a pin—a holdover from how I was raised and the military—but I wasn't taking any chances and, satisfied, I then cupped my hand in front of my mouth and exhaled into it, smelling my breath to see if I should hop into the bathroom and brush my teeth. My breath passing the sniff test, I gathered up my courage and whispered to myself, "Just breathe. It's Lois. It'll be fine."

I left the still-sad-looking room and came out into the main one, where Lois had been industrious while I was being foolish. She had put the laptop away on the coffee table, and then pushed the coffee table all the way up to the television, making room for the pullout, which she was sitting on.

"Hey, you," she said, and I would swear if it were anyone but Lois, I would have called her tone shy. "I got this far, but I didn't know where you keep your clean sheets, or if you even have another set for this. I should have asked before leaving Rose's; this bed is the same size as mine there."

"No problem, kiddo; I've got the spares on the shelf in the closet in my room. I'll be right back." I returned moments later with the first set of sheets I could grab, and two pillowcases, too, and presented them to her, feeling like a knight in shining armor. That is, until we unfolded them to tuck around the corners of the mattress.

"Are these Pokémon sheets?" she asked, trying to conceal her laughter and failing miserably. Now, I could lie and say they were Jonathan's, but the huge, turquoise head of Bulbasaur looking back at me demanded I keep my honesty policy.

"Yeah. And they weren't a gift, I picked them out. Because I like freakin' Pokémon."

"Elsa loves Pokémon," she said, smoothing out the top sheet while I wrestled pillows into the matching Jiggly Puff pillowcases. "That's something you two can talk about when she comes back, in case you were worried. You know, about how to relate to a six-year-old."

I tossed the second pillow onto the bed and looked her in the eye. "Lois Washington nee Jensen, are you making fun of me?"

"No, honest," she said, her eyes twinkling and her mouth twitching at the corners. "I think it's cute that you two have a shared interest. She'll like that, too."

"And we both like Star Wars, apparently. Don't you think she's a bit young for that?"

"Norman Grant, are you criticizing my parenting?"

"No, honest," I said. "I was thinking about nightmares of hands flying everywhere and Sarlacc pits."

"Well, you may have a small point there, but Elsa is a bright kid. She knows the difference between fantasy and reality because we discussed it at length. She's aware it's all pretend."

We put the duvet back on in silence, and I thought of what to say. As the silence stretched, I thought, literally *anything* would be better than this awkwardness that had settled over us.

"Lois—"

"Norman—" she said at the exact same time.

"You go," I said, standing there, feeling like something big was brewing between us.

"Norman, I'm a direct person, you know this about me. So, I'm going to be direct. I want to share this bed with you tonight. I'm not ready for sex, but I want to feel your arms around me and snuggle into you and just… be. Can you do that for me?"

We faced off across the bed, and I gripped my cane like a lifeline. Could I do that for her? Hell yes, I could, if she could.

"You know I have scars," I began, wanting her to understand the full extent of what she was asking.

"That doesn't matter to me, Norman. I want all of you, even your scars."

"And I need to sleep on the left side of the bed, so you don't squish my hip or leg. Not that you're heavy, and not that I would care if you were, but I need to have space on that side because it hurts most nights and—"

"You're rambling. Are you nervous? Did I ask too much of you?" She sounded concerned. She cocked her head, her tongue wetting her lips.

"No," I said, walking around the bed to meet her. "You asked just the right amount." I brought my lips down to hers, then dropped my cane and entwined my other hand in her silky hair. Her body fit against mine like it was made to be there, and in that moment, in the sharing of breath and the glide of tongues, I felt like I was home. I never wanted to let her go; I wanted to feel the press of her breasts against my chest, the curve of her waist under my hand, which had worked its way down from her face to rest there. Her hands had settled over my ass, pulling our hips together, and that was fine by me. We kissed like the world was going to burn and these were our last moments together. I'd never been with a woman so passionate, with so much heat between us that I felt I might get scorched.

After a few minutes, or ten, or twenty—who could count right now—she broke it off, and snuggled under my chin for a moment before murmuring, "Want to climb into bed and watch a movie?"

Panting slightly, I adjusted myself in my pants, which were way too tight at this point, and muttered, "Uh-huh."

She let out a deep, throaty laugh, and then made her way over to her bag, pulling out a handful of DVDs which she plunked down on the coffee table. "We should get into our pajamas before we settle in."

Good idea, I thought. Then I could ditch these jeans, which were still causing me problems. "I'll be right back. The bedroom has its own bathroom, so the one out here is all yours. It should be clean because Jonathan is hardly ever here."

"Thanks, Norm," she said, and I loved hearing the old nickname from her lips again. Like, if the kissing weren't a big enough sign that I was forgiven, that would be.

"No problem, kiddo." I bent to pick up my cane, my back tweaking a bit in the process. Ouch. Well, at least we were going to bed so I could stretch it out. Lois, who must have those eyes on the back of her head that every mother seems to, noticed.

"Did you hurt yourself? I wouldn't have minded grabbing the cane for you, you know."

I bit the inside of my cheek. How to handle this? "I know you mean well, but to be honest, which is my policy with you, I would have minded. I want to do as many things for myself as I can."

"But now you're in pain," she pointed out.

"You could actually help with that." I waggled my eyebrows suggestively. "By giving me some stretching time before the movie," I said in a dirty tone. I found that if you said almost anything in the right tone of voice, it could be filthy.

"Norm! I thought you were going to suggest sexy-times."

"Well, it will be pleasurable for me. Stretching," I continued in the deep, sexy voice. "Anti-inflammatory cream. A heating pad. *Acetaminophen*."

"Rawr," she replied, making clawing motions in the air. "You sure do know how to get a girl's motor running."

"It's a lost art that I personally excel at."

She threw her pajamas at the bed, picked up a silky top and, oh so slowly, walked toward me, lifting her shirt over her head as she did so, revealing a lacy pink bra that did almost nothing to conceal the hard nipples underneath it. She slipped the silky top over her head, and then advanced on me. When she reached me, she stood there, running her tongue over her lips, making them shine in the lamplight of the room. Then, she performed some kind of wizardry where she undid her bra and took it off underneath her top. The bra went sailing back in the direction of the bed.

"Do I get an 'A' in the lost art of seduction, too?" she practically purred, and I swear I could almost feel my pupils dilate. Oh, my God.

"Uh-huh," I answered, my mouth gaped open and the wood in my pants not going anywhere.

"Maybe you should go get started on that routine of yours, Norm. I'll be out here waiting." Well, if that wasn't motivation to hustle, I didn't know what was, but I also knew better than to rush when my back was involved. I slowly moved to my bedroom and closed the door behind me, leaning up against it and letting out a ragged breath. That woman! What was I going to do with her?

CHAPTER 17

LOIS

I grabbed my toiletries bag and entered the small bathroom, which was, much to my relief, exceptionally clean. I quickly did my nighttime routine and left the bag on the counter for the morning. Next, I walked out to the bed where I'd tossed my silky pink pair of sleep shorts. I preferred my flannel granny nightgowns, but I longed to look and feel a bit sexy with Norman, and I knew he would appreciate the way the camisole clung to my bust and the shorts were just a touch *too* short. At least, I hoped he would. I had a thrum of nervousness running through me as I tucked my dirty clothes away inside a laundry bag in my duffel I'd brought. Then I went back to the pullout, sitting down and making several "sexy" poses for Norman to find me in until I thought to hell with it, and climbed inside the Pokémon sheets under the duvet on the right-hand side of the bed. I twisted around a bit to get in a comfortable position where I could still see the television at the foot of the bed and noticed that Norman was taking quite a long time. Perhaps I should help him with the cream he mentioned, or maybe he was having a hard time getting changed after pulling his back?

About ten minutes later, wearing hideous red pajama pants with a Christmas tree theme and a band T-shirt, Norman emerged from the bedroom, a heating pad in his free hand.

"Get in here; it's a bit cold," I complained, sure that Mrs. Potter had capped the heat on the thermostat.

"Shouldn't we pick out a movie first?" he asked, walking to his side of the bed and plugging in the heating pad, spreading it out flat where his lower back would go. It was the exact same brand I used for my menstrual cramps, not that I was going to point that out.

"Yeah, I forgot about that. The DVDs I brought are on the table, or we can watch something of yours, if you like."

"Nah, we'll pick from your pile. Let's see." He sat on the end of the bed and picked through my offerings. He held up *National Lampoon's Christmas Vacation* and proclaimed, "Shitter's full! We have to watch this one, kiddo; it's a holiday classic."

"Go for it. But be warned, I'll be asleep by the time we hit that part."

"That's cool; I like falling asleep to movies or audiobooks. Audiobooks, mostly; I have a huge collection. I put them on my tablet on the pillow next to me and fall asleep to the story. It kind of reminds me of being a kid and being read to by my dad."

As Norman got the DVD going and lay down in the bed beside me, I turned on my side so I was facing him. "I remember you used to be a big reader when we were in high school. Are you still into Sci-Fi and Fantasy?"

"I am, but I read almost anything. Or rather, listen to about anything these days. I finished *A Court of Thorns and Roses* and am reading *Redshirts* next. I also started reading romance after you argued with me so effectively back then that they are books to be taken seriously. I loved the *Outlander* series, though perhaps that's not strictly romance, and I enjoyed the *Bridgerton* books."

"Wow, I'm impressed. I haven't made it through the most recent *Outlander* book; I get so busy with Elsa, and back in New York I was too stressed to relax and enjoy reading. But I think now that we're settling in and things aren't as crazy for me with bills and worrying about being a bad parent, I'll have more time to read again. Something other than the bedtime stories I read to her, anyway, even though she can read them to herself by now. There's still something special in being read to."

"Hence why I love audiobooks so much. I pop them on in the shop sometimes when I'm working there alone. Jonathan prefers to work to music and I don't mind that either, so it's usually some kind of classic rock going on."

I moved my feet over and captured his right foot in mine, gently rubbing up his leg with my foot. As much as I loved talking to Norman, I was getting tired, and I wanted to snuggle my man.

Whoa, where had *that* thought come from? My man? Was that what Norman was? Oh, boy. I'd chew on that for a while before talking about it with him. But for now, it was time for Operation: Snuggles.

I placed my hand on his chest and asked, in a voice a tad huskier than normal, "Do you usually sleep with a shirt on? Because you can take it off if you want. It would be nice to cuddle, skin to skin." And with that, I slipped out of my camisole and tossed it onto the floor, leaving my breasts bared to him. He groaned, and quickly got with the program by likewise sending his shirt sailing.

I smiled and made an appreciative noise as I stared at his chest, and he chewed on his lower lip as he looked at my breasts, and the air felt thick between us. I felt ready to pounce, and then I remembered his back. "Hey," I said, gently pushing on his left shoulder until he was flat on his back. "Stay on that heating pad, okay? I don't want you to hurt yourself because I whipped out my tits."

"But what a way to get hurt," he said, flashing an impish grin.

"Just lie there and I'll cuddle into your side, if that's okay?"

"Yeah, definitely more than okay." He lifted his right arm and I snuggled in to his side, pressing our chests together as much as I could and placing kisses on his collarbone and pecs as I settled in. My right leg was over his, the hideous pajama pants surprisingly soft and comforting. He started running his right hand through my hair and then placed it on my bare back, tracing designs on my skin. If I'd been capable of it, I'd be purring, it felt so nice. He smelled of clean soap and medicated cream, which was part of the package that was Norman. I breathed in deep at his neck and he chuckled low, saying, "I'm not watching the movie at all. Are you?"

"Nope, not a bit." I couldn't help myself; I licked his skin below his collarbone and reveled in the taste of him. He groaned again, and this time he was in motion. Quick as The Flash, he had me on my back and was loosening the string on my sleep shorts, sticking his left hand inside and making his way to my core.

"Is this okay?" he asked.

I parroted back his earlier reply to me, "Yeah, definitely more than okay."

I slightly parted my legs, making this easier for him, and he was there, fingering my curls and exploring me, parting my lower lips. It was my turn to moan, and I did as he worked me over with the experience of someone used to working with their hands. It had been so long for either of us since we'd been intimate like this with someone else that I wasn't surprised when I came with a gasp and a shudder after mere minutes, my back arching off the bed.

"Oh my God, Norm. That was, that was… Oh my God." He touched me gently until I couldn't stand it anymore, and I pulled his hand from my shorts, only for him to stick his fingers into his mouth to clean them off. Holy shit.

"You are hotter than hell itself, Lois Jensen," he said, leaning down and pressing a soft kiss to the corner of my mouth.

"You should lie back down," I said, still gasping for air. "Your back…"

"My back is fine. Or it will be by the morning, don't you worry. I wanted this."

"Do you want some reciprocation? After I can breathe properly?"

"No." He kissed me again, then lay back down flat on his heating pad. "You're delicious."

"Perv."

"Prude."

We both laughed, and I don't know who started the tickle war, but by the end of it we were both naked and curled up with him on his back and me against his side again. I fell into the deepest sleep I'd had in months, and all was well.

~

"Oh my God, Norman, you have to taste this," I said, holding out my fork with a piece of French toast on it. With real maple syrup it was like heaven on a plate, and I couldn't remember a breakfast I had enjoyed so much. Norman leaned forward, took the bite off my fork, and made a noise of satisfaction, nodding his head.

"Yeah, I'm so getting that next time," he declared, returning to his stack of blueberry pancakes. "These are pretty great, too, though." It had been his idea to wake up early and come to Daisy's for a decent breakfast before taking me to work. We had awoken this morning in a mess of twisted arms and legs, wrapped around each other as much as possible. Norman had been sporting some morning wood, and the only thing that confused me was when I tried to go down on him, he softly pulled me up and shook his head.

I only knew David in bed, but I'd never known him to turn down a blow job in the morning, so I was flooded with self-doubt until Norman whispered in my ear, "Not yet, sweetheart. I want us to enjoy what we've had so far and not go too fast. Not when you're still starting to trust me again. Okay?"

"Okay," I whispered back, my heart thudding in my chest. He respected me. He cared for me. He wanted me to trust him. I didn't know how to handle the flood of emotion in that moment, so I put on my proverbial practical Lois panties and got out of bed and called dibs on the first shower.

"What are you thinking about, Lo?" Norman asked, reaching for his coffee.

"This morning."

"It was a nice way to wake up, yeah?" he asked, sprinkling some sugar into his cup and giving it a stir.

"The first time I've woken up to anyone else in almost six years, other than my daughter."

"Well, while Elsa isn't around, you know you're welcome anytime. We never actually did get the movie watched."

"No, we didn't," I laughed, then blushed, remembering what exactly had interrupted us and made me so sleepy.

"As soon as I'm done with my coffee, I'd like to hit the road if that's okay with you," he said, then took a long swig of the drink. I was surprised, as that would put me at the library extra early, but I supposed the maintenance closet could always use a decent reorganizing. I ate the rest of my French toast rather fast, moaning a few times in ecstasy as the deliciousness passed my lips. Breakfast at Daisy's? Definitely one of my favorite parts of living in Green Valley so far.

When I looked up from my plate, I saw Norman staring at me, slack-jawed, holding his coffee cup in the air. "What?" I asked, confuddled.

"Well, I was going to ask if you two wanted to be alone." He pointed at my plate, and then to me. I coughed, half laughing, and grabbed my orange juice and downed the rest of the glass.

"Hey, if you'd had that on your plate, you'd sound like you wanted to be alone with it, too."

"I suppose. Hey, you ready to hit the road?"

"Almost, I need my purse…" I reached out and grabbed it.

Norman interrupted me with his, "Nope, I've got this."

"Well, all right then." I smiled, because I never said no to free food.

We went up front and paid up and Norman led me to his truck, his hand on my lower back, as though he were staking a claim on me in public. I can't say I didn't like it, though, so I said nothing and even kept my mouth shut when he walked me to my side of the truck. He did, however, let me open my own door.

~

"I can't see a thing under this," I complained as we drove along a twisty road, the blindfold thick and keeping me in the dark, literally and figuratively.

"Well, it would be a pretty piss-poor kidnapping if you knew where I was taking you," he said, having produced the blindfold right after we'd gotten into the truck after Daisy's. That was ten minutes ago, and we had to be wherever we were going soon; there weren't many places in Green Valley that were more than ten minutes apart, even with morning traffic. Right on cue, we pulled into somewhere and Norman turned off the truck.

"You ready?" he asked, and when I nodded, he pulled off the blindfold and I saw… The Winston Brothers Auto Shop? And my Sentra! Right there, in front of the truck, glistening like it had been washed and polished. Oh, my *God*. I was going to get Max to drop me by here after work to meet Beau and settle up for the vehicle. I hadn't been sure how I was going to concentrate all day at work knowing what was waiting for me. Well, apparently, Norman had the same thought.

"You considerate sonofabitch." I wiped my eyes, which had filled with tears. What was I going to do with this man? This kind, selfless man who had once broken my heart and was now trying to redeem himself in every way possible. Well, this was a big freaking move in that direction. This everyday thoughtfulness, this way he wanted to make my life easier, even if it were trying to find my dropped towel or get me to my car early so I could drive myself to work.

"Hey, hey, don't cry," he said, reaching over and handing me a Kleenex and holding it up to my nose, like I did to Elsa. "Blow," he commanded, and I did, despite my embarrassment at the overflow of emotion.

"How is the car ready to go now? They weren't expecting me until after work," I managed.

"I called Beau Winston when you were in the shower," he explained, looking cheeky as all fuck.

"You called him at home? Norman!" I scolded, scandalized that he would have potentially woken up my mechanic to arrange my car surprise.

"No, silly, he was already in the shop. I asked him on Friday night at the community center what time he normally got in. He already had the car washed and waxed and ready for you; it was simply a matter of pulling it around front, and now you going in to settle up with him."

"Come with me," I said, pulling on his arm before remembering that he had to exit his side of the vehicle. This was a big moment for me, and I wanted Norman with me to see it. To see that I was building something down here in Green Valley, even if it were friendships, and a job, and now a car. I felt independent and alive and wonderful, like I was building a life.

And yeah, it may have just been a grey Nissan, but when Beau put the keys in my hand, I turned and kissed Norman so hard he practically tipped over.

CHAPTER 18

NORMAN

As I watched Lois peel out of the parking lot of the auto shop, I couldn't help the feeling of pride that came over me. Sure, I'd had nothing to do with her ability to buy a car, but I was proud of her and this achievement anyway, and pleased that I had been able to whip together a sort of surprise for her.

Then, as I was getting ready to hop back into my truck and head to the shop, a man with a slightly chaotic beard approached me. He had the name "Cletus" embroidered on his coveralls, and I assumed this must be another one of the Winston brothers.

"You here to have that looked at? I can fit you in. I heard the sound your truck made pulling in, and I didn't like it."

I let out a puff of air and relinquished the keys, giving in to the inevitable. "Do you guys have a place where I can sit down while I wait? My leg's a bit twitchy today." It flat out hurt from last night's activities for, as careful as we'd been, we couldn't control the rolling around that happened once we had fallen asleep. Lois and I both slept like eggbeaters.

"Why yes, we do; I'll show you where. Come on."

A half-hour later, after my truck had failed to be deemed road-worthy, I was driving a loaner Dodge Neon over to Max's while the staff at the auto shop had assured me they could fix whatever the hell was wrong with my truck. Despite my uncle's efforts to teach me when I was younger, I didn't know crap about cars and how to fix them or what could be wrong with them.

But I knew that the shop had a good reputation, which set me at ease that they wouldn't charge me five hundred bucks for a single screw or some shit.

I didn't finish Lois's Christmas gift over the weekend, but I couldn't be sorry about it given how yesterday and last night turned out. I whistled as I made my way into the shop, bopping my head and then flat out singing "I'm in the Mood for Love." I waltzed my way inside, grabbing a bemused Jonathan and whirling him around in the open space at the front of the shop, dancing with my friend and giving him a twirl. He broke off from me and, laughing, said, "Good night?"

"Oh man, the best night! *I'm in the mood for love,*" I crooned, continuing to dance solo, "*Simply because you're near me. Funny, but when you're near me, I'm in the mood for love.*"

"You already sang that part, doofus."

"Shhh. It's the only part of the song I know."

"I'll put up with your singing for five minutes. After that, I'm playing 'Last Christmas' by Wham! and you're losing Whamageddon like four years in a row."

"My own best friend would do me dirty like that? All because I feel the spirit of lurve moving over me?"

"Dude, let me do you a solid and tell you flat out: never use the word 'lurve' again."

I thought that over for a moment before nodding solemnly. "Duly noted. Any other great advice this morning?"

"Not great advice," he began in an upbeat tone, "but news. Max and I worked in here after arena yesterday and almost all night, getting us caught up on our backorders, and two more rush Christmas orders came into the shop. I told them that there's no way they are getting them on time unless they pay a courier, and they are both down for it so… We've got work to do."

"Sweet, considering I'm pouring my life savings into my truck, Lois's computer, and making rent. I really have to go back to Florida, man. After the holidays, maybe in the spring. I need to clean out Mom's trailer and sell it." I swear, Jonathan almost tripped over himself walking to his workbench.

"You're serious? You think you can let go?"

I scratched my beard and ran a hand through my hair like I did whenever something weighed heavily on my mind, and replied, "Yeah, I do. I'm ready. There was something about getting away from there and those walls around me that was so empowering. And then to find Lois again, it was like… It was like a freaking miracle, man. I'm not going to live in that trailer alone again."

Jonathan turned his attention to the project on his desk and absentmindedly passed me a stack of paper with the specs of the machine I was to build. Lois's present would have to wait; these were super-fast orders, and mine seemed a bit complicated. "Yo, do we have all the parts in stock for these?"

"No, but the graphics card for yours, the processor, and the extra monitors are arriving tomorrow. I got them rushed. Don't ask what it cost; we'll pass it on to the customer anyway in their shipping bill since this was a last-minute thing. They said that was cool."

"Fair enough," I agreed. Then I couldn't resist adding, "*L is for the way you look at me; O is for the only one I see; V is…*"

"Two more minutes man, then we're going to Wham! town."

"I need a date idea for Lois and me," I mused aloud, near the end of our workday.

"Well, do you want to go fancy or more homemade?" Jonathan asked.

"Both, I think. I don't need one date idea; I need a slew. Because I plan on lots of dating in our future."

"Ah Norman, hope springs eternal with you, doesn't it?"

"Hey, after the night and morning we had, you'd be hopeful, too. But I need ideas, man! I don't know this town well yet, and I don't want to take her to my place for a movie or to the jam session over and over. I want to vary it up. Show her I can be spontaneous, or at least a tad imaginative when it comes to these things."

"So, naturally, you're asking me to figure it out for you?"

I scoffed. "No, I'm asking because you had four more whole extra days here than me, and you have an in with Max. You know Green Valley better."

"Okay, well there's the obvious of course; dancing at Genie's, which we've already done as a group, but I think she would enjoy it more with you solo now, a fancy dinner at The Front Porch, and I heard there's a Christmas market she might like to go to."

I grabbed my cell out of my back pocket and opened a new note to myself. "Hold up, let me write this gold down. Front Porch—fancy—Genie's—not so fancy—and a Christmas market—perfect level of schmaltz. Thanks, bro."

"You're welcome. Um, does she like horses? Because there's this place I, uh, know. They do hayrides."

"That might be better after Elsa is back; she loves horses. We could take her there to feed them apples or something, and then maybe in the summer she'd be interested in going riding, the three of us."

Jonathan looked at me funny. "You're already planning for trips or dates or whatever with Elsa, too? That's serious, Norman. You can't get a child involved unless you're, like, super committed to the relationship. They get attached so fast, you know. Have you and Lois even defined what you are yet?"

"No," I admitted. "And I know you're right; I have to be careful around her daughter. I don't want to build up expectations and then have it all taken away if Lois and I don't work out."

"That's assuming Elsa even likes you," Jonathan said, tossing a balled-up rag at me.

"Hey, what's not to like?" I replied, grabbing the rag, tightening it up into as solid a projectile as I dare make here in the shop, and threw it at his head. It pinged off the back and landed on the floor. "Woot! Three points right there! You know, Max's backyard where it touches onto the woods would be a perfect place to play with our nerf gear."

"I take back that element of doubt I might have planted in your mind: Elsa's going to love you, because you're practically a six-year-old yourself."

"Oh, stuff it, Mr. I-Threw-The-Rag-First!" In typical Jonathan fashion, he ignored me and kept working, whistling a tune I couldn't place but would drive me crazy until I did.

I scanned around for the maintenance closet and found it, door open, Lois pushing the cart inside. Perfect timing. I walked up behind her, and instead of scaring the shit out of her like I would do if this were Max or Jonathan, I decided to play nice. I coughed to get her attention, but apparently that was scary enough because she flailed around like a ninja and turned to see who was behind her.

"Norman! You scared the hell out of me!"

I chuckled because I couldn't win with this woman. I held out the latte as a peace offering and she looked at it, to my face, to the latte, and back to my face, her expression softening. "You brought me Daisy's?" she asked, and I mutely nodded. She stepped forward and took the cup from my outstretched hand, then reached up and kissed me on the cheek.

Only for some little shit who looked about twelve to say, "Ooh, Ms. Lois has a boooooyfriend!" accompanied by kissing noises.

"Yes, she does," Lois replied, ignoring the cacophony of kids and turning to lock up her closet for the end of shift. Meanwhile, I stood there stock-still, not quite believing my ears. Did Lois call me her boyfriend? Lois thought of me that way? Holy crap! *Okay, stay calm, stay cool*, I told myself. Confirmation was needed before losing it.

We held hands as we left the building, and as we approached her car, I asked, "So, I'm your boyfriend?"

She flushed red and answered, "What else was I supposed to say back there?" My heart sank like a stone, until she said, "But I would like it if you *were* my boyfriend. I know we've only been together again for over two weeks, but we've got something here, don't you think?"

I literally had to stop myself from throwing my cane to the four winds and breakdancing on the spot. "Um, yeah, I do. Think, that is. About you. I mean, about us. You and me. I've wanted to be able to call you my girlfriend since I was seventeen years old. I never thought I would get the chance, having blown it so spectacularly. Is that what you really want, Lois? You and me? Because I am so there; I'm so ready for you and me to be an *us*."

She gulped down some latte and nodded as we reached her car. "You know that I'm a package deal, right? That it's all well and fine to want that girl I was at seventeen, but I'm a mom now. Elsa must come first in my life, no matter who I'm dating or how crazy about them I am. And I would hope that she would come first in the life of whoever I'm with."

"I understand, Lois. That's how I want it, too. Elsa first, then each other."

"Well, all right then. I guess we're in a relationship. Do we kiss on it to make it official?"

Damn straight we do, I thought as I lowered my head and captured her lips with my own. We kissed like we always did, like it was the last time, or the first; like it had to be savored and appreciated and felt to the very core of our souls. Okay, so maybe I was a bit of a sappy romantic. But honestly, I was feeling things I'd only ever read about, and I was reveling in it.

"Wow, okay," she said softly, panting hard after we'd broken apart. "It's official. Like, really official." She raised her right hand to her mouth, letting the fingers run over her lips, smiling as she did so. "As much as I'd like to stay here and make out in the parking lot of where I work, I need to run to the Piggly Wiggly to get some groceries so we can cook supper tonight. What are you and Jonathan doing? He staying at Max's again?"

"Nope, he's home and I'm making veggie wraps and salad. He can like it or lump it."

"Or go bum food off Max," Lois said, grinning. "Okay, I've got to go. Thanks for the latte, Norman."

"Oh wait! There's a bear claw for you in my loaner car. There was only so much I could carry."

"Sweet! I could use an infusion of sugar right about now." She stood by her car while I retrieved the wayward doughnut and deposited it into her waiting, grabby hands. "I'm assuming the loaner was because your truck needed a bunch of work?"

"Yeah, yeah. Everyone makes fun of it, but it's brought me here safely to you, right?" I knew I was playing fast and loose with the definition of "safely," but if she didn't ask too many questions then the point would stand.

"I believe I've heard you yourself call it a 'bucket of bolts' or something similar," she mused while I cringed.

"Okay, so it's a love-hate relationship I have with it. Still, though, that one Winston, Cletus? He told me that it was worth saving rather than junking it and starting over with a new car. He sounded like he knew his stuff."

"Cletus, I've heard that name before. Oh! He's in Max's book club! A friend of Max's wouldn't screw you over." I felt relief ripple through me, considering we were talking about my life savings here, which were dwindling.

"Well, I won't keep you. The Piggly Wiggly awaits," I said, and I couldn't resist opening her car door for her once I heard her hit the unlock button on the key fob. She stubbornly reached out and wrested the door from me, closing it herself with a mighty slam and sticking her tongue out at me.

That's my girl, I thought, and waved at her as she drove off.

CHAPTER 19

LOIS

The next few days were hectic and I didn't see Norman. No, scratch that, the next few days were hectic for *him* in his shop. For me, they consisted of my usual routine at work, and then playing Cards Against Humanity once with Rose, Max, and Jonathan, reading Rose's historical romances, doing chores for the house with my new car, or doing quests in *Magecraft* with Max.

I knew Norman and Jonathan had picked up some local business, the gossip chain of Green Valley having caught on that there was finally a computer shop in town. They had several Christmas orders, and I also knew that Norman felt compelled to take on the brunt of the workload right now. I wasn't sure why, but I think it had to do with money, and I understood all about needing extra money.

Then, on Friday, he popped up at the library at the start of my shift, looking a tad sheepish, latte in hand. "I know I've been MIA for a while, but I swear I'm not ghosting you. I got caught up in my orders and even had time for a side project. No more crazy late hours for me."

"That's good; you could stand some time to relax," I said, taking the latte from him and planting a kiss on the corner of his mouth. Every time I saw Norman as a man and not the skinny, shaggy-haired teen, I swear my breath caught in my throat that I was allowed to kiss this man, to hold him. He was so gorgeous, with defined muscles in his arms but a bit of a dad bod in the front and a pair of eyes that could ensnare a person. And those hands, mmm those hands. What they were capable of drove me wild.

"Lois, you there?" he asked playfully, and I knew I missed something while I was daydreaming about his incredibly sexy body.

"Yeah, sorry. Just woolgathering."

"I was wondering if you want to go to The Front Porch for dinner with me tonight, instead of the jam session with the gang."

"The Front Porch? Isn't that kind of swanky? Do you even own a suit?" I'd only ever seen Norman in band T-shirts, Henleys, or light sweaters and jeans. The thought of him in a suit was suddenly very appealing.

"Yes, I own a suit. Do you own a dress?" he sassed back, and I laughed.

"Okay, it was a silly question. But of course I'll go with you. It should be fun. I haven't been out to a fancy restaurant since David was wooing me, and even that wasn't *fancy* fancy. I'm actually pretty excited about this." Then, to distract from my runaway mouth, I punched him lightly on the shoulder and took a huge gulp of latte. "I should get in there; the library won't clean itself," I said a tad too cheerfully. Why did I suddenly feel awkward? Was it because I'd mentioned David and wooing to Norman? Probably, I decided. New plan: don't regale your new boyfriend with tales about your ex-husband.

"I'll pick you up at around six, okay? Our reservation is for six-thirty."

"Sounds perfect." With a discreet kiss, I turned and made my way into work.

~

"Oh my God, I own nothing that's appropriate for a fancy dinner!" I wailed at Rose, my room looking like the closet had exploded, flinging all my clothing onto the bed.

"Calm, child. There are three dresses right here and they all would be fine. Especially if you put this one here, the green, with a shawl I have. It would make your eyes pop and look gorgeous with your hair. Now slip into that dress, honey, and I'll go get my shawl. Then we'll do your hair and makeup. When did you say he's coming?"

"In fifteen minutes!"

"Well, I've worked miracles under harsher conditions than this. We'll have you turned out like Cinderella going to the ball. Now, dress!" And with that, Rose left to go to her room and I pulled the green silk dress down over the slip I was already wearing. I next pulled on some hose and picked out my go-to pumps that had seen a lot of mileage but were still in fair condition.

When Rose came in bearing a beautiful green and red shawl that was obviously an antique, I couldn't help but tear up. The dress I was wearing was sleeveless, and this would make it appropriate for both the weather and the Christmas season.

"See, my dear? Nothing to fuss over! Wear this and remember to break out that gorgeous smile of yours from time to time," she instructed firmly. I laughed and nodded, and then we set to work on taming my hair into an updo. By the time Rose had finished slipping a borrowed earring onto my left ear, I heard the doorbell ring and I felt like a million bucks.

"I'll get it!" I hollered, already halfway down the stairs. When I opened the door, I went completely slack-jawed at the sight which greeted me. Norman was dressed in a deep navy suit complete with a waistcoat, and his beard had been freshly trimmed. He held out two bouquets of flowers, and I immediately knew what he was doing.

"Rose!" I said, unable to keep the huge grin off my face as I noticed that one of the bouquets had red roses in it, and the other purple—my favorite color.

"Why, what in the world!" Rose exclaimed when she appeared, and Norman held out the bouquet with the red roses in it. "Thank you, Norman." She then plucked the other bouquet from my hands and said she would get them both into water right away and would place my flowers up in my room. If Norman was out to impress tonight, he had certainly started on the right foot.

We drove to the restaurant, singing along to another of Norman's holiday albums, this time doing a rousing rendition of "Rockin' Around the Christmas Tree." Norman was a surprisingly good singer, whereas I couldn't carry a tune in a bucket. Not that I let my terrible singing voice stop me from joining in. I found I wasn't embarrassed around Norman like I thought I might be. He was, after all, the boy in whom I'd confided all my secrets as a teen, and there wasn't much now that I wouldn't share with him. Bad singing included.

After we were shown to our table by a pretty woman named Hannah, our server, Deveron, gave us the four-one-one that this was *the* place in town to get a steak dinner. I told him we'd need a few minutes, and I looked over to Norman and said, "Let's go Dutch tonight. That way we can each get a nice steak dinner and neither one of us will be unfairly burdened. I know all about money being tight, and now that I can afford a place like this for myself, I'd like to pay for my own meal. Besides, you've paid every time we've gone to Daisy's."

"But Lois, I invited you here. I checked out the menu online to make sure I could afford it before I asked. I won't argue with you about a dinner check of all things, but I will say that I want to spoil you a little. I think you haven't been spoiled enough in your life as an adult, always putting Elsa first, and I think it's time someone stepped in and took care of you. Not that you can't take care of yourself, but that's not the point. The point is, I want to do this for you. For us. Okay?"

I couldn't help the smile that burst out across my face. "Okay, then. But I'm getting the steak and a Caesar salad, and maybe a glass of wine."

"Sounds great," Norman said, grinning back.

~

Dinner was everything I had hoped it would be, with Norman behaving like a perfect gentleman and the conversation flowing as freely as the wine. We talked about comic books—he preferred Marvel and the indie scene, while I could never give up my love for Clark Kent—and movies we'd seen, books we'd read, anything to catch up on the last ten years. I finally told him the whole story about NYU, and he looked sad for me when I said that I had dropped out, but then confused when I told him that I had managed to get my Associate of Applied Science in Business degree by taking online courses while caring for Elsa. He did have one question, though, which I'd been anticipating.

"If you have a degree from NYU in business, even if it's not a Bachelor's, why are you working as a library janitor? I mean, why aren't you working for some company around here, like Payton Mills, or in Knoxville?"

"Would it shock you to know that I actually enjoy being a janitor? Look, I know it's not what everyone dreams of doing when they grow up, but I love working at the library. I love the vibe of it, the faces I get to see every day, the routine to the work and then the not-so-routine stuff. And it was the first job that was on offer when I moved here. I know Max advocated for me, no matter what she says. I was sort of using my degree in New York, and I was miserable at that company. God, I can still feel my ass being pinched when I think about it. Maybe I won't work at the library forever, but for now it's good for me. And I believe in the value of honest work. When I look back, I think that there were some shady practices going on at my last company." I took another gulp of wine from what had to be my third or fourth glass and looked at him earnestly.

"Well, I have to respect all of that, and I do, kiddo. You're something special. But I've been having a brain wave and I want your advice, as a businessperson, before I run it by Jonathan. That okay?"

"Sure, shoot," I leaned forward, paying close attention. The wine was getting to my head a bit, but I wanted to take in what he was going to say.

"Jonathan and I, when we started Supernatural Computers, went with an online business model because, where we lived, there was no place or point in having a storefront. There wasn't the population in our town to support us. But here, we've been getting word of mouth orders from people in Green Valley just by working out of Max's garage. I think if we went into the repair business as well as building, we could manage a real store and workshop. But we would need someone to run the business end and the customers while we took care of the nuts and bolts. Jonathan already does the customer interactions and the finances, and he hates it, how it detracts from his time building. I think within the next year we'd be ready to expand if we keep on our current trajectory. If we did expand, would you be interested in coming on board? We couldn't pay much more than what you're making at the library, not at first, but you'd be using your degree and be integral in getting our venture off the ground." He took a long sip of water and waited for my answer.

"I think that's… That's the most I've ever heard you talk about business, Norman. And it's sexy as hell." I took my foot out of my pump and rubbed my hosed toes over his right pant leg.

He coughed, and almost spat out the water he had in his mouth. "Okay, that's it; I'm officially cutting you off and taking you home. To my home, so Rose doesn't see me bringing you back all loopy. My God, that was three… No, wait, it was four glasses of wine. Geez. I guess we were talking, and Deveron kept pouring."

"Mmmm yes, let's go back to your place," I said, thinking that was the best idea I'd heard, ever. Norman signaled for our check and settled up while I retrieved my wayward pump and then weaved my way to the bathroom to break the seal. I had overdone it with the wine, because even though I wasn't normally a lightweight, I also hadn't had more than a glass or two since Elsa was born.

At length, I emerged from the bathroom and Norman took my arm as I giggled and told him how handsome he was. My own mood swings were making me nauseated. I didn't even complain when he loaded me into his loaner car and off we went to the other side of town to his rental. When he unlocked the door and threw the lights on, a boxer-short-wearing Jonathan thrashed around on the pullout, obviously not expecting us to be laughing and turning on the lights. Cripes, how late was it?

"Ugh, what time is it? I thought you'd kind of creep in, Norman. I mean, I didn't know you'd have company tonight. Should I, uh, leave?"

"No, man; I'm a gentleman and she's way too buzzed for anything like that to happen. I'm going to tuck her into bed with me so Rose doesn't see her like this."

"Better give Mama Bear a call or she'll worry all night," Jonathan offered.

"Already done. She told us to have fun," he laughed. "I know I'll have fun if she doesn't puke on me."

"Hey, I'm right here," I piped up, "and I am not drunk. I'm a bit tipsy. Hey, Jonathan. Norm and I are going to snuggle. And one day, we're going into business together. Have a good night!" With that, I sashayed across the room and entered the bedroom, carefully putting Rose's shawl over the back of Norman's desk chair and pulling my dress off over my head. I could sleep in my slip, but there was no way I was sleeping in the hose. I kicked off my heels, and when I bent to take the hose off, there was a loud thud that I registered before I realized that it was me, hitting the floor.

CHAPTER 20

NORMAN

I learned a few things after our dinner at The Front Porch. First, a buzzed Lois was a Lois that snored like a chainsaw. And second, my bed was not wide enough for two people who rolled around in their sleep. I slept mashed up against the wall, and that meant that Lois was lying on my bad hip and leg for most of the night. I didn't want to wake her by getting up to take pain medication, but at around three o'clock, I couldn't stand it anymore and had to wrangle her to the other side of the bed so I could get out and get to a painkiller.

I decided to take some ibuprofen with it, too, and smeared some pungent anti-inflammatory cream on my hip and leg in the bathroom. I hated that my leg and hip were so sore, because of my plans to go to the Christmas Market with Lois tomorrow—well, later today, actually—and I didn't know how up for walking I'd be. My doctor had suggested I get a walker for the difficult days, but I didn't want to go there yet. I knew it was a stupid pride thing, and there was nothing wrong with using mobility aids, but I felt I could manage with my cane for a while yet.

I went back to the bed and Lois was awake, watching me in the dim light coming from the bathroom.

"Sorry I woke you," I said softly, not wanting to wake Jonathan. The walls in this place were paper-thin, another reason that I saw this as a temporary living situation. At least it was a month-to-month lease, so we could leave whenever we wanted.

"You didn't wake me." She yawned, and I knew she was lying to be polite. "How's your hip?"

"Haven't had any complaints," I replied, trying to get a smile out of her. *There we go.* I'd knocked that concerned look off and she was grinning, patting the outside edge of the bed next to her.

"I think you should sleep on this side. I'll take the wall, and I can sleep on my side. I'm sorry I was smushed onto you, I wasn't thinking about your leg or hip at all last night. That wine went right to my head. It's actually rather embarrassing."

I turned off the light and walked over to the bed, feeling my way across the room. "Hey, don't be embarrassed, kiddo. I had a feeling it had been a long while since you had some real adult time. I mean, French toast at Daisy's in the morning is great and all, but getting dressed up and having a nice steak and wine? That's awesomeness, and I don't fault you for indulging a bit."

"Oh shit," she said as I sat down and got ready to get into the cramped bed. "Did you call or text Rose? She must be worried sick!"

"First rule of my philosophy to life: don't panic. I texted her, and then when she didn't reply to the text, I called her. I'm not sure she knows how to text, come to think of it. We should teach her."

"We should snuggle down for another six hours," Lois replied sleepily. I heartily agreed, but I knew that unless the over-the-counter pain pills had magic in them, I was going to be sore until morning. My body was screaming for morphine, and I was glad I didn't have any left on me because I wouldn't be able to stop myself from taking some if I had access to it tonight. That was the bitch about morphine for me; I'd fought to get off it with the help of my doctors, but I never fully stopped craving it.

The next item to come out of my savings: a new, wider bed. I lay down with my left leg hanging slightly over the edge of the mattress and Lois curled up into my right side. I put my arm around her and kissed her forehead as she fell back into a deep sleep, buzz-sawing it up again.

~

After a splendiferous breakfast at Daisy's, I secured directions to the Green Valley Christmas Market. We were a week away from the big day, and I wanted to get some more of my festive spirit on, and plus I thought Lois would appreciate it because I'd heard that there were all kinds of local vendors set up with items that would make great gifts. She'd admitted she hadn't done any shopping yet but wanted to get Rose, Max, and Jonathan all something small but meaningful, so I figured the market would be right up her alley.

We'd had to go back to Rose's place first for Lois to change, return the antique shawl before some disaster befell it, and to ask her if there was anything from the market she wanted us to look out for to bring back to her. Promising to look for homemade soaps, we took off, the cooler air having us both in coats and me wearing a pair of mittens. I knew this wasn't cold to Lois, but I was from freaking Florida; the light, slowly falling snow Lois called a "flurry" was mitten weather for me.

Mitten handholding was a bit of a challenge, and once we arrived at the market, I took my right mitten off so I could sap Lois's warmth like a wraith. I had to say, Green Valley went all out on this whole affair. The Christmas Market was like something out of a schmaltzy Christmas movie, which was exactly what I was hoping for. I knew Lois missed Christmas in New York, but this held up pretty good. There were plenty of vendor stalls, all looking like log cabins with fake snow on the tops, and wooden cutouts of elves where you could stick your head in a hole and get your picture taken. There was even a beer garden set up by Genie's. The pièce de résistance was the tree, which had to be at *least* fifty feet tall and decked out in lights. While there was Christmas music blaring over speakers right now, apparently carolers came out at night to sing by the tree. There were plenty of activities for children, and I figured that would make Lois miss Elsa, so I focused on keeping her busy.

First, we hit up a drink stand—Lois getting an apple cider and me a hot chocolate so I could warm my hand. There was also the delicious smell of baking bread wafting through the air which we followed to a pretzel stand and each got one. We found a table so I could handle both the pretzel and my drink, not having two available hands. Plus, my leg was aching like a sonofabitch. I'd take any sitting down time we could get.

A boy wandered over to where we were sitting, attracted by the bright stickers I had all over my cane. They were all superheroes, except for a Hello Kitty sticker, and this wasn't the first time a kid had been drawn in to have a peek. I held the cane upright so he could have a look, and he then looked at me with wide eyes and asked, "Are you a superhero, too?"

"Nah, buddy. But I like them. Who's your favorite?"

"Wonder Woman. But I don't see her here," he said in an almost accusing tone, funny coming from what appeared to be a four-year-old.

"I have Catwoman over here on this side, see?" I pointed. "She's pretty cool, too. And over here I have Spider-Man and Iron Man, who are both my favorites." He seemed to consider this and nodded. "Do you have a grown-up you're here with?" I asked the kid, looking around for a frantic parent.

Lois came over, knelt next to the boy, and asked, "What's your name, honey? We should find your family."

"Oh my God, Pat! There you are!" Ah, the frantic parent revealed themselves. A woman came running over and knelt beside Lois, grabbing the boy into a huge hug.

"I wasn't lost this time, Mommy; I was right here. Look at this stick!" He pointed to my cane, and the mother put her face in her palm.

"I'm so sorry; he will wander off the second you take your eyes off him, I swear to God. Did he bother you? I'm sorry if he asked questions that made you uncomfortable."

"No, no bother at all," I answered. "I love kids. We were actually asking him if he was here with a grown-up; we would have kept an eye on him while trying to find you."

"Thank you so much. Pat, were you nice to them?" the mother asked, and Pat nodded solemnly. "Okay, then, you can still have your reindeer ride. Let's go. Wave to the nice people, honey."

Lois got up from where she was crouched on the ground and we both waved Pat and his mother off as they went over to a pen with ponies that had fake antlers attached. "You handled that well, Norm," she said. "I haven't seen you interact with any children except Elsa, and she liked you well enough for the time you were together, but I wasn't sure how you'd be around kids in general. I like men who are good with kids."

"I get attention from kids because of my disability," I explained. "I mean, even Elsa's first real question to me was if she could play with my cane. The stickers are also a draw. I didn't think of that when I put them there, of course; I put them on for me, but cartoons are a hit with the little ones. And I like how kids aren't afraid to ask the questions that embarrass adults, like what's wrong with me and how I got hurt. I usually tell them that I was a soldier and got hurt overseas, if they're old enough to understand that. I went into the whole story with Elsa because she seemed mature enough to handle it, and I also wanted you to know. I didn't want misplaced pity from Max's BFF for being a wounded warrior when I'm only a guy who was lucky enough to escape a burning vehicle."

"Well, speaking of being wounded, how are you feeling today? I've noticed you're walking slower than usual and leaning on your cane or my arm more. Are you okay to stay here? The market is open until Christmas Eve; we can always come back another time this week."

I was crestfallen at her words; I didn't want my disability to be something that held us back from enjoying time out together. "How about a compromise? Let's finish up our food and we'll do one trek around the vendor stalls. We'll also skip the beer garden, you lush. Sound good?"

"Sounds perfect," Lois replied, taking an enormous bite of her pretzel and moaning at the salty, buttery flavor. That moan went straight to my dick, and I felt my pants tighten. *Not here, you dope,* I told myself. There were kids everywhere, and older ladies selling homemade beeswax candles, for Pete's sake! I finished up my own pretzel and wiped my mouth and hands with napkins while I watched Lois fetch out one of her endless supply of wet wipes.

It was tiny reminders like those wet wipes which drove home that Lois was a mom. I wondered if I would be able to keep my promise to her and put Elsa first always, because right now, my heartbeat was practically spelling out "Lois" in Morse Code.

Bogged down with purchases, we made our way to Rose's house, finishing up the last stanza of "Last Christmas"—covers were allowed under Whamageddon rules. We hollered for Rose to stay where she was in the parlor because we had gifts for her in our arms and we made the trek up to Lois's bedroom on the second floor. Curse these older houses that had stairs that were like a goat path—narrow and steep. On a good day they'd be no problem for me, but today it hurt making the climb. Still, I didn't want Lois to know, so I sucked it up and followed along behind her. If she noticed my slower than snail pace, she said nothing.

We'd decided to do joint gifts this year, which was awfully couple-y, and simply fine by me. Max and Rose both got an assortment of homemade items, from soaps to beeswax candles to bath bombs. Jonathan was getting a nice knit hat and gloves, beeswax lip balm, and a book a local author put out about gardening in the region. He'd talked about wanting to do some landscaping at Max's for her, so we figured this would be right up his alley.

I'd debated going back to the market later this week to pick up some items I'd seen Lois cooing over but decided that the computer was a big enough gift, and I didn't want to overwhelm or embarrass her. People got funny about gifts sometimes, comparing who gave and got what, which I thought was ridiculous.

I wondered what Elsa was getting for Christmas, and then remembered that Lois said she had sent some books over with David from the Little People, Big

Dreams series, on Malala Yousafzai and RuPaul. She wanted Elsa to have a variety of role models, so I decided to pick up a few of those books myself to give Elsa when she came back. She could unwrap them under our tree at Rose's since it would still be up when she returned.

We wrapped our gifts to our friends in this wood-blocked paper we found at the market, which was expensive but looked amazing, and then trooped back downstairs to place them under the tree. I noticed Lois giving the branches tugs and declared it was holding up decently, thanks to Rose's efforts to keep it watered.

I kissed Lois long and hard on the porch before driving home, where I knew I had nothing waiting for me but an evening and a night alone in pain. Jonathan was probably at Max's, and while we said we would skirmish in the arena tonight, I didn't feel up to being our captain right now.

I was tired, and my whole left side from the waist down was screaming at me relentlessly. I wanted relief. I wanted fucking morphine, or to down a bottle of vodka and pass out. But I also wanted to stay clean and sober, so I left in the Neon and gritted my teeth as I drove across town, hating my body and driven to the point where I hated the world itself.

CHAPTER 21

LOIS

The buzz of my cell interrupted me as I was dusting the magazine shelving area. I knew I wouldn't catch hell from Thuy for using my cell for a minute during work—she knew we all had lives and families—but I still wasn't a fan of it going off unless it was an emergency.

Jonathan: Hey, Lois. You hear from Norman lately? I tried his cell like a dozen times and he isn't answering, and he didn't show up in the shop today. We're swamped, so I didn't go over to the rental yet to see if he's there. I was hoping you'd heard from him.

Me: No, I haven't heard from him or seen him since Saturday, at the Xmas market. I think he was in pain that day.

Jonathan: Shit.

Me: What?

Jonathan: He used to drink a lot when he would be in bad pain. He replaced that with gaming, but he hasn't come online at all since Friday. I'm worried.

I looked around at my maintenance cart and the almost empty library and made a snap decision.

. . .

Me: I'll be at the rental in fifteen minutes. Less, if I can manage it.

Jonathan: Thanks so much, Lois. The spare key is under the planter on the left side of the front door.

Me: I'll let you know as soon as I know anything.

I wheeled my cart back to its closet with a sense of urgency, and then ran down the basement steps to Max, who had her headphones on and was vibing to something while cataloguing. I tapped her on the shoulder, and she threw up her arms in the air and dropped the book she'd been holding.

"Christ on a cracker, Lois! What the hell? Is something wrong?"

"I don't know," I said, out of breath. "It's Norman. Apparently no one has heard from him since I last saw him on Saturday, and he was in a mess of pain then. Jonathan messaged me, and I said I'd go to the rental to make sure he isn't drinking himself to death."

Okay, so maybe I was exaggerating, but remember the exploding half-empty glass? Yeah, this was the time when stuff like that crossed my mind.

"Oh my God," Max said, putting her face in her hand. "We were so busy this weekend, we didn't check in with him. He can get low when he's in a lot of pain, Lois. The painful spells, the really bad ones? The ones that put him on his ass? He used to be on morphine for those, and when the morphine stopped, he started drinking. He doesn't do it anymore, but maybe… Maybe I should come with you."

I sighed in relief, because that was exactly what I was hoping she'd offer. Plus, this way we could present a united front to Thuy about why we needed to leave in the middle of the workday.

Ten minutes later, with her blessing, I was almost speeding in my Sentra to the rental, my heart pounding in my chest and my hands shaking. Where was the Lois who could handle anything? She had fled the coop, and I was a ball of nerves and tension. The man I loved was in trouble. The man I… loved? Like, *loved*-loved? Yes, I told my inner voice, this was the man I loved, and we were getting to him even if I had to plow through this car in front of me going at least ten miles below the speed limit. I honked on the horn and made a rather dangerous pass, which had Max screeching like a banshee, and had us at the rental in moments.

When I pulled up to the curb, she said, "Who are you, James freaking Bond?"

"When someone I love is possibly up shit's creek? You bet I am."

"Someone you love?!" she said as we ran up to the front stoop.

"Stow it for now, Max. The extra key is supposed to be under this incredibly heavy planter. Help me?"

She leapt into action, us both hefting the planter, and I grabbed the key in triumph then asked Max if she would mind waiting on the stoop unless I needed her inside. She gave me a quick hug and said of course she would, and with trepidation, I opened the door.

The apartment was neat as a pin, but the bedroom door was closed. I heard a small voice call out, "Jonathan? Thank fuck you're here."

"It's not Jonathan, it's me," I said as I opened the bedroom door.

"Well, damn," he responded. He looked as white as the quilt he was huddled under, with sweat beaded on his forehead and his hair wet from it and his body shivering. He looked like hell, and I was suddenly so scared that I started to shake, too. There was an empty water glass on the bedside table, which I walked toward and filled in the bathroom. I went back to Norman and sat on the bed beside him, helping him lift his head to get down some water.

"Tell me what's going on, Norman. How can I help you right now? Do we need an ambulance?"

"No!" he said sharply. "Sorry. They'll want to give me morphine or something like it, and I can't go there again, Lois. I can't. You don't know how hard it was to get off that poison. Yes, it helped take my pain away, or at least took my brain to a place where I didn't care about the pain, but the cravings, the need for it… It wasn't worth it. I weaned off it slowly, over two years. Two freaking years to get off morphine. No ambulance."

"Where are your other painkillers? Your cell? I don't understand how it got this bad." I helped him get to sitting and he groaned a bit but reached for the water cup, took it, and drained it in a millisecond.

"I ran out of pills last night. I had my cell but it went dead, and the charger is in my truck. My hip and my leg, sometimes they get so bad I can't walk that far. And overnight the pain, oh my God, the pain, Lois. Lois, are you here? I hoped Jonathan would come. I've pissed myself because I couldn't make it to the bathroom and back this morning. I fell trying—my leg went out from under me—but I did manage to climb back into bed. You'll never want to be with me now."

"Norm, I'm here. I want you to listen to me, okay?" I pulled out my most authoritative voice. "You are in hell, and I know that. I have some pills in my purse, and I'm going to give them to you right now, and in about twenty minutes you should start to feel better. No morphine, I promise, just Tylenol and Advil, okay?"

At his nod, I rummaged through my purse and grabbed two Tylenol and three Advil and refilled the water glass. He took the pills and drained the entire glass again.

"Okay. Now, this is going to suck, but you're going to have a shower. You don't want to be lying there in your own sweat and mess, do you?"

"Fuck no."

"I'm going to get one of the kitchen chairs and put it in the shower. We get you onto that chair, and if you can't wash yourself, I can wash you down while you sit, okay?"

"Yeah, sounds like a plan."

"Now, wait two minutes while I tell Max to go back to work and put in my excuses with Thuy for the rest of the day. There's no way I'm leaving you like this."

"Max is here? Don't let her see me like this, kiddo. I couldn't stand it. It's bad enough you are."

"Max won't know a thing other than you overslept, your phone went dead, and you're feeling like shit, so she can tell Jonathan you won't be in today."

"Thanks, Lois," he said, his voice sounding like it was coming from between gritted teeth, and I felt he was preparing himself for the walk to the shower. Well, this time he wouldn't fall, because I would never let him.

"I'll be right back." I leaned down to kiss him, and he pulled his head away.

"Sorry; it's only that I threw up in the trash can. I tied off the bag so the smell wouldn't be so bad, but trust me, you don't want to kiss me right now." I leaned down and kissed his forehead instead, gently wiping his brow then clasping one of his hands, tight.

"I'll be right back. I promise."

I first sent Max back to the library, assuring her that we would be fine and asking her to make my excuses with the boss. Next, I grabbed the slimmest of the mismatched wooden chairs from the kitchen and headed to the bathroom to place it inside the shower stall. I turned on the water to a nice temperature and put a washcloth and the soap where Norman could reach them. I noticed my hands were still shaking and I told myself to get it together right the hell now, because he needed me. I knew he said his bad days were few and far between, but this was one of them and I was going to get him through it, damn it.

When I got back out into the bathroom, my composure restored, I found a naked Norman sitting up on the bed, rubbing his left thigh. I picked up his cane from where it was on the floor and handed it to him, and then put myself beside him and heaved his arm over my shoulders. He was a lot stronger and more determined than I gave him credit for, because even though he cursed every other step, he made it the dozen steps to the shower and plunked himself down in the seat, making a noise of relief when the warm water hit him.

"Oh, Lois? I forgot to ask you to get my gabapentin from the medicine cabinet. That will help a lot. It's for nerve pain. Three of the yellow pills, please."

"Sure thing." I got the pills as Norman found the washcloth and soap and started to clean himself up. I cupped my hands and he opened his mouth, and I kind of tossed the pills in while he let water pour into his mouth and then swallowed. He nodded, and then sort of lay back in the chair, eyes closed, so I took that as my cue to take the washcloth and soap from him and finish up as fast as possible. When he said he could do his own hair, I ran out into the living room and pulled open the pullout, deciding that it would be quicker to get him into that bed than to make him wait while I changed his sheets.

With a bit of help from me, he rose in the shower using the wall and chair for support, and I turned the water off, confident that the painkillers I had given him were doing *something* by now, even if it wasn't enough. I grabbed a fluffy towel off a shelf and began patting him down, careful to avoid his left lower side. It felt good taking care of him, treasuring him, and I knew I would do whatever he needed of me.

I handed him his cane and we began the same awkward walk as earlier, this time to the pullout couch. I laid a fresh towel over the pillow so his wet hair wouldn't soak it, and tucked him in under the blankets because he was still shaking a bit.

"Thanks, Lois," he said, grabbing my arm. "I'd have been up against it today if you hadn't come by. And thank you for staying. I know that wasn't pleasant."

"Don't thank me for doing the bare minimum for someone you love, Norman. Of course

I came, and of freaking course I didn't leave you like that."

"Someone you love, huh?" He smiled then, and it was so needed that I didn't even berate myself for picking what on the surface seemed like the worst possible time to drop the L-word.

"Yeah, someone I love. Now, where is the stinky cream you put on that hip and leg of yours?"

"I can do that if you can grab it. And a glove, since I won't be able to get up and wash my hands. It's in the medicine cabinet; gloves are with the first aid kit under the bathroom sink."

"Done," I said as I scurried off, my heart racing. I had told Norman I loved him. But Norman was in a hell of pain, and this kind of situation couldn't continue. We had to focus on what was important here. Just then, I had an idea. I returned and tossed him the tube of cream, got him another drink, and wrote down on a slip of paper tacked to the fridge what time he'd had his meds and what he'd taken.

"Norm, when you moved here, did you investigate finding a new doctor? Perhaps someone with a specialization in pain? My Mormor, she had a pain doctor who would give her injections in her back. Maybe you need injections in your hip."

"I used to get them every four months through the VA. They helped. But I haven't in a long time. I used to have to drive to Jacksonville for them and it was a pain in the ass. I got used to living with how things were, and they haven't been this bad in ages, Lois. I swear, if you think I'm always like this when we aren't together, you're wrong. It hasn't been this bad in like a whole year. I'm not usually so… so… God, I'm trying to think of the right word. Helpless. I'm not normally so helpless."

"You're not helpless now, Norm. You had a run of bad luck. I mean, I know that fall didn't help you any, and that wasn't your fault. Running out of your pain meds was probably more my fault than yours; I've kept you so busy that you haven't been on top of things here. And even Jonathan is at fault because he shouldn't leave you here alone for days on end. I mean, what if you'd been abducted by aliens? How would we know?"

"Jonathan called you, though, didn't he," Norman said, settling down more under the blankets. He looked exhausted, and I hoped that he would be able to rest now that he was clean, in fresher sheets, and had taken some things for the pain.

"He texted me. He was worried sick and was going to come over here himself, but I guess you guys got in a last-minute order that was complicated? I don't know, I don't care. I'm glad I was the one who helped you. And hey, where's that heating pad of yours? You're all dry under there by now, yes?"

"Yeah. And it's out here. Over there on the other side of the couch."

"Well, I'll wrap your hip or leg in it, whichever part hurts worst. Do you need me to run to the pharmacy to get anything else, other than your pain meds?"

"You're leaving?" he asked, suddenly looking incredibly young and vulnerable.

"No, I'm not; not yet. I was thinking about ducking out after you've gone to sleep and had some time to feel better. But I'm not abandoning you, Norm. I promise I won't ever do that. Not when you need me."

"I always need you, Lois. Not because of my screwed-up hip, or leg, or anything. I always need you here." He reached up and touched me lightly between my breasts.

"Dude, are you trying to cop a feel?" I teased, holding his hand in place then bringing it up to my mouth so I could gently press a kiss to his palm.

"No, you fool; I'm demonstrating my love for you by touching your heart."

"You always touch my heart. No demonstration necessary."

CHAPTER 22

NORMAN

When I awoke at what the alarm clock told me was four o'clock in the afternoon, I found fresh bottles of all my meds and a huge glass of water all on the bedside table. Curled up into my side was Lois, who had at some point stripped down to her bra and panties and was loosely holding my right hand and had one arm arced up over my head, like she was protecting me.

My body was due for another dose of meds, I thought, but I couldn't be sure, so I'd have to wake her. That's when I saw the note on top of the Tylenol: *Eat Me at 3 or later.* God, how I loved this woman. She'd seen me at my worst, and instead of freaking out or getting other people involved, she respected me and cared for me, my body, and my privacy. I was at about a four on the pain scale now, which was amazing considering I was at a nine through the night, and reached over, shaking out some new meds to keep them in my system and prevent the pain from ramping back up.

As I was settling back in, I heard the door open and saw Jonathan peek his head inside. "Man, are you okay?"

"Shh," I replied, pointing to Lois, who was now moving and making little moaning noises, reminding me of a kid who doesn't want to get up in the morning.

He nodded and came over, sitting down on the floor by my side of the pull-out, and said, softly this time, "You look a lot better than I figured. We need to do something to make sure this doesn't happen again, man. Like, I shouldn't have left you here alone for so long without checking in. I feel like hell about that."

"I don't need a babysitter. Last night and this morning were the result of a clusterfuck of epic proportions, but I can tell you it won't be happening again. I'll take better care to keep on top of things so it doesn't get that bad again. And I'm going to try to get a doctor up here through the VA in Knoxville maybe, who can start up my hip injections again, since I'm going to be more active than I was in Florida, I think."

"Damn skippy you're going to do all that," Lois piped up sleepily. "Hey, Jonathan. Thanks for the texts this morning. It all went okay; you don't have to worry." Lois brought her hand down and threaded it through my now-dry hair, and it felt amazing. It felt amazing every time the woman I loved touched me, and now that I knew she loved me in return? Even better.

"I got us all caught up at the shop, and I shut down the online order form until after the New Year. We could both use a break, for our mental and physical health," Jonathan said in a voice that would not be argued with. "We tried to do too much, too fast, I think. I know I've been a bit more anxious than normal, with the relocation and then thinking about possibly expanding, and with suddenly having a woman in my life."

"I know." I yawned, and then said, "Sorry, but I am so tired. Do you think you could spend the night at Max's again? She's not sick of your face yet?"

"No, you jerk, she's not. Of course I can. But I expect those sheets changed."

"About that, I want you to take the main room until I get around to buying a bigger, better bed for myself. This one is so much more comfortable. Oh, don't give me that Eeyore look; we didn't know when we were doling out room assignments that you were sending me off to sleep on something with broken springs that was also too narrow for me and my girl."

"Also, in my defense? You didn't have a girl back then."

"Fair points, all," Lois said, sitting up, forgetting that she was wearing only an almost see-through pink bra.

"Um, Lois," I began as Jonathan threw an arm up over his eyes. "Top. You're not wearing one."

"Ack!" she exclaimed and pulled the blankets up around her. "My clothes are here… One sec, Jonathan." I watched her as she got out of bed, this gorgeous redheaded goddess that was all mine. She slipped into the long T-shirt she'd had on under her cardigan from work, and then pulled on her dark jeans. "I'm dressed. You can drop your arm. I couldn't possibly have traumatized you that much; Max has a pair of breasts, too."

"Hey, when it's your best friend's girl it's an entirely different scenario. I mean, do you want to see my bat and balls? I don't think so."

"I see your point."

"As much fun as this conversation is," I butted in, "I need to go to the bathroom, and I'm buck naked under here. Anyone who wants to can watch." I threw back the covers and grabbed my cane, which Lois had thoughtfully placed against the bedside table.

"Man! Give a guy a little more lead time on that, okay? I don't want to see your naked bits," Jonathan protested.

"Oh shush, ya big prude."

After my trip to the bathroom and a thorough brushing of my teeth, Jonathan was gone, so I sauntered around the apartment naked for a while, exercising my leg and hip. I had spent way too long lying on it, and that was also the reason my lower back hurt like it did. Lois was working in the bedroom, cleaning up in there, and I was so freaking grateful. I longed to shout my gratitude to the universe that had brought us together again and given her a forgiving heart. She appeared a moment later, my red fuzzy pajama pants and a plain black tee in her hands. "I didn't think you'd want to get down on the floor to do your stretches in the buff," she explained. Then she unrolled my yoga mat and asked me if I needed a spotter.

"No, this isn't the trampoline. I just need to get down to the floor, and I can do that on my own now. I'm feeling so much better, honestly. If you want to leave, even, I'd be fine."

"I never want to leave you," she almost whispered. Then she got down on the floor beside my yoga mat, crossing her legs and reaching up her arms for me to have something to grab on to if I needed it.

"So, you want to tell me more about your condition? I mean, the prognosis, what I can do to help, that kind of thing?"

"Well," I began, lying on my right-hand side so I could do the left leg raises that were part of my routine. "It's nothing too serious. I live in some level of pain all the time because the drugs I can use aren't enough to kill it entirely. And my balance is kind of messed up. Sometimes my left leg goes out from under me, like when I fell last night. Hence, the cane. But it never gets above a six normally on the pain scale—that's six out of ten—unless I mess up and do dumb stuff like fall, or if there's a big barometric drop."

"Or if you walk around during the cold at a Christmas Market while already in pain, and then push it further by walking up and down the steepest stairs in Tennessee? Kind of like that?"

"Lois, I made those choices because I *wanted* to do those things with you. But, yeah, you're right. I pushed too hard on Saturday, and then I couldn't move so well. I should have tried harder to get to my truck and that charger when I still could have made it, but it didn't occur to me that I was going to be at a point where I *couldn't* make it. I didn't know how bad it was going to get. Like I said this morning, it hasn't been like this in, like, at least a year, maybe a bit more. You don't have to worry about me. I lived alone in Florida; I can take care of myself when I make the right moves." I turned and flopped onto my back, and brought both knees up, bent comfortably. Then I yanked my left leg up and over, so the foot was resting against the right knee. I took a hold of my left knee and gently did pulls and pushes, feeling the stretch in my hip.

"Do you do these exercises every day?"

"Three times, yeah. They're supposed to help, but I don't know if they do or not. Since it's no skin off my back to do them, I'm not going to stop for the sake of finding out."

"I don't want to be pushy here, but have you considered that you might need to be on a low dose of morphine? Or some other drug like it? Or have a supply on hand so you can—"

"No. Definitely not. I know you're trying to take care of me, but you have to trust me when it comes to my own body. Yeah, I got all fucked up this weekend. That was my fault. And I won't do it again, no matter how much I want to see you stick your face through a cardboard cutout of an elf, okay?"

"Okay. It's your body, you're in charge." She leaned over and planted a kiss on my mouth, and I knew we would be all right.

We were on the pullout in the middle of eating pizza and playing a rousing game of Go—something we'd learned how to play together online back when we were teens—when I had a thought. "Let's talk about sex."

She belted out the lyrics to the song, snapping her fingers and bobbing her head.

"Ah, I love me some Salt-N-Pepa. But yes. Because I think this whole experience of today has driven home the point that, yeah, I'm disabled. And that means that when it comes to sex, there are some things I can't do, or maybe I can do on one day, but not on another. I want you to know what you're in for. Because I love you, and, unless I was very mistaken earlier, you love me. Which means there shall be sexy-times in our future."

"Hopefully in the near future." Lois smiled. "Norman, I don't care about the things we can't do; and the things we can, we'll enjoy a hell of a lot. And if we don't enjoy it, we stop and reassess. I'm usually the overprotective worry-wart, but I think, in this, I have to say you're taking up that mantle. Because I'm not worried at all. Sex between us will be beautiful, no matter how it happens."

"Oh?" I raised my eyebrows in challenge. "Want to see who can clean up Go and pizza faster?"

"Heck yeah, I do."

Cleaning up our supper and game turned into ripping our clothes off as fast as possible, with Lois elbowing me in the eye while taking off my shirt, and me getting her helplessly tangled in her bra when I tried to take it off over her head instead of taking the time to unsnap the thing. Finally, we were both naked, panting, and staring at each other on the pullout couch, and I knew this was it. After ten years of regret and longing, Lois Jensen was going to be mine in every way. And I'd be hers, as much as she wanted me. Which apparently was a lot, because she was looking at me with a gleam in her eye that reminded me of something I'd seen on the Discovery channel.

"You look like a lioness on the Serengeti about to leap on to a water buffalo. Slow, that's the first rule. We start out slow and see how things feel. For both of us, but mostly because I don't want to overdo it."

"Got it, slow." She got on all fours and crawled across the bed toward me, that look still in her eye.

"And uh, you can't, um…" Damn, I was losing concentration, fast. She nuzzled her head into my collarbone and licked a line up my neck. "You can't be on top," I panted. "Sorry, but it won't work that way."

"Got it." She peppered kisses along the side of my face. "When's the last time you had a woman, Norm?"

"Sometime around the Nixon administration," I replied, closing my eyes and letting her take control for now. Her kisses were gentle, as were her roaming hands.

"If anything I do hurts you in a bad way, tell me. I mean it. No pushing through because you're trying to please me."

"Okay—oh, wow, yeah, that, do that again," I encouraged as her hands had worked their way down from my pecs. She let out a throaty, husky laugh, and kept moving her hands over me, and I felt like something freakin' precious. I leaned in and captured her mouth with mine, her lips parting and letting in my tongue, which did battle against hers for dominance. No, it was more of a back and forth, a push and a pull that was timeless and scorching. Her scent was all around me, and as I twined my fingers in that fiery blaze of her hair, I felt something deep inside of me come alive, something that I hadn't felt in a long time. With this woman, in her arms, I didn't feel like an orphan who had only two best friends in the world. I felt like I was finally home. I wrapped my arms around her and flipped her, sending her squealing onto her back, and decided it was my turn to make her feel the same way.

Cherished, appreciated, cared for.

Loved.

CHAPTER 23

LOIS

In the days leading up to Christmas, more presents appeared under the tree in the parlor, and Rose began baking up a storm of cookies, squares, and cakes. At first, I didn't know who she was trying to feed, considering we were a total group of five not fifty, but then I was schooled that Rose made up little gift bags of goodies and gave them to her friends who visited her over the holidays. I'd been living with Rose for over a month when this whirlwind of baking began, and I wasn't aware that she'd gotten many visitors, but then I wasn't around during the weekdays. And it was also true that now and then some kind of casserole would show up in the fridge, so I guess Rose did have a girl squad after all.

I had ordered some *League of Magecraft* merchandise for Norman and put it under the tree, but I wasn't sure it was personal enough, considering we were now officially a *thing*. I ran this by Rose, who laughed and said there were many years when she got her husband socks for Christmas, because that's what he wanted and needed. She told me not to stress the presents, that it was the being together that made the holiday.

The only thing that nagged at my heart was Elsa's absence. Our twice-weekly Skypes were fine, but they weren't the same as having her here. Technically, I could keep her year-round if I wanted, but it felt wrong to me to separate Elsa from a father who wanted to be involved in her life. But it was moments like this, like filling up a stocking for her to open in the New Year, that made me miss her *so* much. I longed to tickle her, or chase her around pretending to be a velociraptor, or run my fingers through her bouncy curls.

I pictured Norman doing those things with her, and something inside me felt warm and vigorously alive. Like maybe, one day, we could be our own little family of three instead of us living off the generosity of Rose. I had to berate myself for getting too far ahead of things in my mind. I didn't even know if Norman wanted kids of his own, or if he would be able to think of Elsa as his daughter and not merely another kid. Because Philippe had been all-in didn't mean that Norman would be.

Every day after that disastrous Monday, Norman had shown up at the library in the morning for me, latte in hand. Though there was technically a no food or drink policy in the building, I would decide to take my break at those times, and we would sit together outside if it weren't too cold for Norman, or in my car if it were, and talk. Or rather, he would talk while I drank.

I learned more about how lonely he had been in Florida, despite having Jonathan and the Owen family nearby; how he sometimes hated his own father for being a war hero, because it placed such expectation on Norman's shoulders. And I learned that I was the first woman he'd ever been with who hadn't made him feel inadequate in bed because of his disability. That was part of the real reason he'd given up on dating; finding someone who could love him as he was and not be disappointed in the end felt like finding the ultra-rare Ultimate Weapon in *Magecraft*.

Christmas Eve brought with it a cold front that also meant a bit of real snow, not a flurry that amounts to nothing. When Norman arrived at Rose's that morning, he pulled me out onto the porch and kissed me long and hard, his body molding perfectly to mine. I broke away from him and hustled him around the veranda to the side of the house, not wanting to give the neighbors across the street a free show. He had this almost feral look in his eyes as he pushed me up against the side of the house and pressed our mouths together in that delicious dance that we had basically perfected by this point. The next thing I knew, Norman was growling as he took off his right mitten with his teeth, and then resumed kissing me while also sticking his hand up my ugly Christmas sweater. I sighed into his mouth and let him explore me as he would, until I heard a creak on the old wood and then a feminine cough. Max.

"Oh yeah, Max and Jonathan were right behind me," he laughed, extracting his hand and putting my sweater back to rights. Meanwhile, Max and Jonathan both stood there giving us twin stares of amusement while they were in the middle of carting presents and food into the house. I let out a satisfied noise as I passed them down to… Norman's truck! The Neon was gone and there was the old rust bucket, looking shiny and new. The passenger side door was open, and I could see a few more presents in there, so I grabbed the largest box and hoofed it to the house, lest I drop it.

"Whoa, Lois, you got that?" Norman called, and though the box covered up my vision, I knew the path to the parlor by heart. I deposited it in a corner under the tree and then caught a look at the card attached to the top, almost concealed by an enormous bow. "*To Lois. No take-backsies. Love, N. Xoxo*" Seeing the x's and o's on the card made me feel all twitterpated, and I had to remind myself to stop daydreaming while my friends were lugging in groceries and other gifts.

I moved to the kitchen and found Norman standing in the doorway to it, leaning up against the doorjamb. I wrapped my arms around his torso from behind, and he reached up and held on to my hands where they were linked around his midsection. "Rose, Max, do you need any help in there?" I called, hoping to feel of some use and not like an interloper.

"No, dear; why don't you entertain the boys in the parlor? My Maxie and I can handle all this."

I started to protest, but then stopped myself. This was Rose's home, and these were Max's and her traditions. She also probably wanted the alone time with her daughter, like how I cherished my alone time with Elsa. "Okay, troops, let's move. We've got a huge stack of board games to pick from, and I know how much you enjoy tabletop gaming," I declared.

"Or we could take turns logging on to *Magecraft* and get our gifts from the Yuletide King," Norman suggested, his eyes dancing with excitement. Behind him, Jonathan nodded.

"Okay, Yuletide King, here we come," I declared. Jonathan grabbed a laptop bag from the foyer, and we settled into the parlor for some free in-game collectables from their Santa Claus pastiche.

First, I got this enormous Staff of Wild Healing, a rare gift that would help make my player dominate even more. Jonathan tried his luck next and got a huge freakin' sword that glowed in shifting patterns, making it look like the weapon was on fire. Next up was Norman, and as he logged on to Deathdrop, he rubbed his hands together in glee. A short flight to the capital city, and he was ready to crawl on the Yuletide King's lap. And his gift? A slingshot. A toy slingshot, which would vanish after being used a few times. Oh, and he got a few snowballs to lob, too. Jonathan and I cracked up when Norman said that this was total bullshit, and I whispered in his ear, "It's because you've been a naughty man this year." I then bit his earlobe, and I felt a shudder run through him.

We were in our own world temporarily, leaning in for a kiss when Max interrupted, saying, "On my mother's couch in the middle of the afternoon? Really, guys? And hey, is that the Yuletide King?! I've got to get in there and see what I got!"

Max came along and inserted herself between Norman and me on the couch, a slightly evil grin on her face. She took her turn logging in and visiting the King, making loud "Whoop whoop" noises as she unsheathed a badass battle-axe that looked like it could destroy anything she cut with it. "This is great, guys; we got new weapons for the arena. Almost all rare items, too; except you, Norman. Sorry."

"Yeah, I can sense your utter heartbreak for me," he replied sarcastically.

After some time, during which the four of us were talking at once, Max got up and said, "Okay, huddle up for room assignments." We all came to a hush and she said, "We have two bedrooms upstairs, both with queen beds. So naturally I'll be with Lois, and Norman and Jonathan, you can take Elsa's room. That's what we discussed, right, Mom?" I hadn't even noticed Rose enter the room.

She looked mischievous as she smiled benevolently at the group. "Yup, we did. And no hangdog faces around here! You can go without getting any for one night."

"Momma!" Max exclaimed, her accent coming out a bit more in her voice when she was scandalized.

"Oh shush, Maxie. I've been in love a time or two, I know how it goes. Now, everyone grab your bags and settle in upstairs. I'll be in the kitchen keeping an eye on the mulled wine."

Mulled wine? That wasn't something I thought was on the agenda; I thought everyone was having the homemade eggnog Rose already prepared. As much as I had dreaded drinking that concoction because I couldn't stand the stuff, I was grateful that there would be something festive for me to drink. I grew up with mulled wine on Christmas Eve—I wonder if I had ever told Rose that. I let it go and we trooped upstairs one at a time because of the narrowness of the staircase. Max pulled Jonathan into Elsa's room, which I had made up with fresh sheets, so I figured they wanted alone time. I grabbed Norman's hand and lent him some support for the last of the steps, and then we went to my room.

"Your room is nice, Lois. I love old houses like this; the history, the bones of them."

"The extremely small windows?" I laughed, pointing at my window. Okay, so maybe it wasn't *extremely* small, but it was definitely smaller than it looked from the outside. "You know, this used to be Rose's room when she was growing up. The kicker? There was once a tall oak outside the house on this side, and Rose used to squeeze through that window and climb down to sneak out and hit up the bars or honky-tonks, or whatever they're called down here. When her father found out, he was furious, and the oak was cut down."

"Wow, go Rose. What a rebel," Norman said, grinning. "I bet she could cut a rug even now. It's a shame we always have to leave her behind when we go out as a group."

"Well, there is a piano in that parlor. How about we get down there and you show off some of your skills? Bring the singing and dancing here?"

Norman seemed to think on that for a moment, then nodded. "Let's do it. But first, I'm going to drop my bag off in the right bedroom. I hope they aren't shagging in there."

"Ugh, in my daughter's bed? They'd better not be!"

After some rousing carols in the parlor and a few rounds of *Exploding Kittens*, Rose left the room and signaled for Max to follow her. They returned with identical gleams in their eyes, and I knew something was up.

"Now, we're going to have dinner in the dining room, since it is a holiday. I know you'd prefer to eat in here with your plates on your laps, but do me this one solid?" Rose asked, and I was impressed by her incorporation of slang. We all followed her down the hallway and into the dining room, which looked like something from a Christmas movie. I never came in here, so I hadn't known what Rose had been up to while I was at work.

The table was set with candles burning, poinsettias were placed around the room, and evergreen boughs decorated the highboy. We all looked around in wonder, and that's when I saw the dishes of food on the table. My lower lip and chin started to quiver, because I knew now why Rose had asked all those probing questions about my upbringing last week.

"Now for tonight's treats, we owe a debt to Lois's Mormor, who has passed, may she rest in peace," Rose began, her eyes on me. "Lois let me know that her Mormor tried to keep Swedish traditions alive while Lois was growing up, especially around Christmas. We've got gingerbread cookies and a light cheese to spread on them, there's mulled wine, which is also known as glögg, a Christmas ham with a sliced potato side dish, and another made from cabbage. Meatballs, in the Swedish style of course, and there are also little pork sausages which I have not been snacking on at all—don't look at me like that, Maxie—and in true Swedish fashion, we are having as many toasts during dinner as we like."

We practically fell on the food like a pack of starving wolves once we were all seated and Rose had said a short grace. I tried not to cry as the flavors from home danced on my tongue, reminding me of my last Christmas in Nebraska, before Elsa and when Mormor was still alive. Before life got too complicated and everything fell apart.

"A toast!" Norman shouted, lifting a glass of Coke, while the rest of us had wine. "To Lois's Mormor, and to Rose and Max, for making her dishes come to life for us this Christmas Eve."

"To Mormor, Rose, and Max," we all said, clinking our glasses.

"I would like to make a toast," Jonathan said. "To all of you, for making Norman and me feel so welcome and appreciated. It means the world to us."

"Hear, hear!" Norman said, and we all laughed and clinked glasses again. As the meal went on, and the ham and side dishes dwindled, we all made a toast, and I taught them a bawdy drinking song that I'd heard my grandpa sing when I was young. Then, with a lump in my throat, I made the last toast of the evening.

"To friends who are like family, and to those who can't be here with us tonight." Everyone was a bit more somber at that, and Norman leaned over in his chair and pressed a kiss to my cheek.

"I love you," he said, in a voice just for me.

"I know."

"You're sexy when you quote *Star Wars*."

CHAPTER 24

LOIS

I made sure to set an alarm so I would be up early Christmas morning to make my Skype call with Elsa. With the time difference, they would have already celebrated during their morning. I left a snoring Max—too much glögg—and crept down to the parlor with my tablet. Once I was certain I looked half decent, even though I was still in my pajamas, I brought up Skype and put through the call. An excited Elsa popped up on screen and shrieked, "Mommy, I got a Nintendo Switch from Santa! And books, so many books my room here is full of them!"

"Well, that's why we left extra room in your suitcase, you lucky girl. You can bring home some of your presents and leave some of them there for you to play with or read during your summer trip over. I hope you remembered to thank Santa and Daddy and Philippe."

"Mommy, Philippe gave me the foal for Christmas. She's mine, but we can't fit her in my suitcase." Elsa giggled like that was the most hilarious joke ever, and I was so swept up in her joy that I laughed, too.

"Well, when you get back here, we are going to get some riding lessons for you. So when your horse is old enough, you can ride her without having to wait and be taught. How does that sound?"

"Mommy, do you mean it? I like that idea very much."

"Of course I mean it, you silly goose. Did she finally get a name? I know you were thinking of a few."

"I named her this morning, because today is an important day, you know.

It's baby Jesus in the cradle's birthday. And there were angels heard on high and wise men with camels. I like everything about that except for the camels, because they spit."

I smiled and smelt Philippe's influence there; both David and I were agnostic, but Philippe was Catholic through and through. Well, Elsa could be exposed to all kinds of religions and practices and pick her own path when she was older. David and I both did meditation with her, and I told her the story of the life of the Buddha when she asked questions about why people did it. We weren't Buddhists, but we believed in the mental and physical benefits to meditation, and perhaps Elsa would make that her chosen path. Who knew?

"Well, tell me what name you picked!"

"Bella," she replied, proudly. "Her name is Bella."

"Oh, that's so pretty, honey."

"It's from Twilight, you know." Oh, lord.

"How do you know about Twilight, sweetie?" I probed, my Mommy radar going off.

"Daddy and Philippe let me watch it. It's one of Philippe's favorite movies. I think he liked it when I picked Bella to be the horsie's name."

"Did the movie scare you at all, honey?" I asked, because honestly, letting our six-year-old watch a vampire movie? David was going to hear about this. Not today, though. No one fights or gets their hackles up on Christmas, it's one of my rules.

"No, I thought it wasn't scary, because vampires are like ghosts; they aren't real." Now, I did believe in ghosts, but like hell was I going to tell Elsa that. I heard footsteps on the stairs and realized that the rest of the house was waking, taking showers, getting dressed.

"Honey, Mommy has to go and get dressed and help make everyone breakfast. We all miss you and love you so much. And you know what? This morning, there was a stocking hanging by the tree with your name on it. So, Santa knows you have two homes and came here, too. You can open it as soon as you get back." I got off the couch and walked the tablet over to the tree and showed her the stuffed stocking on which Rose had embroidered "Elsa." "Now, remember to be good for your Daddy and Philippe, and give Bella an apple and tell her it's from me. I want her to like me when I eventually meet her."

"Mommy, wait. I have something I feel funny about and I want to tell you. I heard Daddy—and I wasn't trying to listen in!—tell Philippe that it would be so nice to have us all here living together, in France. He said he was getting special papers to make that happen. But I like Green Valley, and I don't want to live here all the time. I want to live where *you* want to live. And I love Ms. Rose and Ms. Max. I would miss them. Am I bad for not wanting to live here with my Daddy all the time?"

A lump formed in my throat as I tried to process the bomb Elsa had dropped. David wanted Elsa, not in an informal arrangement like we had, but *custody*. I was suddenly cold and wondered if this was some kind of ploy to get me to agree to pack up and move to France without going through the courts. Like he was playing chicken with me. Well, if there was one thing in this world that could take me from a reasonable, cool-headed woman to savage in 0.2 seconds, it was the idea of someone hurting my child. And the thought that someone wanted to take her away from me, father or not. The fear that rushed through me in that moment was making my hand holding the tablet shake, and I fought to stay still and keep a neutral expression on my face, despite the racing of my heart and the sinking feeling in my stomach.

But this wasn't the time for me to focus on my own big emotions about this; Elsa was still on the line and needed me to encourage her, support her. "Oh baby, no. You are not bad for how you feel inside, ever. And you can always tell me how you feel about anything, okay? Mommy loves you so much." With that, I blew kisses at the screen, and Elsa pretended to catch one and slapped it onto her cheek. I giggled, and so did she, and the magic of Christmas was upon us once more.

But as for David? Well, our next Skype would be interesting to say the least. Getting papers, indeed!

Everyone graciously waited to eat breakfast—Jonathan's mother's French toast recipe—until I had a shower and got dressed in yet another ugly Christmas sweater. This one was baby puke green and garish red with jingle bells attached around front, near the bottom. Norman, funnily enough, already had a collection of ugly sweaters, and he wore one of those and made it festive by hot-gluing on battery-operated LEDs in flashing colors. There was a punch bowl of eggnog out on the counter and I knew it had moonshine in it, because Max had brought it with her. With the glögg going to our heads, we hadn't needed it last night, but I guess day-drinking during an adults-only Christmas party was acceptable, so I didn't say anything.

I should have said something. Next thing I knew, Norman was making a retching noise, and exclaiming, "Whoa! What's in this?"

"Norman! I'm sorry, I didn't even think to tell you. That's moonshine eggnog. I have a pitcher of regular homemade eggnog over here for you," Max told him.

"Jesus Christ, are you sure that was moonshine and not paint thinner?"

"Norman Grant! Don't take the Lord's name in vain on his birthday," Rose scolded.

"But Rose, you know that this isn't really Jesus' birthday. It was a co-opting of several Pagan festivals by the Church to try to win over the locals and expand by incorporating their traditions."

"And who told you that?" she demanded.

"Uh, you did, last night when we were talking about Yule logs."

"Maybe that eggnog is stronger than you thought," I muttered to Max.

"Nah, she's being contrary to fuck with him," Max muttered back. We laughed, but I noticed Max slowed down her rate of eggnog consumption.

After some French toast that rivaled that of Daisy's, Rose announced that we would leave the dishes for now and go open our presents. I sat back on the couch with Norman, while Max and Jonathan sat cross-legged on the floor by the tree so they could pass the gifts around.

"Let's do Lois's gifts first," Norman said, and I flushed in embarrassment.

Jonathan pulled the big box out from the back of the tree and walked it over to me, smiling. I gulped down some tears that were threatening to bubble up, because I hadn't gotten an in-person Christmas gift since Elsa was born, other than the homemade crafts she would make for me. Jonathan set the gift down on the floor in front of me and said he could help me with it once it was unwrapped. Okay, whatever that meant. I plucked off the gargantuan bow and slapped it on top of Norman's head, making everyone laugh as he posed for the camera on Max's cell. Shit, she was filming this? Now I *really* didn't want to cry. I ripped at the red- and white-striped paper, and then gasped when I saw the picture of a chassis on the side of the box.

"Norman," I warned, "this better not be what I think it is!"

"Well, I can't control your thoughts, sugar."

My eyes widened as I opened the box, and I found a piece of paper on top inside with a list of amazeballs specs for a PC. I saw that the object inside was surrounded by Styrofoam, and Jonathan did need to help me wrangle it free, placing it on top of the coffee table. It was a thing of beauty; a red chassis, which happened to be my favorite color, and a clear side so I could look in and take in all the parts. It was freaking perfect. It was also too much.

"But Norm, your truck…"

"I can afford the truck and the computer and my rent, before you bring that up, too. It's okay. Say thank you and accept that I like spoiling you."

"But you got me a brand-new computer that you built yourself, and I got you a T-shirt that says, 'Rogues Do It From Behind' and a plush Zebrah," I moaned.

"And I love them both. Or I will, once I unwrap them." He winked cheekily.

"Oh, darn it, sorry for the spoilers. But seriously, Norm—"

"I wanted to give you something I could make with my own two hands. And I wanted you and Elsa to have a proper machine, not simply so you could play *Magecraft* but so that she also has something reliable for school. It's all good, kiddo. Trust me, okay?"

"Okay," I replied, and threw my arms around him, giving him a kiss.

"Open ours next!" Max said excitedly, grabbing another large box from the back of the tree that I hadn't even seen and depositing it on my lap. "It's from the rest of us: me, Jonathan, and Mom."

"You guys…"

"Shh. Open!" Max scolded playfully.

I ripped the paper, and then I was suddenly holding a kickass-looking monitor. "We wanted you to have the best, so the picture quality is high when you and Elsa have to Skype back and forth, or for her when she's on with David and Philippe. It has a built-in webcam and mic." And that did me in. The tears bubbled up and spilled over, and then it was Max's turn to put her arms around me.

"Let us take care of you, okay?" she said softly.

I nodded, wiped my eyes, and told them, "It's just, I haven't had a Christmas like this in a long time, not since I was back with Mormor in Nebraska. It's just been Elsa and me, with me scraping together to get her a few gifts and a stocking so she would believe in Santa." Oops, there came more tears.

"We're your family now, dear," Rose declared as she approached me, holding out a Kleenex box. "And I couldn't have asked for a better second daughter. I know you've only been here for a short while, but that's honestly how I feel. Besides, when we're adults, we can choose our families, and they don't all look alike. I'm glad you are *all* a part of this one."

A chorus of thank-yous filled the room, and then we did the only thing left to do to move on from this: we hugged it out. When Jonathan wrapped me up in a huge hug and lifted me from the floor to make me screech, he said in a low voice as he set me back down, "Nothing has been decided yet about setting up a storefront here in Green Valley other than we know we want you to be a part of it when the time comes. I don't think you know how much you mean to all of us. It would be an honor to work with you." As a final sob ripped loose from my throat, Jonathan released me and patted my shoulder in a big-brother way.

"Good lord, man, what did you do to my woman?" Norman said, wrapping me up in those big arms of his. I breathed in his scent and rested my head against his shoulder, the tears stopping, and the sensation of pure joy washed over me. "Love you, Lo," he murmured, kissing me softly.

"Love you, too," I said, almost breathless from our kiss. Then, there was Max suddenly, camera back in hand, pointing it at us.

"Wait a minute, you're in love?!" she shrieked like she had won on *The Price is Right* and jumped up and down excitedly. "Norman, when did you first realize you loved Lois? Lo, when did you reciprocate? The public has questions!"

"What makes you think I fell for her first?" Norman asked, sounding wounded.

"Oh, come off it, Norman; you know that's how it went down," Jonathan chimed in.

"Did you know about this?" Max turned to Jonathan, still pointing that darn camera.

"I had my suspicions. But that's all they were. I'm sorry I didn't tell you what I thought, but gossip is evil," he said, like he meant it.

"Evil, my ass. You didn't want me stirring the pot," Max said, and Jonathan nodded.

"Yeah, that's about the size of it. Love you, pookie. Now, let's let you and Rose open your gifts. Ladies first, and all that."

An hour later Max, Jonathan, Norman, and I were all crowded around the desk in my room, staring at the stunning picture quality of *League of Magecraft* with my pricey graphics card and monitor. I got a bit emotional when my avatar cast her spells on a practice dummy because the effects were brilliant. And then there was the fact that my whole American-based family had conspired to do this truly kind thing for me. It was too much, and I wanted some Norman time before our afternoon Christmas dinner. Max must have seen my face, because she grabbed Jonathan's arm. "Let's go downstairs and help Mom with the cooking and leave the new lovebirds up here, yeah?"

I mouthed "thank you" to her, and she smiled at me and waggled her eyebrows suggestively as she backed out of the room and shut the door behind her.

"Are you worn out? I am so tired. I think it was the emotional upheaval, you know?" I yawned, and Norman helped me over to the queen-sized bed and peeled back the top blanket.

"Lie down, hot stuff. We want you up and lucid for the movie marathon later. *White Christmas* and *It's a Wonderful Life*, remember?"

Oh, I remembered. I watched those movies every Christmas, and there was no way I was missing out. I needed to rest my eyes for a few minutes. I got in and scooted to the far side of the bed, near the window, which left plenty of room for Norman to climb in beside me. Instantly, I was the little spoon, and I settled in against his beautiful body and breathed in his addicting scent, being cradled in his arms until I fell into a dead sleep.

CHAPTER 25

NORMAN

The days between Christmas and New Year's flew by, and Jonathan and I used the time to settle into Green Valley more, going to another jam session, checking out the hardware store, and bringing treats from the Donner Bakery to Max, Lois, and Rose. We dominated in the *Magecraft* arena and had come together as a team who could anticipate each other's needs and moves. I also used the time to look up doctors in the area who specialized in chronic pain, preferably through the VA. The closest one was in Knoxville, but that was a hop, skip, and a jump from Green Valley compared to my treks to Jacksonville from home back in Florida. I requested an appointment as soon as possible and was put on a waitlist for January.

As New Year's Eve approached, Rose sent out a group text—we had taught her how on the new cell Max had given her for Christmas—that she wanted the four of us to go out dancing and kick up our heels, and not spend the evening at her home like we had planned. She told Lois that we doted on her too much and that she was fine being alone. I honestly thought that all the holiday activity around the house was a bit triggering for her agoraphobia, though she still managed a walk around the block most days.

And so, on December thirty-first, I was hopping into my truck and ready for some fun at Genie's. I picked up Lois, who was dressed up in another gorgeous green dress, no shawl this time, and her hair was shiny and braided like Katniss Everdeen's. We scored the last free table in the joint, and now were waiting for Max and Jonathan to show up. A quick text to Jonathan let me know that they had taken a shower first, and I sensed that they were running late because they were having shower sex.

Speaking of sex, Lois spent most of her nights with me, because once Elsa returned that wouldn't be an option anymore. We fit together like pieces of a puzzle; like our hearts were beating for each other in those intimate moments. We'd gotten quite creative in bed to avoid putting undue stress on my hip and left leg, and Lois never once complained that we had to go slow sometimes, use unconventional positions, or if there was a night when I couldn't perform because I was in too much pain.

And every night we spent together she would snuggle into my side, holding my hand, and tell me how much she loved me. That she had never stopped in the ten years in between, and that with every candle she lit over the years in almost every church she walked by, she prayed to keep me safe and to bring me back to her somehow. I knew Lois thought of herself as agnostic, but she had been raised in a Christian household, and some habits were hard to break, she explained. Like prayer, or talking to God like in *Are You There God? It's Me, Margaret.*

I was snapped out of my thoughts by our waitress and we ordered a Coke for me and a margarita for Lois. Just as our drinks arrived, so did Max and Jonathan, looking sheepish. Our waitress, who bore the name tag "Willa," scurried off to get their drink orders in, too, as well as the pile of chicken wings we'd ordered. Since we had some waiting to do, I got up and extended a hand to Lois. "A dance, milady?"

She downed the rest of her margarita and replied with, "Why indeed, good sir." I guided her to an empty space on the floor and wrapped both arms around her lower back, while she clung to my neck. We swayed and spun around like we were the only two people in the world, and it was seriously hardcore epic. After a faster song came on, she asked, "Norm, where's your cane?"

"Surprise. I don't need it when I have my arms full of you. Plus, it's mostly standing fairly still and moving in a slow circle; I can tolerate that. Didn't you notice the last time we came here and danced?" I leaned in and we fused our mouths together, the heat between us building. We were hours away from midnight, and I swore as soon as the clock struck 12:01 a.m., we were hitting the road. I wanted to be inside her so badly my heart ached for her.

"Hey, lovebirds, save the kisses for midnight!" Max heckled from where she and Jonathan were sitting, drinking beer and laughing. Then, as if she were struck with inspiration, she grabbed Jonathan's hand and yanked him to the dance floor and cut in between Lois and me. Jonathan swept up Lois, and I was facing a Max with mirth in her eyes. "Shall we?" she asked, and I took her by the waist and we were off.

I hadn't had a lot of time to talk to Max lately; I was so busy with work, Lois, and Rose. This was quite nice hanging on to her and having an opportunity to catch up.

"And how is the lovely Maximus_Damage this evening?" I asked, whirling her around a bit on the floor.

"Oh, not bad at all. Jonathan and I are in a solid place in our relationship, and he is taking his medications faithfully and hasn't had any severe episodes of his bipolar disorder since I was in Florida. He's doing his therapy over Skype, and I'm so proud of how far he's come in such a short time. And me? I'm enjoying everything about having y'all here. I know Mom is, as well. It's like our world expanded enormously. But that's enough about me. I was wondering how things were going with two of my best friends."

I looked over to where Jonathan had Lois laughing with some ridiculous interpretive dance thing he was doing, and for a moment jealousy tore through me that I couldn't do the same stupid stunts for her. "We're great; enjoying the time we have together, getting to reconnect as adults. I give thanks every day, you know? Every day, I'm thankful that she's in my life."

"You do know that when Elsa comes back, it's all going to change, right? You won't be the center of her world anymore; Elsa will be. Things will get more challenging. Think you're up for it?"

I thought about it for a split second and nodded my head. "I'll have to be, won't I? I have to convince a six-year-old who already has two fathers that she needs another man in her life."

"Whatever you do, Norman, don't make promises you can't keep. If you aren't a hundred percent sure that you and Lois are endgame, don't let Elsa get too close. She already has two fathers, as you pointed out, but she's torn between them and Lois constantly. She doesn't need another man who's in her life but not all-in for all the responsibility that means."

Just when I was about to tell her that I wanted Lois and me to be together long-term, we were knocked into by a drunk guy who I swear could have a career in professional wrestling. He sloshed some beer on me in the crash, and of course didn't apologize. I widened my eyes at Max and suggested we move a bit further away from where the Hulk and friends were having some kind of drinking contest.

We were in the slow process of pushing in on the crowded dance floor, when Hulk looked directly at us, first to me, and then he set his sights on Max. Oh boy, this couldn't be good. He was so much bigger than me, and I couldn't get Jonathan's attention quickly enough as the brute lumbered toward us through the crowd, which parted for him like he was parting the Red Sea.

Ignoring me altogether, he tried to cut in and take Max away. Lightning quick, he grabbed her by the arm, and she made a small noise of pain. That was more than enough. If there was one thing I hated, it was a man who mistreats a woman. I swung around to face him and told him to fuck off, and for my efforts got gut-punched and landed in a heap on the floor. Max screamed, and then I saw Lois dash and grab one of the almost full beer glasses from our table and fling its contents into the man's face.

For a moment I thought we were about to have a full-out bar brawl, until an older woman hustled over and yelled at the man who towered over her, "Take it out of my place! You want to pull shit like this, you go to the Dragon and drink. Out!" She pointed at the direction of the exit, and sure enough, he shambled out the door, taking his friends with him. Bar brawl avoided, almost over as quickly as it started.

"Thanks, Genie," Max said, nodding respectfully at who I presumed was the owner of the bar.

"Oh it was nothing, sweetheart. I learned how to handle dumb drunks a long time ago. Now, would y'all like another round of drinks?"

As Genie and Max talked, Lois grabbed my cane and brought it over, handing it to me and extending her left arm. Using both the cane and Lois as leverage, I got up off the floor, saying, "Show's over, folks. And thanks, kiddo. You're totally my hero."

"Bah, all I did was give that guy a bath, which he sorely needed. He smelled like a sweaty foot."

We retreated to the table, where Jonathan leaned in and gave me a one-armed side hug and said, "Thanks for looking out for my girl."

"He had like, what, a hundred pounds on me? Easy peasy."

"Guys," Lois said, sliding into the seat beside me, "I think we're going to go back to the rental. I know it's early, but Norman had a fall and he needs to ice that leg, do some hip stretches, that kind of thing."

"Oh, and suddenly you're an expert on what I need?" I teased.

"Yes."

"Well, you aren't wrong. I could use a rub down, too." I bumped shoulders with her.

Max fussed, saying, "I feel like this was all my fault somehow."

"It wasn't, and you're not the one who punched Norman," Jonathan said, leaning over to peck Max on the cheek.

"You should check on her arm, Jonathan," I said. "You couldn't see from where you were dancing, but he grabbed her. Hard."

Jonathan's face paled, and you could literally see the tension and anxiety building in him. Max must have had her Spidey-senses tingle, too, because she put a hand on his shoulder and said, "I'm fine. It didn't hurt that bad. It'll just leave some small bruises."

"That's it; there are too many drunk assholes out tonight. We're leaving, too, if that's okay with you, Max. I don't want someone else thinking they can snatch up the most gorgeous girl in the bar, and I won't see you get hurt again. Why don't we go and celebrate with Rose, if she changed her mind? Or go to your cottage if she prefers to be alone. We can split up the wings and get them to go."

Max acquiesced to this proposition, and within a few minutes we settled our tab and hugged it out in the parking lot. I held both Jonathan and Max tightly, and we parted ways as the snow began to fall at the end of one hell of a year.

~

We were snuggled together on the pullout, naked under my puffy duvet and watching the New Year's Eve Celebrations from Times Square. It made me wonder what life would have been like had I not bailed on Lois all those years ago and had met her at the top of the Empire State Building like we had wanted. But there was no taking back what had been done, and if Lois hadn't met David there would be no Elsa, so I couldn't regret how things unfolded.

Lois grew excited and grasped my hands as the countdown to midnight happened and we watched the ball drop, signaling the start to another year. As "Auld Lang Syne" began to play and Times Square was filled with confetti, we gave each other a New Year's kiss and I gathered her braid in my hands and pulled her in for a deeper connection than the traditional peck.

"Let's make a pact. A resolution, if you prefer," I began, peppering her face and neck with kisses.

"Oh?" she replied with interest.

"Let's seize this second chance that the universe gave us, and not let anything else come between us. Let's never let each other go." I weaved our fingers together and let my other hand rise to her breasts, then to her cheek. "I know I messed up when we were kids, Lo. But I want all-in now. I want you in every part of my life, and I want to be in every part of yours."

"Wow. That's a big resolution. Usually, I decide to drop twenty pounds."

"Oh, don't you dare! I love your body as it is."

She sighed. "Okay, then. Our resolution is that we're all-in. Both of us." She reached for the remote and turned off the New Year's revelers, and we had a private celebration of our own—no clothing required.

CHAPTER 26

LOIS

"Mommy!" Elsa yelled, letting go of David's hand she had been holding, and ran over to me, flinging herself into my arms. A smiling employee followed along and handed off Elsa's luggage to me. After a huge hug, I kissed her cheeks, and she giggled, kissing mine back. David had booked a return flight for later tonight, so he would be crashing at the airport Hilton until it was time for him to board.

One look at his face and I knew he was hiding something from me. It was so funny how my intuition had always been right about David—except for figuring out that he wasn't in love with me anymore.

"Happy New Year, Lolo. Philippe also sends his love," David said, coming in for his usual greeting of three kisses. I pulled back and tried to make it look like no big deal.

"Happy New Year, David. I hope you have a safe trip back. And we are overdue for a

Skype. I have things I need to talk to you about once you get home and all three of us can talk."

He took a step backward and looked me dead in the eye. "Okay," he said and gave a little nod.

Elsa gave David a huge hug, and then he spoke to her softly in French. I could hear her high-pitched reply, "*Oui, Papa!*" and then David was off in one direction, Elsa and me in the other.

Elsa was talking so fast she was practically chirping like a bird—which is where her nickname from David, "little bird," had come from—and pulling along her carry-on while I pulled the bigger suitcase and held her hand. We stopped at a Starbucks, and Elsa looked at me quizzically.

"Why are we stopping here, Mommy?"

"Because I have a surprise for you, and he's right over… there!" I pointed at Norman, who was holding a hot chocolate for Elsa; let's face it, she was already on a high so a sugar rush wouldn't matter at this point. Plus, having Norman waiting at Starbucks would keep him away from David, and I didn't want there to be any awkwardness. Not that I wasn't entitled to date, but I never had before, and I didn't want David all up in my business. "Do you remember who that is, sweetie?"

"I'm six, not a baby," she replied, affronted by my query. "It's Mr. Norman! And he has his pretty cane with the superheroes on it. Can I go over, Mommy?" That's when I realized I was still holding her hand. The moment I released it and let go, she ran over to Norman and flung herself at him, much like she had to me.

"Whoa, careful there. We wouldn't want to spill any of this on you. Especially since it's yours," Norman said in a teasing tone.

"But I'm not allowed to drink coffee. Daddy said that's a grown-up drink."

"It's not coffee, it's hot chocolate." Her eyes went wide.

"What do we say?" I asked as she was passed the cup and Norman took a hold of her carry-on.

"Thank you, Mr. Norman?"

"That's right." She sighed in bliss as she looked from the hot chocolate to me, and back to Norman, who was getting a kick out of her calling him "Mr. Norman" all the time. I took her hand again and Norman brought up the rear, and we headed out to my car. When we got there, Elsa let out a squeal of excitement as she saw our new transportation and didn't even complain about the booster seat I installed in the back. I climbed in the back with her, and my little chatterbox was full of questions.

She began her interrogation with, "Why did Mr. Norman come with you to get me?"

"We're going to talk about that on the way home, sweetie," I replied as Norman navigated the airport's parking lot. Once we hit the main road, it was my turn to ask her some questions.

"Elsa, do you know what having a boyfriend means? Not a boy who is your friend, but someone incredibly special to you?" I could practically hear her eyes roll.

"Like I keep telling you, I'm *six.* I know all about this stuff."

"Of course; you're practically a relationship expert," I said, doing an eye roll of my own to make her laugh. "Tell me what you know about having a boyfriend."

"It's someone who you make kisses with and who brings you ice cream and rubs your feet and calls you love-y names." Norman chuckled, and I unsuccessfully tried to hide a smile. "Well, that's what Daddy and Philippe do, and they're boyfriends. But they're going to be husbands soon, and I get to be the flower girl." Elsa slapped a hand over her mouth, and then slowly lowered it. "Daddy wanted to tell you that himself." I had a fleeting moment of jealousy, which was ridiculous because things in my life were starting to go well for the first time since my divorce.

"I won't tell Daddy that you slipped and told me their surprise, okay, honey? Don't worry about it."

"You aren't mad?"

"No, sweetie. But I have some news, too, and I hope you'll be happy for me, okay?"

"Okay," she said, sounding solemn. I reached over and took her hand in mine, looking for signs of growth over the last month. I hated that we'd been apart for so long, but I'd had time with Norman that never would have happened had she been here.

"While you were in France getting to know Bella and playing with Daddy and Philippe, I made friends with Norman again. He and I used to know each other a long, long time ago. Before you were born. And now we fell in love with each other."

"So, Mr. Norman is your boyfriend now?" Elsa cocked her head to one side, and then looked from me to Norman and back again. "Does this mean that I can play with him whenever I want to?"

"Of course you can, as long as he wants to, too." She was taking this awfully well, and I waited for the other shoe to drop.

"Maybe you could marry Mr. Norman, like Daddy and Philippe are getting married, and I could be a flower girl for you, too. And then I would have another daddy here in America." Shoe, meet floor. Now, how to handle this. I often wished kids came with an instruction manual.

"That's a lovely thought, sweetie, but it takes time for couples to get to know each other well enough to get married. Being married is supposed to be forever, and Norman and I aren't ready to decide that yet. But we *are* boyfriend and girlfriend, which means we will be spending more time together, the three of us. Are you okay with that? With Norman being at our house, or us going to his house?"

She seemed to consider this for a moment because she squeezed my hand tighter. "Do you love him more than you love me now?" Ouch. Why not rip the heart out of my chest?

"No, sweetie. I will never, ever love anyone more than you. Not in a million years. You're always going to come first with me, no matter who else I love. But that's the great thing about love. It can always grow and stretch to let more people in without taking anything away from the people who you already love. So, me loving Norman doesn't mean I love you any bit less. Do you understand?"

She nodded, and then started to cry. Oh, crap. What now?

"I thought that you would get married and I would have another daddy I could see all the time."

"Oh, honey. I'm not marrying Norman today but that doesn't mean I won't someday. You can cry if you need to, but know that I will always love you. You're the most important person to me." I opened my purse and got out some Kleenex, handing it to her so she could wipe her eyes and blow her nose.

After a few minutes, her sobbing had turned to hiccups and she was quiet. That's when Norman shocked me. "So, you know, Elsa, I love your mommy very much. And I already love you, because even though we don't know each other well yet, you were all she talked about while you were gone. I would like it if we were good friends. Can we be friends?"

"Yes," she said softly, and then hiccupped once more. We held hands all the way back to Green Valley.

~

While we were road tripping to the airport and back, singing our favorite songs and answering Elsa's barrage of questions, Rose, Max, and Jonathan were scheming. When we pulled up to the Victorian, there were balloons tied to the mailbox, crepe paper strung around the doorway, and a huge sign that said, "Welcome home!"

Elsa craned her neck from the car to take it all in, and once the engine was off, she hopped out of the car like a bunny to see her surprise better. Inside, everyone was there to give her hugs, ask her about her trip, and offer up some red velvet goodies that Rose had made. But Elsa, ever the sneak, made a beeline for the parlor, where the tree still stood and her stocking was hung by the fireplace.

"Can I, Mommy?" she asked, bouncing from one foot to the other.

"Go ahead," I said, feeling teary-eyed as everyone took their seats to watch, with Max playing cameraman. I sat down on the floor next to Elsa and waved Norman over, too. He could sit comfortably on a cushion and be part of Elsa's second Christmas this season. She was practically vibrating with excitement when I took the stocking down from the fireplace and handed it to her, and then Norman shocked the hell out of me by pulling a gift out from under the tree. What on earth could that be, and how had so many presents gone unnoticed by me under there?

She put the stocking down and accepted the box Norman handed her gracefully, and he explained, "This is a gift from all of us." She tore open the paper and then her mouth gaped open as she stared at the box. I couldn't even be mad that they had all conspired behind my back, because Elsa was in so much shock. "This is for me? For reals?"

"Yup. All yours, kiddo." I loved how Norman had transferred the nickname from me to Elsa. Nicknames were a way of showing affection, and I swear, at that moment, my heart was about to leap out of my chest. She opened the box and there was a brand spanking new Surface Pro. "See, it's a little laptop computer, but you can also use it as a tablet to draw on. I saw your drawings hanging on the wall upstairs and on the fridge and knew you were an artist at heart. Because of that, we all got together and decided on this for you. It comes with a pen for you to draw with, see?"

I didn't know who was more excited, Norman or Elsa.

"Thank you, Mr. Norman. And Mr. Jonathan, Ms. Maxine, and Mrs. Rose," she said, clutching the device to her chest.

"About that. How about you call me Norman from now on? You don't need to call me mister. It's polite that you have been, but if we're going to be good friends then I want us to be equals. And I don't call you Miss Elsa." He reached out and tickled her on the side, causing her to laugh so hard she tipped over and landed practically on my lap.

"Now, do you want to see what Santa brought you in your stocking?" he asked, and when she nodded enthusiastically, I passed her the embroidered sock and she put the Surface down on the coffee table. She carefully took out one item at a time, oohing and aahing over things like a new LEGO kit, bubble bath, pretty necklaces, beads, and of course a large orange in the bottom of the sock.

She sighed in contentment and crawled into my lap, giving me a hug and a kiss. Then she shocked me by going over to Norman and repeating the process, only not climbing into his lap. She remembered that he had pain there, and my smart, empathetic girl wouldn't want to cause anyone extra pain.

"Thank you, everybody. And thank you, Santa!" she yelled at the fireplace.

She then settled back into my lap, and while Norman was talking about the features of her new Surface, she dozed off, probably exhausted from the long trip and the excitement which followed. I carefully picked her up and laid her on the chaise, putting a blanket over her and kissing her forehead.

Norman came up behind me and wrapped me in his arms, and asked, "It wasn't too much, was it? I was afraid if we asked your permission first, you'd say no, and that machine is perfect for tiny fingers to use and learn on. I unboxed it and set it up with parental controls and loaded some games for her."

"She loves it," I conceded, and realized that I was going to have to get used to this group, my chosen family, spoiling me and my daughter. I'd never had this, except with my Mormor, and in that moment I felt loved and genuinely cared for. And I felt like Elsa was, too. But the question Elsa asked me about marriage had rattled me, and as I turned in Norman's arms to face him, I said quietly, "Thanks for being so great with her. I know it freaked you out when she said she wanted you to be her dad, but don't worry. We don't have to rush into anything. I mean, I'm not expecting a surprise proposal."

"I'm not always great at expressing my emotions, Lo, but when she said that, I felt so freaking honored that I felt compelled to drive right to the town hall and get the paperwork. But I love you, and I know you and I are in this for the long haul. I'm not in a rush if you're not."

CHAPTER 27

NORMAN

I was singing the soundtrack to *Rent* in the shower and thinking about my problem. Well, problems. One of them was a huge case of blue balls, but it was more than sex I missed. Being able to feel the soft warm body of Lois next to me at night and hold her in my arms was something that I had almost started to take for granted. Well, I never would again, because of course now the sleep-overs had stopped. Lois wouldn't be away from Elsa for a night, and while I knew that in her eyes, it was proper and all, it was also making me a bit miserable.

The workshop had opened again in the second week of January, and it felt like I'd only seen Lois in person a handful of times that month. I was working hard to scope out Green Valley and figure out what place we could afford to make into a storefront. I was also working on something that was a surprise: a new place to rent, one that didn't smell like it had a mold problem. And one that would have a yard for Elsa to play in, and a place where the three of us could live together like a family. Unfortunately, all the small houses I had looked at were out of my price range at the moment.

At least Rose had invited me over for dinner anytime, and the days when I wasn't zonked out from working and looking at properties, I accepted the invite. I always sat between Lois and Elsa, because they both wanted to sit next to me, which was kind of adorable. Tonight's topic of conversation was riding lessons for Elsa. Max had recommended a guy named Rick who ran The

Cades Cove Chariot Company, and we were going to enroll her in private lessons in the spring.

Wait, did I say "we"?

I meant Lois was going to enroll her.

Problem number two was that Elsa and I were getting attached to each other, fast. Most nights after supper, I would stay for a while and read to her from her growing library. We were currently on *Charlotte's Web.* She trusted me to be around and to care for her, because one night after her bath she asked Lois if I could do her hair. I honestly hadn't the first clue about how to manage a biracial child's natural hair, but Lois guided me through the process and it went fine, if Elsa would sit still.

The problematic part of all this was, if Lois dumped my ass, I could see it being awfully hard on Elsa, because she had in her mind that one day, I would be her American daddy. I never thought I would be a dad, considering the issues I'd had with my own old man, but it was so easy with this girl, and she was sneaking into my heart and making a home there.

Problem number three was that I rarely had time alone with Lois anymore. I couldn't leave work every morning to bring her a latte, because we were getting swamped and leaving Jonathan alone to handle it all wasn't fair. But I longed for some grown-up time with Lois, where she could drink some wine, we'd cuddle on the couch, talk, and make love. Lois was reluctant to take up the others' offers of babysitting, and I had to somehow convince her that everything would be all right if she let Elsa have a sleepover at Max's, or let Rose watch her for a few hours at the Victorian.

Which brought us around to problem number four. Lois had some high walls she'd built around herself and Elsa, walls meant to protect them from the outside world back when it was the two of them in New York. She wasn't used to having someone else around to take care of her and her daughter. Despite our New Year's resolution to seize this second chance, as the weeks wore on and turned into months, I felt her pulling away from me a bit. I didn't know why, and it hurt like hell. I finished my shower and dried off, resolving to call my relationship guru, Elaine.

I sat down in front of Lucille in my boxers, opened Skype, and called Elaine in Chicago.

"Yo yo yo," I said when she picked up. "How's life in Chicago?" I smiled as my old friend ran a brush through her hair. She must be getting ready to go out, and I had caught her.

"Well, life goes. Work, friends, sleep, rinse, repeat." Once again, I wondered exactly what Elaine did for work, because she was always playing cloak and dagger when it came to that question. I'd learned a long time ago to not bother asking, because she'd reply with, "If I told you, I'd have to kill you."

"Elaine, I have some problems I can't seem to sort my way out of, and I can't talk to Max or Jonathan about them because they're too close to the situation. Do you have a few minutes?"

"Hmm, that depends. General topic?"

"My girlfriend, Lois."

"Ah yes, I'd heard you'd levelled up that relationship. Go, Norman. What's the problem exactly?"

"She's stopped letting me in like she used to. No, get your head out of the gutter," I said. "Though, yes, our sex life has pretty much dried up now that I think of it. I feel like I'm in a long-distance relationship, when we live in the same small town. I can't read her easily like I used to. She's guarded herself against me, for some reason."

Elaine put down her brush and nodded, and I gave her some time to mull this over. And then she came out with, "Have you considered talking to her like you just talked to me? Open communication is essential to make any relationship work, Norman. And maybe you should tell her that you've never had a girlfriend before, so you feel a bit lost as to how to navigate things. I'm sure if you're honest and show her your vulnerability, she'll reciprocate."

Of course, it all came back to honesty. "Thanks, Eli. You're a good friend."

She smiled her dazzling smile at me and said, "Same to you. Now, go talk to your woman. I'm off to a work function so I have to go, as much as I'd like to catch up a bit more."

I pulled my truck into Rose's driveway at around seven o'clock that night, figuring that Elsa would be in bed for the evening and Lois and I could have some privacy to talk. When I knocked on the door and she answered it, I swear her face almost fell.

"Okay, that's it. What's going on? I came here so we could talk about our relationship, and you look like you'd rather I was anyone else in the world other than your boyfriend." She flushed a bit red but didn't argue the point, and I felt like I'd been gut-punched again. "Why don't we sit on the porch swing and have a talk, Lo?"

Lois nodded and followed me to the swing, where we sat next to each other, awkwardness in the air. I took her hand in mine and rubbed the knuckles of her hand with my thumb, hoping to soothe her. She reminded me of a skittish horse, and I wanted this conversation to be calm.

"Lois, it's been almost two months since New Year's, and we made a pact that we'd always be there for each other, that we loved each other. What is going on in your head? Why have you been holding me at arm's length ever since Elsa came home?" I inwardly hoped to hell she would tell me that I was dead wrong, that she'd never put distance between us willingly. She looked at me with eyes that were rapidly filling with tears, and then it was as though the bottom went out of whatever fight she had and she was suddenly holding on to me and crying; deep, guttural cries that I felt powerless to stop. I held on and let her use me as a giant cushion.

"You're not wrong, I have been—I've been—I—"

"Hey, shh. Wait until you've got your cry out and then explain. The truth can't hurt me, Lois. Unless you don't love me anymore, and even in that case, you'd have to have a reason."

"I do love you," she said softly, sitting back up and holding my hand. She fetched some Kleenex from her pocket and blew her nose, then turned to face me. "It's David and Philippe, though I sense it's David who's the driving force behind this. I had a call with them the week after New Year's. And do you know what they want? They want Elsa!"

She may as well have tossed a bucket of freezing water over me. Elsa. There was no way Lois's ex was taking Elsa away from her, and if I had to beg, borrow, or steal the funds to hire the best damn lawyer in Tennessee, I was doing it.

"What exactly did you two say?"

"Well, he told me that he respected me and the way I was raising Elsa. He thought I was an exemplary mother." She snorted, and said, "What I said back was something like what would he know about it? Is he here, day in and day out to see it? No, he sees the benefit of it when she's excited and happy all the time on Christmas vacations or summers running barefoot around that vineyard." She paused to take a breath and asked me if I could get her a glass of water.

Water drank, she continued, "He said he and Philippe were a stable set of parents for her. That they had the means to make her life more comfortable and had a large home of their own. I swear, Norman, at that point I felt like spitting. It was like he was crapping all over my life and being so damn… *cordial* about it." Next to me, she was vibrating, her hands shaking and her breathing irregular. I did the only thing I could think of and grabbed her hands in mine, to at least hold her during this shitshow of a conversation.

"I was ready to scream, to yell, to tell him that I was doing my damn best and there was no better than that. Instead, I asked him to tell me exactly what he planned to do." Tears were rolling down her face at this point: my Lois, with her core of steel, was crying, and I don't even think she knew it. "And here I am ready to strangle him, and he's so fucking *calm*. He said they want to formalize a custody agreement, where they either get full custody or joint custody of her for half the year. My baby, Norman. I'm going to lose my baby. He had points that sound good for a judge—a set of stable parents, owning their own home, everything they are able to give her."

Before Lois could beat herself up more, I squeezed her hands and asked, "What kind of papers has he served you with?"

"None, yet. He said he wants us to work this out between the two of us, like we did when he first left and I agreed he could be a part of her life, only now they want it in writing, and they want me to cheerily sign off on giving up my daughter for more time in France. Now I'm terrified of sending her over this summer, because I'm afraid he won't send her back. How can all this be happening? It's just... It's always been Elsa and me. I've never had a boyfriend since David, and losing him almost broke me. I can't imagine what it would feel like to lose you, to both me and her."

"Lo, look at me, okay?" She turned her head back in my direction and met my gaze, tears pooling in those vibrant green eyes of hers. I gripped her hand a bit tighter. "I'm not David. I'm not going to walk out on you for someone else; I'm not going to bail when things get tough. And if for some reason we mutually decide this relationship isn't going to work, I will not cut Elsa out of my life. I love that kid."

"You love her because you've always seen her on her best behavior. What about temper tantrums, or her stubbornness when she doesn't get her way, or when she gets sick and projectile vomits on you like in *The Exorcist*? Having a kid is a full-time job, Norm. And I worry that you want me but don't understand what it means when I say I will always put Elsa first. Even if that means trying to get a bit of distance between you two so she doesn't get too attached so fast. She prays, you know. Philippe is Catholic and told her how. And she prays that one day, very soon, you will be one of her daddies. Can you imagine for a minute what that's like for me, feeling that pressure? And then I wonder, what if David somehow uses our relationship as a reason to take away Elsa?"

I held fast to her hand. "Okay, I can see your point of view. But I already told you, I want all-in. I want the cranky kid, the door-slamming kid, the pea-soup-vomit kid. Because, as I recall, you told me from the start you two were a package deal, and I said that I wanted it that way. And I'm not scared of

David, Lois. I will do everything in my power to make sure that if David wants a formal custody agreement, he gets no more time than what he already has. We can't let this shitstorm with David ruin our lives or hurt our relationship. I refuse to give anyone that kind of power. The option we have is to move forward, and I want us to move forward as a team. I've been looking at rental properties; nicer ones than I have now. Cottages, mostly. I have a list of them saved on my phone because I wanted to show you which one could be our future home. The three of us."

She now held my hand in an iron grip, and those tears that had threatened to spill came down her cheeks. I grabbed my handkerchief and wiped her face. "You were doing all of these real estate showings, but I thought that was for the shop's new location. I didn't imagine… A house? For the three of us?"

"If you would be okay with us living in sin for a while. I don't think you're ready to take the big plunge into marriage yet."

"Oh, but you are?"

"I've been waiting for you for a long time. I can wait until you're sure." I flashed a grin at her and brought her hand up and kissed the back of it. Just then, a harried-looking Rose came out to the porch.

"I hate to interrupt you kids, but Lois, Elsa is asking for you. She had a nightmare, poor wee lamb. And she feels like she's running a fever." Lois stood up immediately and started toward the front door. Then she looked behind her, right at me.

"You want to get in some parenting practice?" she asked. I shot to my feet and followed Lois inside.

It was a fever, and Elsa cried and hiccupped her way through the retelling of her dream, in which she never got to see David, Philippe, Rose, Max, Jonathan, or me ever again. Lois had moved them back to their shoebox-sized apartment in Queens, and we all forgot about her.

Lois kissed her daughter's sweaty forehead and said she'd be right back with the thermometer, a cool cloth, and some Tylenol. That left me on Elsa duty. I sat down on the edge of her bed, and before I knew it, I had an armful of crying child, begging me not to leave her. I wasn't exactly sure what to do, so I decided to wing it. I hugged her in return and rubbed her back in small circles. I made shushing noises and told her that it was okay to let out her tears, but that a bad dream wouldn't hurt her and there was no way all those people who loved her would leave her.

"Even you, Norman?" she asked, wiping her eyes and looking up into mine.

"Especially me."

CHAPTER 28

LOIS

I calmly but quickly got all the supplies I needed to make Elsa feel better, and when I returned to the room you could have knocked me over with a twig. She had gone from crying and scared to giggling as she sat up on the bed, Norman at its foot, and the pair were having a… thumb war?

"Okay, this time I'm going to cream you!" Norman said. They joined hands and chanted in unison, "One, two, three, four, I declare a thumb war. Five, six, seven, eight, try to keep your thumbs straight." After some back and forth which should have earned Norman an acting trophy, he was out. "Ah, vanquished again by Elsa 'the kiddo' Washington."

"Mommy, I beat Norman three times in a row," she stated proudly.

"It's true; she did. My thumbs may never recover. Now, kiddo, we should get you back into bed and let your mom help you out with that fever, okay?" She looked disappointed, but reluctantly nodded. I went over and tucked Elsa back in, and Norman straightened up the blankets which had gone awry during their games. Next, I asked Elsa to open wide, and slipped the thermometer under her tongue while putting a cool washcloth on her forehead. The thermometer beeped and I took it out, shaking my head.

"102. I've got some medicine here that will make that all better, okay?"

"It's in the sorbet you brought?"

"Who taught you the word 'sorbet'? Never mind, not important. What is important is that you eat every bit of it, okay? It will make your throat feel nice and cool, too. And it's strawberry, your favorite."

"Can you and Norman stay with me until I fall asleep?" she asked as she accepted the bowl of the cool treat, laced with liquid medicine.

"Of course we can," Norman said, looking to me. "I'll even read you one more chapter of whatever book you have hidden under your pillow."

"I was only going to read a little of it tonight with the flashlight, Mommy," Elsa explained in between bites of the strawberry sorbet.

"I'm sure you were. Grab the book, and Norman will read to you. *One* chapter, okay?"

"Okay," she said glumly as she pulled *The Lion, the Witch, and the Wardrobe* out from under her pillow.

"Ah, excellent choice, kiddo. Did you get this at the library?"

"Mommy brought it home from the library for me to keep, because someone was bad and ripped the back up," she explained. "It was probably some kid who didn't know yet that books are magic, and you can't *rip* them."

"You know what, I think you're right," he agreed, opening the book to where the bookmark was in place. "Oh yes, I remember this part. Edmund gets his just desserts."

"Desserts? Like the Turkish Delight in the early chapter?"

"It's an expression, honey," I supplied. "It means that Edmund was not kind to others, and then something bad happens to him. You know, how we talked about what you put out into the world is what often comes back to you."

"The karma boomerang," she said sagely, and nodded as she finished the sorbet. And so it was with a smile that Norman read about the fantastical, with lessons tucked in here and there. I stood in the doorway, now holding the empty sorbet dish, and watched as he did different voices for the characters, moving his hand around, mimicking what was going on in the book.

Who knew Norman would be a natural at reading to kids? I put the empty dish on the dresser and moved over to the other side of the bed and lay down next to Elsa, wrapping an arm around her tiny waist. Soon she would be too big to think that hanging out with her parents was cool. Hold the phone, did I just think parents? I meant parent. Me. Except when she was in France, then she could have time with her fathers. And the less I thought about that, the better.

I thought about everything I knew about Norman. Would he make a good father? All evidence pointed to yes, but I still felt protective about my kid, considering the various abandonments I'd been through. My father, whoever he was, my mother through illness, Norman, Mormor, whose heart gave out, then David. The people who were supposed to love me had all left. But Norman came back and was here now and doing his level best to prove himself. As he finished the chapter and put the book on her night table and turned off the lamp, I thought, yeah. He'd be a great dad.

~

The Cades Cove Chariot Company was tucked away not too far from Green Valley, and Max insisted on calling Rick Smith and asking if we could bring Elsa to meet the horses. She had been pining for Bella—even to the point where David did a Skype from the barn so Elsa could see Bella in real time. The foal was growing like a weed, and Elsa moaned that by the time she visited in the summer the young horse would be all grown and have forgotten her. How could I reasonably keep Elsa from David and Philippe, and Bella, and everything she loved about France? And the people in France who loved her?

The Chariot Company—which did not have any actual chariots, much to Norman's disappointment, as he wanted to reenact part of *Ben-Hur*—offered mostly guided tours on horseback, but they agreed that Elsa could come down and give some apples to the horses and say hello to them. When I told her what we were doing that Saturday, she vibrated in excitement. I had originally debated asking Norman to come along, but in the end, I said to hell with it and yielded to the fact that he was becoming a permanent fixture in our lives.

Rick Smith, the proprietor, met us in the parking lot and Elsa bounded out of the car, a bag of apples in hand. She had already pre-approved these apples, going through the ones we had bought and selecting the most perfect-looking ones for the horses.

"So, this here's the little lady who loves horses, yes?" Rick said, beaming down at Elsa who was clutching her apples close to her chest. "Have you ever been riding…"

"Elsa," I said.

Rick nodded. "That's right, Elsa. Ever been on a horse before?"

"No, my horsie Bella lives all the way in France, and she's still too small to ride yet."

"What a nice name for a mare. I bet you miss her lots."

"I do. But Daddy Skypes me with her so she won't forget me," Elsa said, now fully drawn into the conversation.

"Well, how about we meet my horses, and you can pass out those apples. They'll be happy to see you when they see what a treat you brought."

I watched as Norman took Elsa's free hand and she skipped along to the stables, chattering about Bella and how she wanted riding lessons so when

Bella was big enough, she could ride her right away. I wondered how expensive those lessons might be, but realized it was time to enroll Elsa in some kind of sport or activity. And if she wanted horseback riding, I'd do everything in my power to make it happen for her.

"Now," Rick began, "when you give the horse your apple, you need to put your hand out like this, so you don't accidentally get bitten," he demonstrated. "Think you can do that?"

"Yes. I'm six, you know."

"Of course, what was I thinking? Now, first up is a mare, Buttercup. She's really sweet, so if you give her an apple, you'll be friends forever." As the tour through the stables continued, I hung back and watched Norman and Rick help Elsa give the horses their treats. One apple each, with an extra for Buttercup, because she was the horse Elsa wanted to ride one day. While they were busy with Elsa fawning over the horses, I was going over a mental list of things I had to do today.

Oh my God, the eggs! I'd almost forgotten, and I promised I would get them from this one particular place, too. Rose wanted to make a meringue dessert to celebrate Jonathan's birthday and said that the best eggs in the whole state came from one place: Mr. Badcock's farm. She gave us directions, and after getting lost a time or two, we found the farm. I made my way up to the main house to see if anyone was around that would sell me two or three dozen. By the time I'd struck a deal, shook on it, and was making my way back to the car escorted by the farmer, I could see that the car was empty.

Where in the world… Aha! I'd recognize that delighted shriek anywhere. Elsa was plastered against the fence outside of a coop, where a lone chicken proudly stood inside. It was a real beauty, with a bright red comb and wattle, and black and white speckled feathers. Elsa looked to Mr. Badcock and asked, almost in awe, "What's her name? She's so pretty."

Mr. Badcock practically beamed with pride. "Well, that's actually a he, which is why he's not with the other chickens right now. He's a Plymouth Rock Cock named Sampson."

"Sampson," Elsa said, trying out the name. "I love him. Mommy, can we get a chick—"

"Honey, there is no way we are adopting chickens. I'm sorry."

~

After supper, Norman and I had our usual private time on the porch swing, a tradition we sort of fell into when it was clear that Rose didn't mind watching

Elsa for a while. We usually held hands and made out like desperate teenagers in the backseat of a car, and if anyone was watching, well, we decided that was their issue, not ours. Elsa's return had essentially thrown a bucket of cold water on our sex life, and I felt bad that it was mostly my fault—Max and Jonathan said that they would take her anytime overnight if we wanted to be alone, but I felt that I had just gotten her back. And I was reluctant to let her go again, with the specter of David and Philippe hanging over me. I was being a helicopter parent.

That was a whole other kettle of fish—Max and Jonathan. Norman had told us at dinner that Jonathan was going to move in with Max, because he spent so much time there already and because he couldn't stand being apart from her when they were a few minutes away by car. The only problem was that it left Norman at a loose end. Jonathan had offered to pay his half of the rent for the next three months, or until Norman found something a bit more affordable.

I secretly wished that Norman could move in here—he was over almost every evening anyway, and there was that room on the third floor. But as much as I wanted that, I couldn't ask Rose to invite him in; I felt that since this was her home, she had to be the one to bring it up. Her agoraphobia was improving every week, and she would either walk further or she would sometimes come on trips with me to the Piggly Wiggly but stay in the car. My concern was that inviting someone else to live with her would roll back all the progress she'd made.

So, making out on the porch swing was our thing now, and I was glad we at least had this.

"Gods, I've missed you, Lo," Norman breathed into my ear when we had broken apart for some oxygen.

"I know; I've missed you, too. Maybe… Maybe it's time I took Max up on her offer and let Elsa stay with her this weekend. I mean, I'm only a phone call away, and I could stay with you in the apartment, right?"

"Fuck, yes," he replied, running his hand through my hair with one hand and cupping my cheek with the other. "Elsa will be completely safe at Max's, and she'd have a blast with that huge movie screen and all the gaming systems Max has. And the books. So. Many. Books. And costumes, too."

"Actually, speaking of costumes, I've had an idea."

"Yeah? Are you going to dress up for me?" There was a twinkle in his eye, and I swear he was having naughty nurse fantasies right about now.

"No, not me. But I have a feeling that Jonathan is going to pop the question to Max when he moves in with her."

"What?! Why would you think that?"

"Because he told me he was going to. Oh, drop the mopey face; he likely didn't get around to telling you yet. Plus, you can be bad with secrets, Norm. You get all excited and give things away."

He seemed to ponder that. "True. Okay, so what's the idea?"

"I'm calling it Operation: Cobra. Don't ask why, just roll with it. Anyway, Jonathan was thinking of setting up that tent they used for that Medieval Day Max and some of the other librarians had in the woods behind the cottage back in the fall and have a bit of a Medieval twist on his proposal. I was originally thinking that there could be two tabards in there—you know, the sign of what House you belong to, that you wear over armor? But they could be matching tabards, to signal the unification of their houses. We'd have to come up with a sigil for House Owen and House Peters. Or at least, that's what we'll tell Jonathan."

"Ooh, I like scheming Lois. What are we actually going to put in the tent?"

"Well, keeping with the Medieval theme, we will give them one tabard. But only one. You know those head cones that ladies in olden times would wear, like the pink ones with the gauzy train?"

Norman laughed. "There is no way that the infamous Maximus_Damage is going to wear a girly head cone."

"Well, of course not. It wouldn't be there for *her* to wear." Norman flat-out giggled and bent over, holding his side. "Sounds like a craft project the three of us can work on, yeah?"

"Definitely," he managed.

CHAPTER 29

NORMAN

At Max's cottage, the assembled group—which shockingly enough included Rose—was getting antsy. We had managed to get all of Jonathan's things into the cottage that afternoon and ate a quick chicken dinner from Genie's. Now, Jonathan and Max had gone for a walk, and we were all holding our breath, waiting to see if his proposal would backfire or not. Max was a very independent woman and, as Elsa had said, she believed in "cohabitation" before marriage. If Max did want to cohabitate before getting engaged, Jonathan was screwed.

My good leg bounced up and down at the table, and no one had much to say. Elsa finished her lunch and went to play with Max's twin black cats, She-Ra and Catra. Rose had gotten up to poke around the massive library of books in the main room, saying she was shocked at how much the cottage had changed since the last time she was here, years ago. That left Lois and me at loose ends, so we decided to go out back to the lawn chairs and sit and wait.

Soon enough, we were greeted by the sight of Jonathan and Max running out of the woods like a pair of kids, their excitement palpable. Jonathan was wearing the pink head cone, Max had tied on the Peters-Owen tabard, and their hands were joined. We stood, and they stopped running when they got to us, Max talking so fast that it was almost hard to understand her.

"Look, look!" she exclaimed, putting her left hand on display. On it was a rockin' ring of white gold and a sapphire. Lois snatched the extended hand and held it up to her face, so she could get a good look.

"Oh my God, it's gorgeous, Max. I wish you both nothing but happiness." She then hugged Max tight while Jonathan and I hugged it out, bro-style, with a lot of back slapping.

"I have to go in and tell my mother. This might come as a big shock to her."

"Nah, she was in on it the whole time." Jonathan grinned. "Everyone knew, except you."

"Well, Elsa didn't know," I pointed out. "Or that secret would have been out in two seconds."

"Truth," said Lois. "My daughter is a blabbermouth when she gets excited about something."

"Let's go in and tell the others. Rose must be dying to find out how this went," Jonathan pointed out.

And so, as a foursome, we went back into the cottage to well-wish the newly engaged couple and toast to their health and happiness.

~

I skipped the big group dinner that night at Rose's place, using my pain level as an excuse, and insisted that Lois stay. I was thrilled for my friends. After fighting for ten years, they had found their happily ever after in each other. Part of me, though, was feeling morose and wanted to be on my own so I could figure a way out of my situation. See, I knew I wanted that to be Lois, with my ring on her hand, living together with me in a little house with a yard big enough for Elsa to play in. I wanted them to be my family, not my family of choice with everyone else, but really *mine*.

I was lying down on my yoga mat, doing my physiotherapy stretches, when I heard a knock at the door. I bellowed, "Be there in a minute!" and then grabbed my cane and used it as a support to get back up off the floor. When I opened the door, there stood Lois, a small duffel in her hand.

"I thought about it and realized that leaving Elsa with Rose wouldn't be the worst thing. Rose did raise Max, after all, and there should be no reason for them to leave the house tonight. You want to have a sleepover?" As if I would say no!

"Get in here, gorgeous." I held the door open for her and grabbed her around the waist, kissing her with everything I had, pouring all my pent-up feelings into that moment. She pushed her body up against mine, and I heard the door slam and realized she had shut it with her foot.

My pants grew tight as she rubbed herself against me, and then she broke off the fusion of our mouths long enough to gasp, "Bed. Now."

Clothing rained down around us as we made our way from the front door to the pullout couch, which I always left out since it was my bed now and I never had company. When we reached the bed, I put my cane against the bedside table and sat down to take off my pants and boxers. Lois stood before me, gloriously naked and hopefully ready for a short performance from me, considering how long it had been.

Once I was naked, I opened my arms to her, and she walked forward and I held her, nuzzling at her belly while she stroked my hair and we murmured words of love to each other. We clumsily toppled backward onto the bed, which made a groaning noise in its springs. Laughing, we sorted out the jumble of arms and legs, and I began to kiss every inch of her, making sure she was good and ready for me. She was delicious everywhere, and I never wanted this feeling to end; I never wanted her to leave.

She would be gone tomorrow, but for now, we had tonight and that would have to be enough.

~

"Lois… Psst! Lois?" It was seven a.m., and I couldn't hold it in any longer. I had to be open with her about what I wanted. Somewhere along the way I had slipped up on my vow to keep it one hundred percent real with her, and if I didn't slam things in reverse right now, I was never going to get what I wanted.

"Ugh." She rolled over, and I saw an adorable line of drool from her mouth going down her cheek. "What time is it?"

"Around seven. I was hoping to talk to you about something important. No, I *need* to talk to you about it." I supported my head with one arm and looked down at her. *Please don't push me away*, I thought. "It's about Elsa and you and me."

She sat up in bed, not caring that her breasts were exposed, and suddenly looked all business. I didn't know if this was a good sign or not. I sat up, too, and took her hand in mine. "Lois, ever since Elsa came back from France, and this crapbag of a situation with David, it's like you've been using her as some kind of shield to keep us apart. Last night was a huge step, but I don't want to rely on babysitters for a night here and there. I guess what I'm saying is, I've been looking for a new place to rent, as you know, and I finally found a nice two-bedroom cottage. It's out of my price range alone, but if we shared the rent, we could live there. You, me, and Elsa, together. Like a real family."

Her eyes went wide and she looked stunned, to be honest. "Are you serious?" she asked in an even tone.

"Completely. I want both of you in my life; I want you to be mine. And I want to be yours. I feel like we could make a go of it, you know? Jonathan doesn't need me anymore, and Rose is doing so much better that you shouldn't feel any obligation about holding up your whole life to see to her. She'd hate that, anyway."

"But Elsa…" She trailed off.

"Listen, Lois. You've already given me the parenting lectures about Elsa. I know it won't be easy all the time. I know she'll have bad days and good ones. But so will I, and I trust you to handle the bad days of mine, and surely you can trust me to handle the bad days of hers. Or yours."

Lois held my hand and leaned up against me. "I guess we need to go see a cottage."

CHAPTER 30

NORMAN

Today we were swamped at work, and I felt terrible about calling Lois to cancel the viewing of the little cottage I had found. I couldn't wait for her to see the inside of it, but our business was growing in leaps and bounds, especially after that cool dragon-headed-shaped build Jonathan had put together in December made a splash on the internet. It wasn't until around ten p.m. that I took off my headset blasting my latest playlist and saw that someone had called me several times in the hours since I had sent Jonathan home.

I picked up my cell, and it was Lois—damn it! I listened to my voicemail, and in the first one, she sounded okay, asking me to call her when I could. In the second message, she sounded almost frantic, saying she had gotten into it with David on Skype and she needed to talk to me ASAP.

I decided to drive over there and see what exactly was going on. If the house was dark, I guess I could always toss some pebbles at her tiny window. The image made me smile, even though I knew with my luck I'd break the pane. Well, it wasn't *that* late, so there was still a chance she and Rose might be up watching TV. I grabbed my keys, locked up the shop, and was out the door, humming as I went.

By the time I crossed town, I was full on singing *Ob-la-di ob-la-da.* I stopped cold as I

turned the corner to Rose's street and caught a whiff of wood smoke and something acrid. Instinct told me to hurry, so I pressed on the gas. Then, like a scene from a horror movie, orange flames lit up the night sky, coming from the third floor of Rose's house. I skidded to a halt right on the lawn, threw the truck in park, and didn't even turn it off so I could see the house with the headlights. I threw open my door, not bothering to close it because I should be seeing three women on this lawn, and I saw no one. Could Rose make it out with her tricky knee? What about little Elsa? And Lois… Lois!

I jumped out of my truck and knew I was a fool for forgetting my cane, but I didn't even need it at this point; I was running on pure adrenaline. The smoke was cloying, even outside, and as I looked up to the fire, at the ashes and embers swirling in the air, I swore I could feel the heat of the flames, burning me as I tried to get out of the Jeep, leaving scars on my skin forever. The ground was rocky and a bit uneven, and I could tell even now that something was seriously fucked in my pelvis and legs. It was all I could do to drag myself free from the wreck, and I could hear the screams of those who couldn't escape… No, no, don't go back there! Then, I was snapped out of my memories by a panicked voice.

I saw Rose stumbling out of the house, Elsa clutched to her chest and wrapped in a blanket. She looked at me with wild eyes and lurched in my direction. "Norman, thank God! I got the baby, but Lord help me, Lois is still inside! I couldn't wake her, and I had to get Elsa out!" Rose would be screaming if not for the smoke inhalation, I knew.

Holy flying fuck. *Lois is still inside*. Lois! I was gripped by terror, but I couldn't let that rule me. Not now. I looked at the fire that was quickly becoming an inferno and didn't hesitate. How could I? My very heart was about to go up in flames. I reached inside the truck and grabbed the two bottles of water I had in there, soaking the front of my T-shirt with one and putting the other on the truck's hood for Rose and Elsa.

"Elsa—how is she?" I hollered as I advanced to the house as fast as possible.

"She's fine! Where are you going? Norman!" Rose exclaimed, as I broke into what for me passed as a run, pain shooting through my hip and down my leg and across my low back with every movement. It was like my whole body was in sync, moving to the tempo of LOISLOISLOIS.

The only noise that broke through was the distant sounds of sirens, but they were too far away, and I couldn't stand here doing nothing and wait for them. I was getting Lois out, for Elsa, for Max and Rose, for everyone who loved her, and, God damn it, for me, too. Where would Lois be? Rose had said she couldn't wake her, so I took that to mean she was in her bedroom. I knew Elsa often crept over to Rose's bed for snuggles, and that must be why Rose was able to get her out.

I pulled my T-shirt over my mouth and nose, for all the good it would do me, and took those achingly steep stairs two at a time. My leg roared and I roared back, fighting with everything I had, every bit of adrenaline coursing through my body. When I finally made it to the top of the stairs, I could hear the crackle of flames and knew I had to pull a miracle out of my ass if I was going to stand a chance of getting us both out of here alive.

It was a good thing I knew the layout of the house, because the smoke was so thick, I was forced to feel my way along the hallway wall to get to Lois's room. I coughed and felt like I was suffocating but continued my awkward journey, bent over so low to the floor I was almost crawling. Lois's door was cracked open, and smoke filled the room. After I entered, I closed the door behind me to slow the influx of the bitter smoke. I made my way to the bed and felt around, finding her unconscious. I didn't waste time trying to rouse her; she needed oxygen and we both needed out before the ceiling collapsed on us. I could hear the fire burning, the crackle and sound of wood breaking as it gave way to the fire.

The window. Where the hell was the window? I reached out and found a pillow on Lois's bed, then felt around the walls of the room until I hit the window. I used the pillow to soften the blow on my fist as I bashed open the pane, quickly clearing the glass. I let the pillow sail down to the ground, and for a precious few seconds, I considered my options.

There was no choice but to make the jump, but I didn't see how I could do it with Lois in my arms. The window simply wasn't big enough. And there was no way with the condition of my leg and hip that I could make the return journey through the smoke-filled house carrying or dragging Lois—assuming that there weren't flames blocking the way by now. I'd have to drop her from the window and pray that she didn't break her back or her neck.

Good God, how could I make this choice? While I waffled on the decision I was faced with, I could still hear the flames now licking at the wood somewhere closer and time was officially up. I picked her up in my arms and leaned down, kissing her and silently praying this wasn't the last time I would get a chance to do so. I heaved her up to the window ledge, getting ready to drop the love of my life from a high second story window when suddenly arms reached *in* and took her from me, and as fresh air cleared some of the smoke at the bottom of the opening, I saw the edge of a ladder. I helped those hands get a good grip on Lois, pull her clear, and forgot my fear of heights as I was assisted out onto that miraculous ladder, scared the whole time that I wouldn't fit through the window.

My head was pounding, and I felt tightness in my chest. The next few minutes were pure chaos as I tried to keep my feet under me and get to the stretcher Lois was loaded on before the ambulance left.

"Lois!" I croaked as I collapsed into the arms of a firefighter.

"Whoa, boy. Let's get you on some oxygen and into an ambulance. You inhaled a dangerous amount of smoke while playing hero."

Her words swam in my head, and I tried to make sense of them. "Ladder?" I asked as someone put an oxygen mask to my face.

"Mrs. Peters told us which window was Lois's, and we saw smoke pouring from a window and the girl said she saw a pillow fall. We did find a pillow on the ground, so we assumed it was you trying to get out. Our guys were on point; they moved as fast as humanly possible. No one wanted to see that kid lose her momma tonight. And you! I should be reading you the riot act. In fact, I will. You don't go into a burning building, no matter who's inside or what kind of military training you've got behind you. You leave that to our team. We can thank the good Lord above that you didn't get the pair of you killed."

I couldn't help but take my mask off for a second and say back to her, "Had to go." I coughed, and she softened her expression and put the mask back, placing the elastic around the back of my head. I let my eyes close and felt myself being half-guided, half-lifted onto a stretcher and then loaded up into an ambulance.

I heard Rose's voice before I drifted off, hoarse but calming. "We'll meet you at the hospital. Elsa is fine, and you're going to be fine, too, and thanks to you, so will Lois. Rest, Norman. We all love you."

"Love you, Norman!" Elsa called in a voice that wasn't entirely hers, and I could tell she was crying. I wondered how much smoke she had inhaled and hoped they were going to do their due diligence on her and Rose. In fact, why weren't they already on their way to the hospital? I tried to take my mask off again to tell Elsa I loved her, when hands batted mine away and the ambulance doors closed, the siren turning on.

I was in a hellscape of heat, of fire and brimstone, of thick, curling smoke. I was so low to the ground that my belly practically touched the floor, and the water from my T-shirt had evaporated ages ago. I sat up, panting hard and clutching my chest, willing the nightmare away. *Lois*. Where was Lois? What about Rose and Elsa? Where was my family? I had to find them, now. I was no expert, but Lois had been unconscious, and she might have serious consequences from all the smoke she inhaled. As much as I wanted to hop out of this bed and demand to be told what was going on, I knew they wouldn't give me any of her medical information because I wasn't family. The only blood family Lois had was Elsa.

Elsa! If I didn't look for her first, Lois would never forgive me, and rightly so.

I was in a bit of an awkward situation because I was tethered to an IV pole via my right hand and I didn't see a cane anywhere, or a walker even. I was going to have to do this the old-fashioned way—suck up the pain, soldier, and keep moving. I gingerly stood, and at a snail's pace, put one foot in front of the other, clutching the IV pole which was thankfully on wheels. When I got to the hallway, I held on to the wall and looked both ways, seeing an empty corridor with a sign pointing toward the nurses' station. That was where I'd start. My progress was pathetic, but I was more determined to get there than my pain was to stop me.

"Whoa there, Mr. Grant; you shouldn't be out of bed!" a scolding voice came from behind me, and I turned to find a male nurse giving me a disapproving expression.

"Cane. Lois?" I managed. My throat was dry and my voice hoarse, but I had gotten my point across.

"I can get you a cane, but not if you're going to be running roughshod through this hospital when you need to rest. Wait here and I'll be right back." I nodded then started coughing, and once I'd started, it seemed impossible to stop. "There's a pitcher of water and some disposable cups at my station. I'll get you some of that, too."

"Lois?" I repeated, and the male nurse let out a puff of air.

"I'm not supposed to give out patient information to anyone who's not family or listed as an emergency contact. I'm sure you are aware of that." The nurse then went to the station, poured me a drink, and brought it back to me. Then he went to a closet and emerged with a cane, which I accepted gratefully.

"If you don't tell me where she is, I'm going to look in every room in this building," I said, feeling a bit lightheaded and short of breath after getting out that full sentence.

"Mr. Grant—"

"Norman!" Thank God it was Elsa. She came tearing out of a room a few doors down from where I was and ran straight for me. I kneeled on the floor, set down my cane, and held open my arms for her. She fell into them and we held each other for what felt like the longest time, with her making hiccupping noises from crying, and tears running down my own face. Thank God and

Rose that she was okay. "I thought that I heard you, but Ms. Max said you wouldn't be up and walking around yet," Elsa explained.

"Is Max in that room with your mother?"

"Yes, but Mommy can't talk yet. She's on a ventilashior."

"A ventilator, I think you mean, sweetheart." Oh god, she was on a vent. It was that bad? Of course it was that bad, I berated myself. She had been sleeping and then became unconscious in a room full of smoke. It was a miracle she wasn't dead.

"That's what I said. And it looks scary, but the doctor and the nice nurse over there said that it's helping Mommy to breathe, and that it's a good thing. Ms. Max and Mrs. Rose asked me to be brave, and I've been trying so hard but —" She burst into full sobs, her body shaking. I held her tighter and rocked her back and forth a bit, making cooing noises and holding the back of her head with one hand, her face mashed into my chest.

She gripped me tightly and I said, in a low voice, "You were so brave, Elsa. So, so brave. I know what happened scared you a lot because it scared me, too. But you don't have to be brave anymore. You can cry as much as you need to. I've got you. I'll always have you, Elsa. I love you so, so much."

"I love you, too," she choked out, releasing her grip on me. "You should come see Mommy."

Then a familiar voice called out, "Elsa? Where are you?!"

Max. She was probably freaked out enough as it was with her mother's house on fire, and so many people she loved involved. Max dashed out into the hall and saw me on the floor, with Elsa pulling on my hand that wasn't tethered to the IV, and I could see her heave a sigh of relief.

"Norman, you're awake! How are you feeling?"

"Like I ran through a burning building," I said, coughing. "Tell me about Rose and Lois."

"Okay, first let's get you up from the floor and maybe get a robe. Your butt is probably sticking out back there."

Now that she mentioned it, I did feel a bit of a breeze. Oh well, at least if people were going to see my behind, they would see a fantabulous one.

The nurse, who had overheard our conversation, went back into the supply closet and came out with a mint green robe, meant to go on over the johnny shirt I was dressed in. There was one problem: the IV.

"Hey, can we take this thing out? I'm not even sure what I'm hooked up to."

"Yes, we can disconnect you from the bag; it's saline right now. But I'm keeping the line in your hand in case we need to administer medication quickly."

Well, that made sense. The nurse helped me to my feet, disconnected the saline, and wrangled me into the robe. Max picked up the cup of water I had set on the floor when I was hugging Elsa, and I finished it in one long gulp that felt amazing on my throat, which was as dry as the Sahara.

Now, cane in hand and properly dressed, I was itching to get into Lois's room. Max must have seen the desperation in my eyes, because she said to Elsa, "Why don't you hold Norman's hand and take him to your mommy, sweetheart."

CHAPTER 31

LOIS

I was floating; floating through dreams of heat and smoke, of a sleep I couldn't shake and an awareness that something was definitely *not* all right. I dreamt of David and about arguing with him about something. I dreamt of Norman and us taking the first dance at our wedding reception. I dreamt of Elsa's upcoming seventh birthday, and of her blowing out the candles on her cake. The candles which were on fire.

Fire… Elsa!

Awareness crashed into me, and the first thing I knew was that there was something in my throat. I couldn't breathe, oh God, I couldn't breathe! In my panic I tried to dislodge the object, until firm hands held mine down and another set of hands stroked my hair and made shushing noises in my ear. My vision was a bit blurry, but when I looked, it was Jonathan holding me down and Norman holding my head. A nurse was injecting something into an IV, and I almost immediately felt calmer. *But please*, I thought, *please don't send me back to the dream world of smoke and fire.*

"Lois," Norman's voice said, speaking almost right into my ear. "Elsa is safe and healthy. Everyone is safe. You're in the hospital, honey; there was a fire at Rose's house, and you were asleep and then unconscious, and took in a lot of smoke. You're on a ventilator, so that's what you're feeling. You've been out for a few days, and it has been breathing for you, so it's important that you don't try to remove it. The doctor said that they'd wean you off it once you woke up, so I'm going to stay right here with you until the doctor comes and explains everything better than I can. Jonathan is going to let go of your arms now, and again, trust that the machine will give you oxygen. You'll be okay." He kissed my temple and I faded out a bit, no doubt due to whatever I had been injected with.

The nurse returned with the doctor and a mini whiteboard and a marker. He gave the board to me so I could write down any questions I might have. I did feel half loopy, but I wrote to Norman, not the doctor. I spelled out the word "Sorry," and he looked at me like he was going to cry. "Lois, you have nothing to be sorry about. The fire wasn't your fault; we think it was the old electrical work up in the attic and third floor. We'll know for sure soon, but it seems like it was just worn out. And it being late at night, you were all asleep; no one noticed until it was almost too late."

I tried to shake my head and wrote "Sorry msg."

At that point he kissed me gently again and held my hand that was free from the IV, and I think he was crying a bit. "Those messages were the reason I came over to the house that night. We don't have to talk about this now. It's not as important as you getting better. I love you, and I know you love me; everyone is safe and right now that's all that matters."

I nodded and then drifted for a bit, while the doctor explained about the ventilator and how they were going to wean me off it and see if I could steadily breathe on my own. Most of what she said went right over my head, but that was okay. Norman was here, and he would look after me. Before I fell asleep again, I wrote on the board, "Where's Elsa/Mom?"

"No need to worry; Rose is staying with a friend of hers from church, Beaulah Howser, who happens to live next door to Max. And Elsa is staying in the gaming room at Max's cottage. Jonathan and Max have been spoiling her rotten, but the kid deserves it. She's been very brave. A chip off the block, one might say."

I felt relief coursing through me that my daughter was safe and with people who loved her, and that Rose had a friend who could understand her anxiety disorder. But something nagged at me, and I couldn't quite put my finger on it until I reached out and felt the material Norman was wearing. He was in a hospital gown, identical to what they had me wearing.

"Why clothes?" I managed to write, fighting now to stay awake.

"Ah, my shiny new duds; I wondered if you'd notice that. I'm here until I'm sprung for good behavior. I'm already running a sideline of contraband. I have gummy worms for you once that thing is out of your throat. Um, but seriously, they're keeping me for observation, now. I think they'll discharge me today or tomorrow. I inhaled a fair bit of smoke, too."

"How?" I wrote. Norman hadn't been in the house when I went to bed, I remembered that clearly. Oh, God. Please don't let this go where I thought it was going.

"About that… I kind of ran into a burning building to save you. But before you act all impressed or get angry, the fire department was a few minutes behind me and would have eventually rescued you without my help. I got you to the window, and they took care of you from there."

"My hero," I wrote, but I don't know if it was legible. Within a few minutes, everything faded to a crisp white.

~

Days went by and I wandered in and out, kept under some mild sedation. I felt Norman's hand in mine whenever I came up to the surface of my mind. Once, I was lucid and he wasn't there, and I started thrashing about, trying to find him through the haze of medication. When the nurse ran in and told me to stay calm, I reached for my board and wrote "Norm?" The nurse said that it was past visiting hours and that he had been discharged, so he wasn't able to be with me all the time. Tears burned in my eyes, and I wrote, "Need Norm."

I then threw the board away from me and writhed on the bed, trying to rip my IV out and get up. The nurse buzzed for backup and I was given more sedation, but the next time I awoke, Norman was there, holding my hand and asleep in a recliner by my bed that hadn't been there before. He was covered in a blanket and had a pillow under his head, and I didn't have the heart to wake him. My room was dim, and so I assumed it was the middle of the night—I guessed those visiting hour rules could be flexible, after all. I wove our fingers together and fell back into a sleep full of nightmares about wandering in smoke so thick no one could see or save me.

~

I lost count of how long I had been on the ventilator, but Norman only left my side to grab a bite in the cafeteria or go to the bathroom. My doctor had started the process of weaning me off the machine, and each time I was able to breathe a bit on my own. Then, the big day was finally here: extubation, the doctor called it. In other words, they were taking the tube out of my throat. They gave me something for anxiety and Norman held my hand tightly, saying I was a badass warrior who could get through anything. Having the tube removed was both freeing and hellish at the same time. But I could breathe on my own and Norman whooped for me until a nurse told him to be quiet, that this *was* a hospital. As if we didn't know.

My throat ached but I didn't even care, because I was one huge step closer to getting out of here and back to Elsa. I wasn't sure what that would look like, because we obviously couldn't stay at Rose's anymore. I tried to speak and, in a croaking voice, asked Norman, "Elsa?"

"She's still fine, as she's been every other time you've asked. Max and Jonathan are taking care of her, remember? And Rose is right next door. She's been here twice to visit you, but you were out of it both times. Elsa cried the last time, so Max decided that she wouldn't be coming back until you were off the vent."

I nodded and was glad that my child wasn't seeing me in such a vulnerable state every day. I had so many questions, though. Questions about where we would go, what the future might hold. Everything seemed so uncertain except those steady brown eyes that looked into mine.

I was released from the hospital on a Wednesday, and still had no idea where I was going. To Max's cottage with Elsa, I assumed. But no, Norman drove me straight to his rental and put me in his bed to rest. Apparently plans had to be made, and some ideas had been floated around. Originally, the plan Max had come up with was for Jonathan to move back into the rental with Norman, and for Elsa and me to stay in her gaming room. Once I had my sensibilities about me, I squashed that plan. First, we had just moved Jonathan into Max's, and I didn't see the point in moving him back out. Second, I needed to be with Norman, whether we stayed in the rental or found a larger place; it didn't matter where. I knew there were big conversations that had to happen between him and me, but the three of us staying together as a unit was imperative.

"Lois, there's something important I have to tell you," Norman said, perching on the edge of the bed and taking my hand in his. It was like our bodies craved even the smallest amount of contact, and I was more than willing to give it to him.

"Oh Lord, the last time a man said that to me the next words out of his mouth were, 'I'm gay'," I moaned.

"No, not gay. I did kiss Jonathan once years ago, but that was because he was questioning his sexuality and I was trying to help him out as, like, an experiment. But I'm sure Max already spilled the tea about that incident.

Anyway, the night of the fire, I was coming over because I got your messages. But it was also to tell you that I love you, and that I love your daughter, and I want the three of us to be together. I know I missed the showing at the cottage, but I want us to live there. I also know it's early to call us a family, but that's how I feel about you and Elsa.

"I'm ready to sell my trailer in Florida and move on, here in Green Valley with you. *Both* of you. I don't know how that kid got to me so fast, but when I thought of losing either of you, I thought I was going to lose a piece of my own soul. And the night of the fire, when I saw Elsa cradled in Rose's arms, I've never known relief like that in my life before. Or terror because you were still inside. See, I need both pieces to be complete. You *and* Elsa." At my silence, he said in near desperation, "Please give some thought to what I'm saying, here."

"I have to warn you, as sweet as Elsa can be, she can be a tough kid to parent. She has a strong will of her own and can lay down the logic like nobody's business. And she's messy, and loud, and—"

"Lois? I know. Trust me, *I know*. And I still want it. I want all of it. I promise you. Now, I know this rental isn't exactly the homiest place, but can we backtrack to the cottage I found? I think we could make it work if we both chipped in for rent. I'm not sure if you're in a position to do that, but—"

"I am," I answered bluntly. Thuy had saved my job for me, hiring someone temporarily to fill in for me until I was ready to come back. I had socked away money after buying the Sentra before Christmas, and I was ready to take this leap of faith with Norman. "I went to the cottage showing alone that day. You're right, it's perfect. A bedroom for you and me, one for Elsa. It has a beautiful kitchen, and the yard is great for Elsa. What's going to happen to Rose's place?" I asked, wondering why I hadn't thought to ask that before.

"Oh, it's being rebuilt and renovated; all new electrical going in, that kind of thing. Rose is excited, I think, about the restoration of the house. Only the attic and third floor were destroyed by the fire, but there was water damage throughout the place. But they managed to save most of the house. We can go there and check on the construction if you're curious."

"No, I'm not quite ready for that."

Norman said he would call the realtor right away and see if the cottage was still available, and we could sign the lease and be in as early as two weeks from now, as the realtor had originally said. That was, of course, too long for me to be away from Elsa, so she was going to move into the bedroom at the rental unit and the three of us would start our journey as a family, together, no matter what life threw at us. There was one lingering issue: to convince David that the best place for Elsa was here, with us.

~

Norman

"Lo—Norman?" the man asked over Skype, obviously expecting Lois since I called him from her account, with her blessing.

"Yeah, this is he. Me. Norman. Look, I think we have to talk."

"Okay, but I'd prefer to deal with Lois directly," he said. "Unless… Oh God, is she okay? Did something more happen to her? Can I see her?"

"No, no; she's fine, she's right here." I tipped the laptop so Lois was in the frame, too. "You should fetch Philippe, and we can have a real family discussion."

"Family? Is that what we are now?" David asked, raising his eyebrows.

"Yup, we sure are. Lois and I signed on the dotted line for our own place this morning, and we're moving in in two weeks. I'm all-in when it comes to her *and* Elsa, and I know you want more time with Elsa than you've been getting. I'm hoping we can talk it all out as a group of mature adults, without resorting to needing a judge to decide this for us."

"Maybe… Yeah, I like that. Let me grab Philippe." There was a moment when the tablet was placed down and I heard a loud "hon!" After some rapid-fire French, the tablet was picked back up and I saw two faces looking in.

"How are you feeling now, Lolo?" David asked, concern on his face. "I'm sorry I didn't come over; I should have come when you were in the hospital. I didn't want to add to a potentially charged situation. I figured your friends and family weren't too pleased with me and I'd be—Oh hell, I almost said adding fuel to the fire. You know what I mean."

"Yeah, I do," Lois said, her voice still a bit croaky from the time on the vent. "And I'm fine. Thanks to Norman. Did you hear that he actually ran into a burning building to save me?"

"*Non*, really?" Philippe broke in, awe in his voice. "So you have found yourself a man with the heart of the lion to be by your side, Lo. And a strong protector for our little princess, yes?"

"If you mean Elsa, then yes, there's nothing I wouldn't do for her," I answered. I had a hunch that if we were going to come to an agreement here, it would be because of Philippe's influence.

"Lois, I feel so bad about the fire," David said. "If you want to put off this discussion until you are feeling bet—"

"No," she broke in. "I want this settled. I don't want to live in fear each time I go to the mailbox, wondering what kind of legal papers might be waiting for me. I don't want to worry about how I'm going to afford a lawyer to settle this. We should be capable of seeing reason here."

David bit his lower lip and looked lost for a moment. Then he nodded. "I did consult a lawyer, Lo, I'm not going to lie. And they said that we should have a formal agreement in place, instead of this honor system we have going on."

"David," I said, knowing in my heart this was a reasonable guy, but also wishing I could reach through the computer and give him a shake, "what exactly has been wrong with the honor system? You're listed on Elsa's birth certificate as her father. You're interested, you're involved. She loves you. If something were to happen to Lois, Elsa would go to you. Is that what you're worried about? That I would fight you for custody?"

"Lois has never had a partner before," Philippe said. "Now that she has one as brave and true as you, we are concerned about what will happen as she grows up. Will we still see her every summer? Every other Christmas? Or will these things fall by the wayside as you become your own family?"

"Philippe," Lois interjected, "I will never, ever stop Elsa from seeing you and David. But I have to say I haven't loved the stress I've been under for three months. That's how long it has been since Elsa told me she overheard you guys talking about paperwork and her visits. Now, if you want your lawyer to create, in English, an agreement that solidifies what we're already doing and have been doing for years, then I will gladly sign. But if you want Elsa to live with you full-time and have a visitation schedule with me, then you can forget about it. I raised that baby, alone, while David chose you over us. He was always welcome to stay in America and be a part of her everyday life if he wanted. He knew what he was giving up: his daughter for the man he loved. And I have learned to not bear a grudge over that, but again—he made his choice. And he chose you. He's not getting our daughter, too."

There was a silence I could only perceive as awkward as Philippe murmured into David's ear. He gave what looked like an imploring look at the other man, and then David sighed. "Lo, I'm sorry. I can't regret Elsa, but I'm sorry for the rest of it. How you were hurt by me. I'm not going to hurt you again. I was going to ask for a fifty-fifty split of her time, but I don't think, I mean, I know I haven't earned the right. I will have my lawyer draw up a document that says every other Christmas, and six weeks every summer. And that I'm Elsa's next of kin in case something does happen to you. Does that still work for you?"

Lois nodded, and I could feel her body quivering next to mine. She was going to cry, and I didn't want them to see it. "Thank you, both of you," I said, and then remembered something else. "Are there any other documents you've already sent that we should be on the lookout for? Because if there are, they're meeting the fireplace."

"*Non*, we didn't go that far yet," Philippe said.

"Okay," I replied. "Then I think we're done here. We'll keep an eye out for the paperwork. It was nice meeting you both."

"Perhaps next time it will be under better circumstances," David said. "Lois, I feel like shit over this. When you have time to think about it, please consider forgiving me."

Lois managed a nod, and then I disconnected the call. She fell into my arms, her body wracked with sobs.

"I thought I was going to lose her, Norman. That he'd pursue custody and they'd find out how much better off he and Philippe are than I am, and, and—"

"Shh, it's okay." I wrapped my arms around her tightly. "No one is taking Elsa away from you. It's going to be okay. I promise you, with our new home, and with Elsa, with all of it. It will be okay."

EPILOGUE

NORMAN

"Welcome to Supernatural Computers! How can we help?" I heard Elsa chirp from where she was out front helping Lois. Normally she'd be at daycare until five, but Lois had taken up picking her up right after school and bringing her to the new shop—a storefront not quite on Main Street, but good enough for our needs. I think the fallout from the fire was making both Lois and Elsa extra clingy, but with therapy and lots of love, they were working through their fears.

I heard the male customer laugh. "Well, hello there. I brought my laptop in because the screen has gone black. I think it needs a new cable in there, but I'm too afraid to rip apart my laptop on my own. Can y'all help?" I listened as Lois took over.

"We can certainly try, sir. I make no promises, because I'm not sure what the problem is exactly, and we won't know until we get in there. But if it is fixable, our team will repair it. Just leave it with us and we'll fill out some forms on our computer and go from there."

"Sounds amazing. I thought I was going to have to go to Merryville or Knoxville to get this thing worked on. Then I heard we had our own computer shop, and that certainly makes it all the more convenient."

I could practically hear the smile and the pride in Lois's voice. "That's excellent to hear, sir. The folks here in Green Valley have certainly made us feel welcome. Might I get your name?"

I tuned out the rest of the conversation and continued to work on the project in front of me. With our new, slightly steady stream of Green Valley customers looking for mostly repair work, and our online orders for new, custom builds and matching custom desks, we were busy. I couldn't complain. This was our dream, and the three of us—well, four if you counted our little greeter, Elsa—were making it happen.

Thuy and the rest of the staff at the library had been sad to see Lois go, but when Jonathan and I put our heads together and realized we could match her salary, she jumped ship like it was a no-brainer. She wanted to help us make our business succeed, and with her educational background in business she was all too happy to be able to apply those skills. She even completely redesigned our website and took over our social media accounts, something that was outside the scope of her job but helped us immensely. Our online orders had never been higher, and with Lois managing all the paperwork for the business end of things, Jonathan and I were free to do what we loved —build.

Plus, I got to see my Lois every day. It was #winning all around, and I'd never been happier.

I was lost in thought when I heard a little voice say, "Papa?" My heart lurched every time Elsa called me that, and I immediately stopped what I was doing so I could see what she needed. She held up the laptop that the customer had dropped off and I took it from her, thanking her profusely. The "Papa" had started in about our second month of living together in the new cottage, which wasn't too far from Max's place. I never once asked her to call me that, but one day at dinner Elsa had said out of the blue that she was so glad that she had a daddy here all the time, but she didn't know what to call me, since David was already "Daddy," and Philippe was "Père." Lois suggested "Papa."

It had started as Papa Norman, and then morphed into plain old Papa. I felt such an upswell of love for her every time she said it, and I took a minute to place the laptop on my workbench and then leaned down and gave her a huge hug. Elsa had grown clingy after the fire and needed a lot of positive reinforcement that the people in her life she loved weren't going to leave her. I understood exactly how she felt. I could barely keep my hands off Lois, and not even in a sexual way; more in a way that meant safety and comfort for us both.

There was one more thing that lurked over me—my mother's trailer in Florida. I knew it was time to let it go and put that part of the past to bed. Jonathan had offered to shut down the shop for a week and come with me, but I didn't want to overwhelm us with orders when we got back or push ahead the promised completed-by dates we had given our customers.

What we wound up doing was a bit of a compromise. We shut down online orders for ten days or so, and Jonathan and Max, during her off hours, would complete the jobs we already had. Then we could open for orders again when I returned. Lois was coming with me so I could show her where I grew up, and so Lois could help me make the hard decisions about my mother's things. And we were bringing Elsa because, after the work of emptying the trailer, we were going to make the long-ish drive down to Disney World. I wouldn't be able to walk all over the park for three days, but they apparently had wheelchairs available, so I would suck up my issues with mobility aides and wheel along if being there would put smiles on my girls' faces.

I did think of them as mine. I knew that Lois was gun shy about the idea of marrying again, plus we were only twenty-seven, so there was plenty of time. For now, I was happy with what I had, and gave thanks every day that it had not all been ripped away from me in smoke and ash. I heard Lois lock up the front door, and through the entrance to the workshop portion of the store, I could see her turn the open sign around to closed. She then sashayed her way into our workspace, and said cheekily, "Do I get a hug, too?"

"Always," I replied, and turned around on my stool and took her in my arms. "Do you have any idea how incredible you are, Lois Jensen?" After the fire, Lois had changed back to her maiden name. I placed my head against her heart and took comfort in the steady rhythm.

"About as incredible as you, Norman Grant."

"Nope, not an acceptable answer. Now you will face the wrath of the tickle monster!" I tightened my hold on her with my left arm, and that left my right hand free to tickle her side. She laughed a deep, throaty laugh, which was music to my ears.

"You're such a goof, Norm," she said, wrenching herself free and straightening her shirt. "But I wouldn't have you any other way."

"Why thank you, milady," I said in an atrocious English accent.

"You are welcome, good sir," she replied, her accent as terrible as mine.

We looked into each other's eyes and in hers I could see it all: our home, another child, a dog and a cat. Gardening out back, and lazy days where we barbequed and invited the whole crew over. Weddings, graduations, birthdays, and Christmases. Everything I ever wanted was there in that beautiful universe of color I was gazing into. In her eyes, and in her arms, I was finally home.

ACKNOWLEDGMENTS

Just as I discovered in writing my debut novel, Dewey Belong Together, it really does take a village to produce a book. Once you are done with that first draft, it can feel like the journey has just begun.

First, I'd like to say that I have nothing but respect and gratitude for everyone mentioned below, who all helped bring this book to fruition. Thank-you to Penny Reid for believing in me and my stories. She is an amazing mentor—even when my anxious Canadian comes out and I apologize constantly! Getting to play in the world of Green Valley once again was both a joy and an honor. I also want to thank her for the creation of Smartypants Romance. This group of amazing writers have become at times my shoulders to lean on, a wealth of information, people to laugh with, and my friends. Fiona Fischer, thank-you for answering a multitude of questions from me at least every Friday. Brooke Nowiski, who has listened to me vent more than I'd like, you were once again an absolute joy to work with, and an amazing beta reader.

To my other betas, Ashley Levy and Katy Nielsen, and my wonderful sensitivity reader, your insights were invaluable in shaping this story, and I appreciated your feedback so very much, even when it was critical (especially when it was critical!) because I know this turned into a better story because of your work.

To my editors, I appreciate every comment, every suggestion, and even every red mark in Track Changes. Kim Huther of Wordsmith Editing, Emerald Edits, and Reina of Rickrack Books, this book is what it is now because of the times you pushed me, encouraged me, and believed it could all come together.

To my dear family and my amazing readers: for lifting my spirits when they faltered, to supporting me, and for encouraging me, thank-you.

AUTHOR'S NOTE

I have a similar cluster of injuries that Norman has, though I acquired them in far less of a traumatic fashion—I never served in the military, though I have great respect for those that do. As for Norman's borderline disdain for mobility aids, and his struggles with getting off morphine, these are things that I have experienced in my own life. I think that is important to note, as I was able to draw on my own experiences in creating the character of Norman. I also wrote the character of Rose as having an anxiety disorder because I live with generalized anxiety disorder, and know many others who struggle with it daily. Rose's agoraphobia, for example, was something I once shared many years ago, and I know how difficult going for those walks around the block were for her, as well as how necessary they were.

I believe that the more we show people what living with a disability can look like, the further we work to de-stigmatize having a disability. That we show these characters as people with wants, goals, dreams; with people who love them and who they love, the closer we get to removing the veil of silence or shame that may embrace these conditions.

ABOUT THE AUTHOR

Ann Whynot is pursuing her lifelong dream of being a published author. She is a voracious reader and book collector, and used book stores are her kryptonite. She also is passionate about video games, crafting, baking, laughter, and travel, especially to Sweden. She lives with her family and two cats on the Canadian east coast, and is inspired by both the forest and sea.

Find Ann online:
Website: www.annwhynot.com
Email: ann@annwhynot.com
Facebook: www.facebook.com/AnnWhynotWrites
Goodreads: www.goodreads.com/annwhynot
Twitter: @AnnWhynotWrites
Instagram: @ann.whynot

Find Smartypants Romance online:
Website: www.smartypantsromance.com
Facebook: https://www.facebook.com/smartypantsromance
Twitter: @smartypantsrom
Instagram: @smartypantsromance
Newsletter: https://smartypantsromance.com/newsletter/

ALSO BY SMARTYPANTS ROMANCE

Green Valley Chronicles

The Love at First Sight Series

Baking Me Crazy by Karla Sorensen (#1)

Batter of Wits by Karla Sorensen (#2)

Steal My Magnolia by Karla Sorensen(#3)

Fighting For Love Series

Stud Muffin by Jiffy Kate (#1)

Beef Cake by Jiffy Kate (#2)

Eye Candy by Jiffy Kate (#3)

The Donner Bakery Series

No Whisk, No Reward by Ellie Kay (#1)

The Green Valley Library Series

Love in Due Time by L.B. Dunbar (#1)

Crime and Periodicals by Nora Everly (#2)

Prose Before Bros by Cathy Yardley (#3)

Shelf Awareness by Katie Ashley (#4)

Carpentry and Cocktails by Nora Everly (#5)

Love in Deed by L.B. Dunbar (#6)

Dewey Belong Together by Ann Whynot (#7)

Hotshot and Hospitality by Nora Everly (#8)

Love in a Pickle by L.B. Dunbar (#9)

Checking You Out by Ann Whynot (#10)

Scorned Women's Society Series

My Bare Lady by Piper Sheldon (#1)

The Treble with Men by Piper Sheldon (#2)

The One That I Want by Piper Sheldon (#3)

Hopelessly Devoted by Piper Sheldon (#3.5)

It Takes a Woman by Piper Sheldon (#4)

Park Ranger Series

Happy Trail by Daisy Prescott (#1)

Stranger Ranger by Daisy Prescott (#2)

The Leffersbee Series

Been There Done That by Hope Ellis (#1)

Before and After You by Hope Ellis (#2)

The Higher Learning Series

Upsy Daisy by Chelsie Edwards (#1)

Green Valley Heroes Series

Forrest for the Trees by Kilby Blades (#1)

Parks and Provocation by Juliette Cross (#2)

Story of Us Collection

My Story of Us: Zach by Chris Brinkley (#1)

Seduction in the City

Cipher Security Series

Code of Conduct by April White (#1)

Code of Honor by April White (#2)

Code of Matrimony by April White (#2.5)

Code of Ethics by April White (#3)

Cipher Office Series

Weight Expectations by M.E. Carter (#1)

Sticking to the Script by Stella Weaver (#2)

Cutie and the Beast by M.E. Carter (#3)

Weights of Wrath by M.E. Carter (#4)

Common Threads Series

Mad About Ewe by Susannah Nix (#1)

Give Love a Chai by Nanxi Wen (#2)

Key Change by Heidi Hutchinson (#3)

Educated Romance

Work For It Series

Street Smart by Aly Stiles (#1)

Heart Smart by Emma Lee Jayne (#2)

Book Smart by Amanda Pennington (#3)

Smart Mouth by Emma Lee Jayne (#4)

Lessons Learned Series

Under Pressure by Allie Winters (#1)

Not Fooling Anyone by Allie Winters (#2)

Out of this World

London Ladies Embroidery Series

Neanderthal Seeks Duchess (#1)

www.ingramcontent.com/pod-product-compliance
Lightning Source LLC
Chambersburg PA
CBHW030618310726
48979CB00003B/776

* 9 7 8 1 9 5 9 0 9 7 5 5 6 *